A Hypocrite's Diary

RELEASING
TOXIC PATTERNS
AND
RELATIONSHIPS

TARAH TALES

MILTON & HUGO L.L.C.
4407 Park Ave., Suite 5
Union City, NJ 07087, USA

Website: *www. miltonandhugo.com*
Hotline: *1- 888-778-0033*
Email: *info@miltonandhugo.com*

Ordering Information:
Quantity sales. Special discounts are granted to corporations, associations, and other organizations. For more information on these discounts, please reach out to the publisher using the contact information provided above.

Library of Congress Control Number: 2025909636
ISBN-13:

979-8-89285-547-1	[Paperback Edition]
979-8-89285-548-8	[Hardback Edition]
979-8-89285-549-5	[Digital Edition]

Rev. date: 08/21/2025

Contents

Dedication

I dedicate this book to my dad, Reginald Dwayne Johnson. His absence from my life precipitated the experiences detailed in this book! I do not blame him, but I am ready to acknowledge the trauma so that I can begin to heal internally in order to manifest the life that I truly deserve to live. I am forever grateful for all of the experiences that I have gone through and grown through. Behind many smiles and laughter is pain being disguised or suppressed. The fact that my father has not yet been able to recover from his childhood trauma has had a significant impact on the pain he has experienced and continues to experience. We can only be our best selves when we're able to get to know who we are, and analyze why we are the way that we are. Those mentioned in the pages to follow subconsciously molded me into a person I no longer identify with. In order to empower myself and give voice to childhood trauma, I'm calling back the energy and love that I have left behind with these men. For all those experiencing scenarios similar to the ones detailed in this book, let this serve as a blueprint on how to decode your life so you can begin to trace the root cause of your pain and begin to heal for a better tomorrow! Endless Love Y'all! Peace.

Prologue

This is the story of a young woman with daddy issues, and mommy, aunty, and cousins' issues. These bitches in my family, —and I mean that with the utmost; respect; it just sounds funky when you add the B -word in there. Well —they did a number on me. That's all I'm gonna say. I learned a lot, and I saw a lot, which helped me avoid, understand, and grow a lot at a very young age. The subconscious trauma, on the other hand, I was completely unaware of! All I know is that certain things seem to keep manifesting with these relationships that I have had. I can only attribute it to the things that I learned consciously from others' lessons and the things that were subconsciously programmed into me as a child.

Now that I'm aware of what subconscious programming is, I can clearly see how I have been magnetizing these experiences in my life because of a lifestyle that lacked many things during childhood. Don't worry, it will all become clear soon.

There wasn't a heavy male presence in my maternal family, not even uncles. I didn't even have uncles on my daddy's side. Everything I learned about how a woman should be treated, I learned from the women on my mother's side. The good, bad, and indifferent. So it took for me to examine their qualities and characteristics to see what could have been impressed upon me and sincerely question whether or not those same attributes are being expressed in me now!

I was given an awesome framework riddled with holes, but I also chose those holes so that they could do exactly what they did: help me to awaken and open my eyes to the fact that I am the one who is in control of my life, and if I wasn't, I wanted to be. It never quite made sense to me that I was born to have no control or very little control over my life. I constantly searched for the answer as to how to gain more control over my life. By revisiting the experiences that have traumatically shaped and formed me, I now understand how it was all done for my greatest good. While simultaneously I am learning to forgive myself for the mistakes that I've made, which weren't mistakes; they were just lessons. My mother was correct when she heavily impressed upon me how perceptive I was as a child. I never really acknowledged that about myself, but she was right. I am very perceptive. My discernment was off though, especially when it came to matters of the heart! I would fight tooth and nail for the most toxic shit because of what I've been exposed to. On the flip side of it, my upbringing has made me financially astute and prosperous at a young age. Once I began to ask myself what I was doing wrong, the answers started to flow. Ige. Once I began to ask mys

Along my spiritual journey, I have rediscovered the seven Hermetic Principles that affect all of creation, either consciously or not. The first principle is that the mind is all and the universe is mental. My understanding of this principle tells me that anything in my personal reality is a refl ction of what my mind believes to be what I want. Since my love life, especially, was no refl ction of what I consciously said I wanted, it was high time I addressed my mind and learned how it works. In order to do that, I had to remember through research and intuition who the fuck I really was, but that came at a price. My ego—it had to suffer. Relationships had to be reanalyzed. I was ready to move out of my struggle-love era of life! According to the way the brain works, it is really the subconscious mind that runs the show. The subtle part of your awareness that notices all things at once and stores them deep down in your memory. The stronger the emotional attachment, the heavier the impact on the mind. Emotions are attached to the reactions, which are also stored in the same way.

In order to change my romantic outcome, I must change my mindset. And that was the hardest part! I have been living this way my entire life, not to mention that thus far I thought I had been doing it right. That's the part of my ego that had to die in order to learn a new way of thinking and then make just as strong of an impact to replace the previous input.

I was born a Scorpio on a two of diamonds day with an eight-life path number. Metaphysically speaking, by tapping into my intuition and using my emotions for the greatest good, I'm supposed to be abundantly living! Numerology says a life path of 8 will do well in business. Financial abundance is my birthright. In cardology, the 2 of diamonds is also a deal-maker, a master negotiator, and the card of the word *billionaire*. I was destined for abundance, and it was time I stopped sleeping on myself. I'm ready to collect all the time, energy, and emotions that left scars and transmute that into positive energy to thrive *now*! I'm tired of living off pain! That was all I knew. So the beginning is where I had to start. You must address the foundation of any temple so the rest of the house doesn't crumble. It appears that I was desperately trying to fix those cracks within me, yet failing miserably. So if you're brave like me, take the sincerest journey with me on how I began to address the limiting beliefs that have been ignored by me, both indirectly and directly.

I hope that after you read this book, you will understand how to better uplift yourself emotionally to the frequency of love. Holistically, I am here to release myself from the shackles of my shadow side by acknowledging the light gained from the darkness. My goal is to impart growth and development to myself and everyone else. *Ase'*!

Part

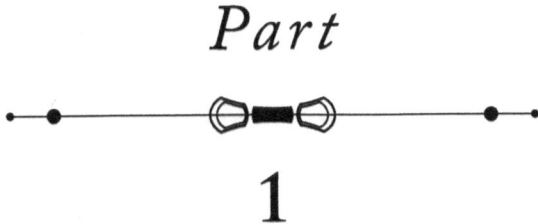

1

Houston, We Have A Problem

*Intuition is perception via the
unconscious that brings forth ideas,
images, new possibilities and ways out of
blocked situations.*

—Carl Jung

Chapter

1

Yeasty Intuition

I went looking for God and found myself! I just might be the biggest hypocrite I know, with the best intentions. The more pain I put myself through, the more it causes me to go within to search for answers. I was searching for the true meaning of being here. When life seems to go horribly wrong, most people turn to "the Lord." However, I gave religion up almost two decades ago, but that's a whole different story. So when I went in search of answers from God, the answers all seemed to come from me, pointing back to me! I was the person creating the problems in my life. I don't remember exactly when I came to this conclusion. What I do know is that when my life began to fall apart, the only common denominator was me.

I had an excuse for everything and for everyone who came and went in my life. Every failed relationship. Hell, even the fact that I was poor at one time, I felt, had to be my fault. Like, really, how could God be so cruel? What was the point of making me suffer? Why not just give me all the answers so that I can live a happy, prosperous life?

I was frustrated. Here I am, on the cusp of a new decade in my life, and what did I really have to show for it? I couldn't seem to keep a man long enough to get on track toward forever. I had no kids, which

I considered a bonus, although I thought I was ready for children. I have a handful of people I could call on in a time of need, but none of them ever seemed to give me advice that completely touched me. It lit sparks of light and gave me ideas and routes to take. Still, it wasn't until I had made enough mistakes based on the opinions of others and started actually listening to my advice that I began to notice I was the common denominator of my troubles. I had to stop living my life as a victim of my own bullshit!

My fault. I guess I should introduce myself. I'm Precious, but I prefer to go by Jewel, which is really my middle name. I think I started doing that just to spite my mom. My dad gave me my middle name; and most people, including my mom, say I look like him. Since his ass was hardly ever around, I missed and longed for his love so deeply that I began going by the name he gave me just to have some sort of connection. I could tell it got on her nerves 'cause she couldn't help but mention everything about me that reminded me of the man who walked out on the family she tried so hard to create with him. To keep it simple, though, my friends call me PJ, so you can too.

Meanwhile, I'm up at 2:00 a.m. furious at myself! I woke up knowing that I had let myself down to a point so low that I was able to catch an STD. Well, not exactly. I have a yeast infection. My pussy was on fire! Literally, it was burning so bad that it woke me out of my sleep at two in the fuckin' morning! If you know me, you know I like to get my sleep when I want it! So for this to be disruptive so late in the night, I was pissed off! I knew what the cause of this terrible pain was. I have been paying attention to myself and my energy this year after acquiring some ancient knowledge. I was going through a metamorphosis during my spiritual reawakening. So, for my pussy to be on fire was absolutely an attempt for my higher consciousness to get my attention. When you dream, it's the subconscious that is giving you messages for growth. When awake, your higher self is guiding your consciousness; therefore, I knew this required some further analysis.

Being a Scorpio is not what they have grouped us to be. I myself am a sapiosexual! There must be a mental connection to get to my panties off. We typically pride ourselves on being alluring and seductive rather than promiscuous; that is, if you have morals, boundaries, and values, which I do. So for me to be sitting here with my pussy on fire was unacceptable. By the way, I call her Miss Mocha. Pussy sounds so low-quality and readily accessible.

Miss Mocha was very unhappy with me and the decisions I had been making, and my higher self desperately wanted to get a hold of my attention. It desperately wanted to let me know that what I had been doing with my temple was unacceptable! I had been misappropriating my most valuable asset, which is myself! My body, my energy, my money, and my time.

My Bama Boo was the toxic energy that I allowed to enter my vessel that was disrupting my energy, my aura, and my hormonal and physical imbalance. Yet I couldn't just be mad at him. Ultimately, I was mad at myself because I invited him in. Boy, oh, boy, it was a hell of a ride. But by the time I knew I should've left his ass alone, the thought of him knee-deep in me, followed by oral disrespect of my labia, held me hostage!

My intuition is telling me I need to get up and soak my love box in a goat milk bath with those bath bombs that are in there. That way I'll tame the fire down there long enough to recharge. I'm learning to recognize how my spirit speaks to me. Instead of ignoring the overwhelming urge to use those milk bombs I haven't thought about in over four months, I'm going to listen to my intuition, knowing that this will help me get relief so I can sleep.

Just because I have birth control protection does not mean that having unprotected sex was a wise decision. Being all willy--nilly with my Yoni has caused my self-worth to be quite low if I'm being perfectly honest. I'm feeling as though I just keep making the wrong decisions. I know what I said to manifest this man in my life wasn't of the highest vibration, but I was only looking to protect my heart. My spell went something like, "I want to have fun, no strings attached. I'm tired of attracting men who lead me to think they want more from me than just sex, only to find out all they really wanted was sex. He must make good money, have a few rough edges, and be ready to blow my back out often! Somehow, I still allowed myself to get my heart strings attached. It seems like thereonly to find out all they res Mocha and my heart.

Especially when the vitamin D is good. The better he fucked me, the more strings formed to my heart."

I should have been a prostitute! I was already misappropriating my most valuable asset around here. Passing out high-class, grade-A services for free. If I'd sold it, I would've been a billionaire by now. At least, hoes get paid for this shit, especially the high-class ones. They are paid to provide an experience; and I'm 'round here passing out the therapist, girlfriend, sometimes the wifey, and even the stepmom experience for free!

This dude was toxic to me and Miss Mocha! To add insult to injury, on top of being inconsistent, arrogant, cigarette-smoking, and always -needing -a favor ass mofo in my life, now he owes me money! It may have felt good for a little while, but being a part of his life has become a chore.

I have been a hypocrite this entire time. From the moment I found out he smoked cigarettes, I should've been walking away. I'm entitled to my preferences. But I'm learning more now, as I sit here on fire, that it's bigger than a preference. His smoking is a refl ction of his mental state . I and a refl ction of how well he takes care of himself and his health. He should have never been allowed to penetrate me. We don't share the same views on health, and that was my first indication —or red flag, as they say. I don't even like that my dad smokes cigarettes. I'm so glad my mom quit, but yet I'm allowing myself to make it okay for me to be romantically and intimately involved with someone who smokes. That was me being hypocritical about my values. I knew I didn't want this, but once again, I made it all right in my mind because I said I didn't want anything serious. It shouldn't matter if he doesn't meet all my boyfriend standards, whether we're on the path to forever or we're just here to bust a nut at night. Why go backward rather than forward? Yet it took for me to have hell between my legs to figure this shit out.

All the pimps, players, and panty-slayers in my family have always told me, the game is to be sold, not told. So if you really want to know what happened, buckle up for the ride mutha-fuckers it's time to roll.

I thought I had healed from my upbringing because I had accomplished so much for myself. I didn't consider myself to be angry or bitter! I was a pleasure to be around. Not to mention, I was the ultimate bad bitch. In this modern time, that simply meant that you had a nice shape, wore designer clothing, and were abreast of most things trending. Those who truly know, know that the baddest bitch embodies everything that she wants and she is moving in the direction of her purpose. She's satisfied with her life! It has nothing to do with whether or not her shape coincides with America's next top model or if her closet is filled with names owned by companies that do not look like her and who don't endorse or support people who look like her. But for me, a bad bitch is the one with a brilliant brain; a phat bank account; an awesome credit score; and a personality that's able to entice and motivate, captivate, and comfort all at the same damn time!

At the age of twenty-eight, I'm pulling that shit off quite masterfully. I have two bachelor's degrees. My waist is 26 inches, nicely snatched, with a curvy proportioned backside. My 38 double Ds sit up nicely! I'm down -to -earth. My friends love me. My family may criticize and ridicule me, but they admire me even though they may not say it.

The first time I knew that I should get rid of the man who gave Miss Mocha the kiss of death was when he asked me for $250. Now, $250 is not particularly a lot of money, right? But it was the fact that I had only known him for, like, three weeks, if that. By now, I think he had put it on me a couple of good times. At the end of the day, why would he feel so comfortable asking a woman he's barely known a month for $250? From my perspective, as a man, I thought he should be embarrassed to ask me for money. It never occurred to me that he was on some scheming shit.

Furthermore, why doesn't anyone you know or are currently working with have $250 to give you? He was a construction worker and traveled for work, so he was with a group of guys in the same home who worked at the same facility. So why isn't anyone within your crew able to loan you this money? He had a reason that slightly made sense, and he promised to return it to me within three days when he got paid. Now, my ego was activated, and heartstrings began to form. Not only had he been to my home, which caused him to believe I could afford to loan him this kind of money, but my heart said, "OMG, he needs some help. I can help him." He knows that I got a little bit of money. He's been to my house, which was a mistake! I don't know if I neglected to mention that I built a 3000 three-thousand-square-foot, half-million-dollar home.

I should be acknowledging the fact that I am the one who manifested him into my inner sanctuary. This is me repeating cycles. I am repeating the fact that I am neglecting to acknowledge my intuition, which tells me when to go in a different direction. It would make the journey a whole lot smoother. Yet, for some reason, I chose the hard route. I'm done doing that shit because this right here is ridiculous. How many times am I gonna make the same mistake? Especially if I got to go through all of this bullshit, I definitely should have been getting paid! I want to tell you more about this nigga right now, but I must get some sleep before the relief from the goat milk bath wears off, but don't worry, I got you.

Sometimes you meet a person and you just click—you're comfortable with them like you've known them your whole life, and you don't have to pretend to be anyone or anything.

—Unknown

Chapter

2

Ten Toes Down

When I awoke the next day, there was a missed call from my best bitch. Let me go ahead and call her back. Now, my main bitch is Lisa. I've known her since I was fifteen years old. Twelve going on thirteen years now, and we've been tight since day one. We met in the parking lot after her ass almost ran into my mom's car. I was actually on my way to an interview. It was the second job of my life. It was a telemarketing company, and I was running late as usual. As I sped through the parking lot, it appeared that she was also running late because she was maneuvering her vehicle in and out of that space as if she had been driving for an eternity. Seriously, she was whipping it so fast that she almost hit me in the parking lot. I didn't trip because, like I said, I was running late; so I hurried to park my mama's gray Honda, and then went inside. To my surprise, there she was in the group interview room, waiting to be interviewed right along with me.

We both grew to hate that job, neither one of us really knew what we were getting into. At the time that I met her, she was pregnant, so I don't really think she cared too much about the job, the finances was what she was after. I needed a little bit of independence and some money to do whatever I wanted to do on the weekends without having to depend on my mama or hear her mouth about chores. So there we were in this training group. We pretty much worked the same shift, so we got pretty close over the few months that we both worked there. She quit before me. I probably didn't last any more than three weeks or so after she left.

I call her my ghetto best friend. Actually, she gave herself that title. I'm her bougie friend that does ghetto shit, according to her. Now, to be honest, I want to be pissed at her ass, but I can't. Why should I be pissed at her, you ask? Well, this was the friend that started all this madness that got me into the situation as to why I'm waking up at 2:00 a.m. with my pussy on fire. Now, did she directly cause Miss Mocha to be on fire? Absolutely not! However, she did introduce me to the negro which set my confidence into a downward spiral of confusion and emotional upheaval. I vowed that I did not want anything serious after dealing with him. I was enjoying my new life in a new state with a new house and a banging career. Since she knew me well enough to know what I liked and what I had previously dealt with in my past relationships, I figured he must be a catch if she was bringing him up to me. Not only did she vouch for him, he damn near lived up to the words that came out of her mouth. But anyway, I'm skipping ahead a little bit, so let me go ahead and hit her back real quick and see what's up.

Ring, ring, ring! She is the only person that I FaceTime or that FaceTime's me first, and I absolutely love it because I get to see and hear her funny ass laugh and crazy ass expressions, all while she gives me the latest scoop. Let me prepare myself, because it's too damn early for her shenanigans.

"Bitch, I got something to tellllll you!"

See, I told you! She keeps the tea hot and ready to serve.

"What's up, girl? This better be good and juicy because it's early as shit! Well, I guess it's only too early for me. I forgot you're three hours ahead of me. But anyway, what's up?"

"Girl, Sweetz is going through it. His bitch-ass baby mama just called the police on him. He just caught another case with this broad."

I won't lie, I was so confused at this point because, to my understanding, they're supposed to be on good terms, doing the family thing and working everything out. Sweetz is the ex-boyfriend of mine who she introduced me to, which caused me to vow not to be in anything serious after our relationship ended on New Year's Eve last year. The main reason I was pissed at Lisa for introducing me to Sweetz was that she neglected to tell me that he was her ex-boyfriend from fucking elementary school.

Elementary school relationships really don't matter, but I don't wanna date my friends' exes, no matter how long ago. That's like breaking the girl code. Not really, though, since not only did I have her blessing, she was advocating that we would be a good match.

Yeah, Sweetz is her childhood best friend, her male best friend whom she dated in elementary and high school. Did I know this before I gave him a chance? Hell no! She knew there would've been no way that I would even consider him, but because they're best friends and she is in a happy, committed relationship and there are no lingering feelings. I guess she wanted him to be happy when she first introduced me to him. She only told me that this was her homie, who's a good guy, hardworking, and sweet, who was getting dogged by his baby mama. She felt, knowing me, her best friend, who kept getting played by different males, and knowing the challenges he had faced, that maybe we could come together and be happy!

So let me tell you how we first met each other, because it was kind of cute. It was the last few days of my Chicago visit, and she asked me to meet her downtown at a club. I put on this nice bodycon black -and -white sweater dress with chic calf-length black suede boots. When I touched down in the city, I got a sew-in, which I could not even believe because I can't stand to have hair on my neck. The burgundy ombre' sixteen-inch weave was spiral curled and blowing in the wind. My silver bangles and choker necklace complimented my outfit and highlighted the brackets on my braces! I was feeling myself, you know, looking majestic as always! We pulled up to this little side street downtown, and this big black truck—I want to say it was a Yukon, but at this time, I really don't remember—pulled up with two dudes in it. She tells me, "That's him, bitch! Let's hop in the backseat."

At the time, my home girl was with me, so all three of us hopped in the backseat. Sweetz was driving, and his homeboy was in the passenger seat. They both turned around to greet us, so I was able to get a better view of this man she wanted me to meet. He was what I would call a dark caramel. He had some stylish eyeglasses on with his long locks pulled to the back, which caused me to pay more attention to his big ass forehead. I was down to take a quick ride. I mean, what's the worst that could happen? I'm just observing at this point because, hey, I'm only here for a short time and a good time. I could really care less about whether he made an impression or not. I only came to get a little high, flash a little bit of my million -dollar smile, and, you know, laugh a little bit. Some may say I'm naturally flirty, but it's really just my charisma that draws people in. I only flirt when I'm interested in getting to know someone. This wasn't exactly that kind of situation.

He wanted to have a little small talk, so we left the group and went back to the car to get in the back seat while they stood outside to finish smoking. Apparently, Lisa must've put him up on the game as to what I had going on in my life because he basically knew everything. He knew I lived in Arizona, was about to graduate from nursing school, had no kids, and had been single for a while now. At the end of the little rendezvous that we were having in his car, he wanted to exchange numbers. He told me that he was going to come see me out in Arizona so we could get to know each other better. That statement went in one ear and out the other. He would have to show and prove these words before I got excited. I'm not paying too much attention to this man because I couldn't care less if he came or not. I wasn't really feeling his low budget 2 Chainz appearance at this point. I mean, he wasn't ugly or anything, just different from the type I usually go for. Not to mention a dude from Chicago saying he's going to fly to see me. I have not yet been flown out, and nobody has flown to come see me, so I'm taking it with a grain of salt.

I was getting sleepy, so we concluded our meet-up. He dropped us back off at my car, which was still parked at the club. As soon as we hopped in the car, I gave Lisa all the tea from our private conversation in his truck. The entire time I was sounding quite unimpressed by her homeboy that I just had to meet until I told her what he said about coming to see me! That's when she told me that he worked for the airline. He probably did mention it in the car, but I was half-ass listening after he told me he had a daughter. I have a rule about dating people with kids. I don't, ever! I'm single with no children, and to be quite honest, I'm still in my selfish phase. I'm not looking to share their time, attention, or financial resources.

So I'm pretty sure you're wondering what happened between me and Sweets after that night. How did he become my man, only to turn into my ex? Why did I say he was the catalyst that sent me on a downward spiral, which led to the burning inferno currently between my legs, right? Well, since your nosy ass wanna know, I'll tell you!

*Have enough courage to trust love one more
time and always one more time.*

—Maya Angelou

Chapter

3

Sweetz

I guess it really began about four months after I returned from my trip home. I was working full-time as a security guard and a CNA for this home health company while I studied for my NCLEX. I remember it like it was yesterday. I was relaxing in the sun room of this elderly man's house while he took his midday nap, and out of the blue, an unsaved Chicago number texted me. It read, "Hey, beautiful, how are you doing?" He had to remind me of who he was because, by this time, his number had been erased. The last time we spoke was when I was in Chicago, which pretty much led me to have no confidence that he would actually contact me, let alone come out to see me like he said he would after all this time had passed. But here he was on my phone, just asking how I was doing. I gave him my sarcastic banter, as I usually do when guys come out of the blue. However, he had a good explanation as to why it took so long to reach out. He said he had been working a lot of overtime and taking care of his daughter. Things were becoming more hectic for him with the baby mama, so he was just taking care of business and staying low-key. I decided to accept his reasoning at face value! Logically, he had no reason to lie to me, so I thought.

I was a complete stranger who lived thousands of miles away. So it really was nothing he could get out of me but some conversation in my mind. His conversation was much more intoxicating now than it was in the back seat of his car. He complimented me on everything. He used words that displayed his intellect, which was a huge turn-on. These days, shorthand text and acronyms were all folks spoke in as if they had not completed school past the ninth grade. He wanted my time and my attention, and he was well on his way to earning it.

I had been more than frustrated with this new location. I didn't really have many people to hang out with outside of school. After being here for almost two years, I had not met a man I could enjoy spending time with who wasn't only looking for friends with benefits. So for him to be showing interest, I welcomed the attention.

He wanted to know everything. When was I going to start working, or what job was I going to have? He had more questions than I had answers. What I did know was that it was time for me to take my test, and I told him that. Over the next two months, we were in constant communication! Either he was texting me with cute, encouraging messages or Face-Timing me when he had some time to spare. He became a part of my daily routine. If he ever skipped a day, that would be the longest day of me checking my phone to see if I missed a call or text. I would miss him, but my ego wouldn't allow me to check on him! I had to continue to tell myself that I wasn't becoming attached to someone I could not have. He had two major red flags that prevented me from being honest with myself about the fact that I had started to like this guy! He lived in another state, and after my last long-distance relationship went awry, I was no longer willing to do that. Secondly, he had a child. Which, by his own mouth, came with baby momma drama that I wanted no part of.

Two days went by, and I hadn't heard from him, which had never happened until now. So I put my pride aside and called him. His phone went straight to voicemail. Two days turned to two weeks, and by now, I had taken my exam, and I was waiting to get the results to see if I had passed. Of course, I reached out to Lisa to see what was going on with him and to see if she knew why he had ghosted me. She said she hadn't heard from him in a while, but she would reach out to see what was going on.

The day before the results of my exam came back, a call from Mr. Sweetz came through on my phone. I let it ring damn near until the voicemail kicked in. I was perturbed and missed him, but I played it cool. Before I could even say hello, he began apologizing for the fact that he hadn't contacted me. According to him, his screen was cracked, and he was unable to see anything. The charging port on his phone had a shortage, so he was barely able to keep a charge. He said he had just gotten paid and ran to Apple to get his phone replaced. He was more than apologetic and seemed to be genuine, so once again, I dismissed his lack of communication. Primarily because I had to remind myself that this was not my man! He had no obligation to check in with me, and I had no right to feel entitled to daily communication. I mean, we were just enjoying "casual conversation," no matter how much I enjoyed it. Of course, he wanted updates on all the things he had been missing out on in my life. I told him I was frantically waiting for the State Board to post whether or not I was officially a nurse now! He was so positive and encouraging with his words. His confidence was refreshing. He told me that he knew I had passed and that he'd be flying out to see me before the month was over so he could take me on a celebratory dinner date. I wanted to believe him. By now, I was absolutely feeling his vibe. It wasn't like he had much competition for my attention. Once again, though I played it cool, I didn't want to get my hopes up, just in case he had another mishap and went MIA on me again.

I was still living with my mom and stepdad at the time, and as I sat on their bed and the morning sun came in through the window, I listened to this man talk sweet nothing for at least the first two hour of his shift. My cheeks were hurting from smiling so hard! My heart was racing with excitement and infatuation from the feeling I got every time we talked. He seemed to be someone that I had been wanting on for a long time! Someone who was consistent despite the two minor occurrences, someone who showed effort. A man who went out of their way to show my importance to him instead of the other way around. I have been caught up so many times before where I tried so hard to prove my love to men because they were broken and shattered and had all of these mommy issues and trust issues, when all I wanted to do was show them how loyal I was, how supportive I could be, and how loving and understanding that I was. Somehow, it seemed to never matter. And here he was, somebody who didn't really know me from a can of paint, the same man my best friend of over fifteen years vouched for, saying all the right things, even when he knew he messed up. He didn't try to defl ct or ignore his fuck-ups! This was a completely new version of a man that I wasn't used to, but I was definitely getting comfortable with the feeling he provided. He was a good, hardworking, responsible guy who took care of his daughter even though the baby mama is crazy; and that just really tugged on my heartstrings. I didn't know how crazy my mom was toward my dad, but it didn't seem like he did too much fighting to be in my life once they separated. I'm pretty sure my father's inconsistency in showing his face had a lot to do with the fact that I looked for a mate that would make me feel differently than my farther did growing up.

I was starting not to care that he had a child. From my vantage point, hell, he was a better dad than I had. He talked about her constantly! He sacrificed his time for her on a regular basis, and on occasion, when we would Face-Time, she would be over there, and I would be able to see how they interacted. Yes, I initially envisioned starting a family with someone special, and ideally, our first child would be a shared experience. However, as I considered the prospect of dating him, I had to come to terms with the reality that my original life plan might need an adjustment. At twenty-eight, going on twenty-nine years old, it had been challenging to find a partner without previous parental responsibilities. Given that he had only one child, I chose to overlook that aspect. As he expressed his desire to see me, reminisced about our connection, and eagerly planned enjoyable moments together, I appreciated his refreshing presence. Despite the positive aspects, the distance factor, with him residing out of state, prompted me to maintain a certain emotional distance and simply cherish the time we spent together.

We decided to set a date! He will be flying in next weekend. I gave him an address close by where the airport is so that he could find a hotel.

I anticipated his visit! I never had a guy fly to come see me, even though he was flying for free. The effort is what I was impressed by!

The day had finally come, and I was excited. I told my mom a friend was coming to town to take me to dinner. I was excited to be able to brag about a guy in my life for a change because she seems to have an opinion about every guy that I date, and no one ever fully meets her standards. So just saying that he was flying into town just for me made an impression on her too. She lent me her car for the evening so I wouldn't have to depend on him for transportation, especially since this was our first real time hanging out alone. Better to be safe than sorry.

He took a cab from the airport to the hotel, and I met him at the hotel. Dinner was scheduled, followed by an evening on the town, most likely to a nightclub, for dancing and enjoying a few drinks. Then I would see him off the next day. When I got to his hotel, he was still getting dressed. He had on pants, a wife beater, and was ironing his shirt. He was looking good and smelling even better. He was clearly happy to see me. His over-sized, juicy lips were spread as far as they could across his face as he flashed all thirty-two of his teeth from smiling. Of course, I was looking great and feeling even better. I had on some blue, black, and white-heeled slippers. My attire was this over-sized, baggy black jumpsuit with a waist belt to give a little shape to the outfit. It was giving my booty the infamous sundress jiggle as I walked. Just in case he couldn't see what I was feeling, I added a little stank to my trot to enhance the view. The girls were sitting up with just a touch of cleavage. Everything was flawlessly delicious, with a whole lot of class. I was absolutely feeling myself.

Once he was fully dressed, he asked me where I wanted to go for dinner. Little did he know the hotel he was staying in was less than five minutes from one of my favorite restaurants.

"Let's go to Pappadeaux," I said, "since it's less than five minutes away."

I didn't know how much the airline was paying him, but since he was flying to town for free, I figured he should have enough money to spend at least $100 or $150 on a nice dinner. It was a habit to sell myself short with guys because I constantly thought that maybe I was asking too much or thinking of what they could afford. Fuck that! It's not gonna kill him, and if it is, he definitely couldn't afford to date me. So we went to Pappadeaux.

We get to the restaurant, the waiter seats us. It was approximately 6:30 p.m., and the sun was setting. Yet this man was sitting across from me with his sunglasses on at the table! I was starting to feel embarrassed. He was licking his lips and trying to grab my hand, all while talking real suave as if we were on the set of a video shoot and his lips-synching was being recorded in HD. The waiter brought us some bread and water and asked if we were ready to order. I'm pretty sure it took him so long to order because he was trying to read the menu through some fucking Ray Bans.

Meanwhile, I'm sitting across from him with the etiquette and attitude of a forty-year-old woman while looking like I'm twenty with the body of a thirty-year-old video vixen. And this clown, in sunglasses and smelling like the finest a bag of dope, is seated at the table across from me. I mean, he was literally embodying the persona of 2 Chainz! That's who everyone says he looks like, and I think he was convinced this is how 2 Chainz would act at dinner. He then proceeds to order the surf and turf. Why would someone go to a seafood restaurant and order a steak? But that's not my business to understand. It is a nice, upscale restaurant. They have pretty good quality food, so I'm sure they're going to do well with his steak.

The conversation was limited as we waited on our food, probably because I had all these thoughts running through my mind. I wasn't really in the mood to ask him any questions, so I basically sat there, answering his questions. His filet mignon and shrimp arrived, and it became apparent that he probably had never had it before because he didn't realize how thick it was going to be as he made sarcastic complaints with every bite. See, that's what he gets for attempting to be impressive rather than simply being himself. I was internally laughing. Mind you, I was thoroughly enjoying my red snapper! The dish was perfectly cooked, and the lemon caper sauce was delivering precisely what it was meant to. I had a few shots of the white Hennessy he bought with him, so my Dirty drink had me on the level I needed to be on to deal with his fuckery! He took his glasses off to examine the bill, LOL, then paid it. He pulled out my seat, and we headed back to the hotel.

We decided we were going to go back to his hotel and get in the pool. We didn't want to go to a loud club. I'm pretty sure he wanted to see this little sexy body in a bathing suit. While I was changing, I could hear him on the phone with his friends, inflating how much fun he was having out of state with my "pretty ass." This was boosting my ego for sure! As he walked behind me on our way to the pool, he was on FaceTime with one of his homeboys, and he politely shared his view, LOL.

The pool water was warm, and nobody was there! We had the pool to ourselves. Ohhh baby, we tried not to cut a fool. The vibe had changed, and I was actually starting to enjoy his presence. My hair was pent up just enough, so it didn't touch the water. Sweetz undivided attention was on me as we approached each other so closely that I considered the possibility of a kiss. The flirting was now mutual, as he continuously complimented me on my appearance, energy, and now my swimsuit. Not even two minutes after telling me how much he liked my one-piece black -and -white bathing suit, I guess the universe decided it was time for a Janet Jackson Superbowl moment. As I walked closer toward the deep end, the strap holding up my 38 DDs came loose. I immediately dipped down in the water, so all of my breasts weren't on display. The surprise was all over my face. In true gentlemanly form, he acted as if nothing had happened and offered to tie the strings for me. I'm sure he appreciated the short preview of the boobs. We both had a good laugh about it. Little did I know my top would come undone two more times. That was my indication that maybe we shouldn't be in the pool because my top doesn't seem to want to stay up.

We shared a couple of kisses before we got out. His jumbo lips were well moisturized, and his breath didn't have an odor. He was actually a really good and passionate kisser. We went upstairs, and we took some more shots of the white Hennessy that he brought specially for me. The taste was pretty decent, seeing as how I prefer Remy Martin. I was definitely feeling a buzz, and so was he. It was late, and all he kept doing was trying to touch on me. I didn't want him to get any ideas, seeing as how we were in this hotel room. He could easily think that something was going to go down if I stayed too long. So I got dressed and told him I would see him tomorrow. After some meaningless conversation and some cuddling that just got a little too uncomfortable, he fell asleep or passed out from being intoxicated, and I crept out and headed back home.

The next morning I came to pick him up, and he apologized for making me feel uncomfortable after having such a good time. At this point, the antics at the restaurant, getting overly touchy -feely in the hotel room, and passing out drunk, he was nowhere near on my good side anymore. It felt like all of the talk over the phone, the texting, and all of the effort it took to come to see me was merely a front to get what he wanted. I was no longer interested in him whatsoever. If he wanted a fuck buddy or some exotic experience with an out-of-state girl, I would have preferred for him to say that upfront! Instead, he spent months communicating with me as if he was interested in me as a person, and I actually started to like him. I felt foolish. As soon as he exited my mom's car at the airport, I blocked him and went on about my life. I couldn't wait to tell my main bitch, Lisa, what happened with her potential setup.

Now, if I were smart, I would've realized that old saying my momma once told me when I began dating. "The way it begins is the way it's going to end." When I say it started with drama, I should have known it wouldn't end well. Stay with me now, because this right here gets crazy.

Lisa came down here to Arizona for her birthday a few weeks later. The date with Sweets all happened in August, and she came down in October. So when she came down, all she had to talk about was how he wanted a second chance. He knew he had acted like a fool and asked her if he could have my number again. Against my better judgment or intuition, if you will, I told my home-girl that she could give him my number again. I was willing to talk to him because I really did enjoy our conversations, and I was very disappointed that he acted the way he did when he came here. Her explanation made sense by saying he was excited and was trying to impress me, but he went overboard by not being himself. That's exactly what it seemed like to me, to be honest. If I was listening to my intuition and being more honest with myself about what I knew I wanted, and the fact that I shouldn't even allow the opportunity to get reacquainted with this dude, I would've understood that even if she gave him my number and we connected again, I should only have him as just a friend. I shouldn't be looking for a future with somebody who lives out of town anyway. I wanted to get to know somebody on a deeper personal level, but that was my mistake. I still hadn't learned my lesson yet.

He decided to text me, and we began reconnecting. He apologized and swore that he would make it up to me. On my next trip home to Chicago, which happened the following year in May, he pulled out all the stops! I put on the fliest, sexiest dress in my bag. This was either going to be the best night he ever had on a date or the last time he saw my fine ass. I chose a black dress that had this fishnet design on the chest, with some black stiletto heels. When he picked me up, baby, not only was he just as clean as I was, he was no longer in that black truck. He pulled up in a silver Mercedes. When he stepped through the door, he was wearing blue jean slacks, a striped button-down shirt, and a navy-blue suit jacket. He was looking and smelling so good that I wasn't even paying attention to his forehead this time. LOL. I needed a little help getting dressed, I couldn't completely zip my dress up. Since I was staying at my home-girl's house and she wasn't there at the time, I asked him to come up and zip up my dress for me.

He was definitely starting this date off right! After zipping up my dress, we headed to the car. He opened my door the entire time, just smiling hard AF! Yeah, he was impressed! As he drove, he did that sexy couple thing women love. He put his hand on my knee, rubbed it, and held my hand the entire time! I couldn't even hold my excitement —it was written all over my face. He was making me feel in person the way he made me feel over the phone. I had his undivided attention the entire night. I don't remember him checking his phone, not once! He had a way of making me feel like the only person in the world.

The first destination was an upscale bowling alley in the heart of downtown. He pulled up and even valeted the car! Ohhh shucks, he was trying to impress me for real, but this time he was doing it right! I thought to myself, we were about to be the best-dressed people in this bowling alley. Since our date was a surprise, I wondered why he was so fancy for bowling. I had an excuse: I didn't know where we were going. After about two hours of kicking his ass, he said we had to go. It was almost time for the next destination! Now I was really smiling hard.

I got my phone out and started taking selfies and recording bits and pieces of my experience. I love surprises, and he was serving them up left and right! Sweetz was earning his name with each passing moment. The next location was a comedy club! Boy, oh, boy, did he do well with this selection! The night felt like we had been dating for years. I was comfortable with him, and he was with me. Even the people we passed on the street felt our vibes and complimented us on how good we looked together! We didn't want the night to end, but the comedy show was over. We went back to his house for a nightcap.

The house was quiet; no one was home. It was just before midnight by the time we pulled up. He lit a couple of candles to set the mood and made us both something to drink. The ambience was very sexy, but this time, he had self-control. He told me to get comfortable. He took off his jacket, took off his shoes, and then proceeded to take my shoes off. I felt my heart melt with every stroke of his hands. He was rubbing all up and down my legs and caressing my feet. I was more than relaxed. He was turning me on. I could feel myself getting wet and wanting him inside of me, but he had not yet earned it. I felt like a lady whom a true man desired. I wanted to enjoy this moment all night. We kissed a couple more times, and I felt like I was sixteen again, with butterflies in my stomach. From that night forward, I knew I was going to see him in a different light. Sweetz made sure to make a lasting impression, and it was one that got him a whole lot more than he bargained for. Neither of us wanted to leave each other, so we cuddled for a couple more hours, and then he took me home.

We continued to communicate like crazy. He was damn near my man in my head. I looked forward to his conversation every day, but not so much so that I was willing to entertain the possibility of making this a serious relationship. However, I was definitely willing to entertain him until something else came along.

His second trip to AZ came pretty quickly after I returned home. By now, I was in my new home, and when he came, I made sure to make his ass sleep on the couch. In my opinion, even if I decided to give him a taste, after his track history, he had to prove himself a little more before the panties came off. I had every right to feel like it was okay for him to sleep on the couch the first night. Since he was only in town for two days, I knew exactly where I was going to take him. On his first trip here, we never actually made it to the club, and I knew just the spot not too far from my house. What he wore was perfect attire, and I slipped into this blue jean dress and blue jean wedges, and we headed to Bobby Q's.

It was Thirsty Thursdays, so the club was packed, and the drinks were strong and cheap. The music was on point, and it didn't take long for us to get on the dance floor. We were about three songs in moving like we were on the set of Love Jones. People were walking by, giving us compliments. We were flowing and moving with each other's rhythm, like the black merengue or some shit. We were the complete black version of *Save the Last Dance*!

If I thought that man was gonna sleep on the couch again after the connection we just built on the dance floor, I was absolutely wrong. I wasn't against him lying next to me on his last night in town. But baby, that man's third leg was damn near touching my knee cap as we spooned. We couldn't stop rubbing and touching each other, to the point when he gave me three small kisses on the back of my neck, I couldn't help but let out a soft moan. All the while, I thought, *If he tried it, I would let him, but I wasn't going to offer it.* Those three kisses traveled down to Miss Mocha, and things were on like Donkey Kong. His oral stimulation left much to be desired, but I knew there was no way that snake I felt behind my knees could disappoint me. Yeah, he rocked my freaking world. I mean, that shit was good, good. I was so glad he had on a rubber because the way we were going at it, neither of us wanted him to pull it out. Do you hear me! The man had a motherfuckn' monster in his pants. I was very confused about how he had such a large pipe, but his oral game was weak, so I asked. He confessed and told me that he didn't really eat pussy often. The women he had been with didn't require it. Probably because of what's between his legs, they were just happy to get a taste. But this was a different scenario because this cat was a top-tier catch for him, so he decided he wanted to go all in and show me what he could do. I appreciated his honesty, but I had to put him up on game. "Baby, you need some help in that department, but I'm willing to teach you," I said.

My heart was wide open, and Miss Mocha would pulsate every time I heard his name or thought about him after the night we shared. I couldn't wait to tell my friend how he laid down some major D and how good of a time we had. Lisa was excited to hear that someone was finally willing to openly show me affection and treat me like the lady I am.

He was absolutely different from the guys I was used to dating thus far. I didn't have to go above and beyond to prove to him that I was worth his time and attention. He openly told me how he felt. He was attentive to the most minute details of my day and even went above and beyond with his actions to show me he was listening. For example, when he returned home, he called on a random Wednesday, and he could hear that I was probably napping in my voice, knowing that I worked nights. I told him I was off that day and was just taking a nap before I had to be at my hair appointment in two hours. He told me that he was on his break and just wanted to say hi, and then we got off the phone. Exactly 1.5 hours later, my phone rang again, and it was him calling to wake me up for my hair appointment. He told me he had set the alarm to make sure he didn't forget to wake me up, as if I had asked him to do so. There were many little things like that that kept me smiling and prevented me from even engaging in conversation with any other guys, all on my own accord, of course. I fell for it, and I fell for it hard! I fell for the attention. I fell for all the things that I didn't know were the basics. To me, he had exceeded my expectations. That's due to the fact that I lacked knowledge of what I should expect from a courtier because of my history.

A few months passed before he asked about being together and what I thought about him moving in. I was apprehensive and curious as to why he was willing to leave his child in another state? That was the first red flag. Why was he so willing to move in with me? I could be crazy. He had an answer to every question. He explained that as much as he currently works, he mainly sees his daughter on the weekend. He would apply for a transfer from his job and fly home twice a month to see her. Okay, that made sense, but something felt strange about making this an actual relationship, even with the butterflies he gave me on a daily basis. My intuition was trying to warn me. However, my ego was telling me to give him a chance. I was subconsciously convinced this was the best it was going to get. If I'm being honest, I was in a rush to be in love. I was tired of getting my heart broken. With each day, Sweetz seemed to mend the pieces left by previous suitors.

My birthday was around the corner, and he decided that he was going to come see me right before Halloween. When he arrived, we sat down and made our relationship official, and he decided he was going to start looking for jobs. At this point, I'm now planning a future with this man. I'm thinking that we are about to make this long-distance relationship work for no more than six months because that was my stipulation. It seemed like it was all happening too soon, but it was flowing, and any little bumps along the way, we fixed them. I was still hopeful. At this point, my heart was wide open.

After his trip for Halloween, he stayed. Now that we're pretty much living together, I wasn't giving him up. Every single day, we wake up to each other. He makes my lunch before work and packs it for me. He even told me he loved me. I couldn't lie; I felt as if I loved him too. I love the way he made me feel, for sure. I loved the consistency that he showed. It helped me to be the softer, naughtier version of myself. That feeling had me sucking dick in the kitchen for no reason, just because he's looking good sitting on the couch. For me, a Scorpio, I was in heaven. He was checking all of my love language boxes.

A month had passed, and he was now living off his savings, trying to find work here. He was on the waiting list for the airline, but that line was long. Even with all of the good that he does, I started to notice some things, like the fact that his conversations with his daughter always seemed to be in private. I understood it was going to be a bit of a transition, with him informing his daughter he was moving out of town. But why did he always need to be secluded to talk to her? It made me feel as though he didn't want me to hear his conversation. I decided not to trip about it because the relationship was still fresh, and maybe he was not ready yet to do that, or maybe he didn't know how to. I thought I was giving him the benefit of the doubt, but in actuality, it was at this moment that I began to make excuses for the things that weren't sitting right with me intuitively. I also began noticing his social media habits. He had been down here playing house, making me feel special, but he wasn't sharing his happiness with the world. We followed each other on different apps, and all I saw were mountain views and desert scenery. Why wasn't he flaunting the little fine ass woman he was telling all his friends about? I hadn't seen one post from him yet of us doing things together. It was weird, you know. I thought we were moving in the direction of us being together long-term. Simple things like showing how he was happy living in AZ, in a new place, with his new boo. For me, things like this were becoming second nature.

The main reason he was in my home playing house so quickly after we decided to officiate our relationship was due to him being suspended from work pending an investigation. On his last trip to see me, he forgot that his pistol was in his backpack while entering the airport for work. Of course, he lost his flight privileges and was placed on suspension without pay. With this time off of work, we decided to see the direction of where things were going and if he could actually find another job here in case they decided to let him go permanently. This is how we got into this shacking-up scenario.

December was approaching, and so was his court day. I had to wrap my head around the fact that this may or may not go the way we wanted. If he was convicted of intentionally bringing a firearm onto the premises, it was possible he would be placed on probation best case. This would definitely cause us to date long distance for more than six months. Mentally and emotionally, I was fully invested in making this work. I enjoyed having a man around. He did all the manly things without me having to ask. I wanted to keep my man, and I wanted to do what I had to do to support him. It was my prerogative to be the best woman I could to help my man keep his head held high during these times.

His court date was December 6, and as long as things went well, he decided that he was going to stay home for Christmas and have those holiday moments with his daughter before packing up to come back here for the new year. I was all for it! The charges were dropped, and now we are waiting for a response at his job.

Two weeks had passed, which seemed like two months. We continued to live life as we planned until I received an unexpected call, which shattered my entire understanding of what we were really doing. I was getting dressed for work when an unknown number came across my screen for a FaceTime. I immediately answered because it had been a whole day since I heard from Sweetz, and he was just about the only person who religiously FaceTimed me. I figured something had happened to his phone, and he was calling to give me the new number. Boy, was I wrong? On the other end, there was a faceless voice. I could hear a woman talking, but she didn't show her face, so when I asked who she was and I didn't get a response, I put the phone down so she wasn't able to see my face. In the most sarcastic tone she could conjure up, she explained that she was Sweetz BM (baby momma) and that I hadn't heard from him because he was with her and that's where he was going to stay. Before I could give her a piece of mind, she hung up the phone. When I called back, of course, she didn't answer.

Pissed was an understatement! The next number I dialed was Sweetz. Again, it went straight to voicemail. The entire ride to work, my brain replayed the last six months. Had I been paying more attention to my instinct and my head wasn't in the clouds of love, I wouldn't be feeling so foolish right now. Was she the reason why he's not posting me on social media? Is she the reason why he would only talk to his child in a secretive manner? How did I not see this coming? Why did I believe he would give up the woman he has a child with for me? All of these questions are swarming around in my head.

Before my shift was over, he called me. I didn't give him the response he was expecting; I was damn near mute. I allowed him to do all the talking. And what does he do? What any cheater would do. He lied to keep the baddest bitch on his team happy. He claimed, "my BM is crazy, and she is causing drama because I told her about you and about my plans to be with you. Now she's trying to break us up and will say whatever she needs to say to get to you." I was primed and ready to accept all of the lies he concocted. It made logical sense to me. Not to mention, my best friend had already told me before introducing us two years ago that his baby momma was loco. I convinced myself for the moment that he wasn't fucking around on me. I just didn't want to believe that was true. But deep down in my gut, things weren't sitting right. So what did I do? I decided to fly home. I wanted to believe in my man. I know women can do some spiteful shit when they still have feelings for someone who has moved on, but I wouldn't be able to really decipher this thousands of miles away.

For the next two weeks before my flight, he made sure not to miss a call. In retrospect, because he knew my schedule, it was easy for him to navigate and appear as if everything was copacetic. My flight was scheduled for December 30. I arrived just before 9:00 p.m. He picked me up from the airport. As usual, I was looking good with a powder-blue dress on and some thigh-high gray boots. I was excited to see him, but I had a plan. I was going to use the powers of Miss Mocha to put that man in a coma and go through his motherfucking phone! What he failed to realize was that my memory is impeccable e, especially when I needed it to be. He had given me the code to his phone back when he was living with me, I guess to prove he had nothing to hide. I would soon find out if that were still true after being home for a little bit over three weeks. I carried out my plan masterfully. I played the role. Once we finished, I politely went through his phone. He was fast asleep, snoring and slobbing on the pillow. You know what the old folks say, "Seek and you will find." I'm pretty sure that it is a biblical verse. And man, they were right!

Their text thread confirmed everything his baby mama said. How much he loved her and missed her. I was staring at all of the messages that they were sending back and forth while he was still in my home. He was clearly making plans to go back to be with her so they could be a family. It was all making sense now. When it was time to start talking about him coming back to be with me after the court case was settled, he had to figure this out and that out. He had to break the news to his child as if he had not already thought of this before telling me he was ready to relocate. The man who had all the answers to convince me to be with him now seemed to need more time to make it a reality. The whole time he wasn't planning to do any of that shit, according to these messages. He was back home, being a family man with the bitch that he truly loved.

When he rolled over, hoping to taste Miss Mocha again, I let his ass have it! In the calmest tone I could muster up, given the situation, I made it very clear that I knew everything. I confessed to looking through his phone the entire time he slept. I even pointed out that he was not only cheating on me with his BM, but I also saw several other random numbers and females in his phone that he had been conversing with. He was caught, and there was no reason to continue to lie! At this point, I just wanted him to be real and explain to me why he would go out of his way for all these months to make me fall for him, just to cheat on me the first chance he had.

We sat there on New Year's Eve in my hotel room and had a real-ass conversation! He explained to me that none of this was part of the plan and that he hadn't been lying to me the entire time. However, after he beat the gun charges and was back home and able to see his daughter, he realized he wasn't ready to not be in her life full-time. He wanted to make his family work, and he was sorry that I got caught in the middle. I listened to him, and nothing but rage was building inside of me. Not because of what he had done, but because I had gone against every standard I set for myself when dating this man, and look at how this shit had backfired on me! I didn't date men with kids because nine times out of ten, there was still something lingering with the child's mother on one side or the other. I didn't date men out of state because my high school sweetheart had shown me that wasn't a good idea. I don't share men with my friends, but since it was an elementary -school fling, I made an exception. And to top it all off, I initially wasn't attracted to him, but the way he treated me and made me feel made him more and more appealing!

Clearly, we broke up that day! I felt as though I was incapable of making smart decisions when it came to love; so instead, I decided to focus on myself, my career, and decorating my new home. Now you see why he was the straw that that broke the camel's back, which led to me manifesting a fuck buddy that gave me a yeast infection! All the pain and disappointment I felt within myself for even getting into another scenario with somebody that I wasn't even feeling like that in the beginning came rushing back to my mind each day I woke up and Miss Mocha was on fire. How did I get myself into another unfavorable situation; all because I wanted to avoid getting my feelings hurt? I didn't want to be in love, so I manifested a fuck-boy who fucked me well and treated me horribly. But anyway, that was the fairy tale with the tragic ending!

Cousin by blood, friends by choice.

—Darlene Shaw

Chapter

4

New Blood

My uncle loves to call me early in the morning, as if he doesn't know that there's a time difference between him and me. Let me call him back right quick to see what's up.

"I hope all is well, sweetheart. I just called to see how you were doing and to let you know your cousins are moving down there soon. My granddaughter and her kids are relocating to AZ from Dallas in a few weeks, and I wanted to know if I could give her your number. She reminds me a lot of you, and I think y'all are about the same age. I think y'all should connect."

He probably could tell I had just woken up when I said to go ahead and give my number to her and have her call me because he reiterated that he knew I worked the night shift, so he wasn't going to hold me. I told him to tell her to call me after 3:00 p.m., which was around the time I got up most days.

"Absolutely! Okay, sweetheart, that sounds like a good idea. Love you. Talk to you later."

My cousin called me later that day, and the connection was instant! The conversation flowed freely. Cool, down to earth, a little ghetto, but you could still tell she has some sense about herself. She was moving here for a promotion at her job in the next few weeks to begin training. The apartment she had secured wouldn't be ready for almost two months, and she wanted to know if she could stay with me until that time. I had the space, and another cousin of mine was already staying with me, so what's one more person. I was happy to help, so I let her know that she could come on down and we could get to know each other.

We talked for over two hours on our very first conversation, talking about the state of our relationships. We both went into detail about how we got ourselves into our situations with these guys. That's when I began to seek validation from her to convince myself to keep seeing my Bama Boo. Although Miss Mocha wasn't yet on fire, this nigga appeared to be having some sort of impact on my daily life. I was frustrated, so I gave her the entire rundown about how I met him on this dating app and how he had that mysterious, nice gangster mystique about himself. You know, the type you could just look at and tell his stroke game was magnificent. Little did I know how toxic it was.

I recall telling her about the moment I realized I ought to have stopped fucking with him when he requested a $250 loan. Despite the fact that he gave it back, the principle was simple. My fuck buddy had taken money from my pocket, but he never put any in there that wasn't already mine to begin with. We barely went on any dates, and now I had to go to him, to see him due to a lack of transportation. His calls were not consistent. I didn't realize that I had relationship expectations from a guy I swore I was supposed to only have fun with. I had no idea why I was continuing to allow this dude to have access to so much of my time and energy. Deep down, maybe it was a fetish of mine to be the exception to the rule. You know what I mean, being the girl who always gets what she wants from the guys that you would least expect to give it to you. It was like I was always chasing a fantasy in a romantic rom-com meets Disney movie from a thug. Someone who had little emotional intelligence. Clearly, I wasn't thinking about what was best for me. I just wanted to have a little fun, have some sex, go out on dates, go to dinner, and go to other fun places, —all without an emotional attachment. Logically, I saw this as impossible from all the people before me who had tried and failed at this feat. That's how your ego gets you! It convinces you that you are the exception to the rule.

What I didn't know at the time was that it has been scientifically and metaphysically proven that Miss Mocha has a direct connection to my heart. This is why the better he fucked me, the more excuses I made to convince myself to ignore all the red flags logically.

It felt good to express my frustration to my cousin, who didn't see me as being judgmental for wanting someone who could give me all the things I could give to myself. I had trained myself not to expect someone I allowed in my space to be equally yoked mentally, emotionally, and financially. I told myself that not everybody has the drive that I have, which resulted in them not materially having all that I have. I was wrong for not looking for those people. By surrounding myself with people who had less than me because I wanted to be a shining light for them, what I was truly doing was neglecting myself and what I truly wanted, just to have people around. Subconsciously, I thought that was the way it was supposed to be.

Nobody reached their hand back to help me up. I got to this place on my own with hard work, struggle, and sacrifice. It wasn't a walk in the park, which contributed to why I was so eager to share everything I have with a man. How did I allow myself to be so hurt that I relinquished all of the things I have learned, especially from past situations that have not worked out right? But I digress. As I listened to my cousin open up to me about her current relationship with the security guard from her last place of employment, and how he made her feel very comfortable, well-loved, and protected, I knew it was innate for a woman to desire these things from a man regardless if they had committed themselves to a monogamous relationship or not. Then she hit me with a whammy! She decided to be in an open relationship now that she was relocating. I'm not really sure how that's gonna work out or why that was a consideration. One thing I know for sure is that when I decide to be with somebody, "open" is not one of the words I want to use in that same sentence.

Girls just wanna have fun! We want to have carefree laughter while falling for someone who likes us, makes us feel special, and blows our backs out! Now that I was trying out these dating sites, I had to decipher between someone I could build a connection with who looked appealing and would treat me well and someone who was selling me a bridge in Brooklyn. Now that I was done complaining about Bama Boo, I couldn't wait to tell her about the second guy I had met on the same site. He was the total opposite of Bama! To be honest, I gave him less attention because he actually embodied many qualities I wanted in a relationship, and as of now I had convinced myself to "only have casual fun."

He had the body of a Greek God! Every inch of him was chiseled. His face was a little rugged. His beard was thick and slightly mangy. Although he lived in southern Cali, he clearly wasn't one of those metro-sexual types. He kept himself well maintained, but if we were both getting dressed at the same time, he wouldn't take longer than me, ya know. He very much gave manly man vibes, like Melvin from *Baby Boy*, just a few shades lighter and minus the criminal record. He speaks well and has an excellent career, which was the first indication that he had accomplished some things in life. He is a border patrol officer for the government. Talk about someone being more equally yoked! We connected on the app during one of his short trips to Arizona. Cuzn' he finna fly me out to come see him! He basically lives in the airport and wants somebody whom he can spend his time with and who has the fl xibility to fly to different places on short notice. Say motherfucking less. Okay! I'm about to have some fun, bitch! Bama ain't actin' right. Even though I want to give him a chance to get his shit straight so I can keep allowing him to lay that D and receive that *gggggreat* head, in my Tony the Tiger voice, but hell, he is not my man, and I deserve to have someone waiting on me for a change.

According to my cousin, there's absolutely nothing wrong with me exploring different options! It's probably why she's currently in an open relationship. It does make logical sense, after all I joined the site with a purpose. My previous relationship with Sweetz didn't work out for various reasons, and that's a whole conversation on its own. In short cuzn, it ended a few months ago; and right now, emotionally, I'm just drained. I've moved past the point of feeling the need to prove the existence of good women to these guys. Can't a man, for once, go above and beyond to demonstrate how good of a partner he can be and what he can do for me? On the topic of good men, I'll catch up with you later cuzn, Mr. Border Patrol is trying to FaceTime me right now! Hopefully, he's calling to gather the information he needs to fly me out. Talk to you later. Bye!

Guard your heart, mind, and time.
Those three things will determine the health of
everything else in your life.

—Andrena Sawyer

Chapter

5

Catching Flights, Not Feelings

I become extremely timid whenever he attempts to FaceTime because he looks so motherfucking good! Okay, okay, let me answer his call. Jay is a man of few words though. Whenever we FaceTime, it seems like he just enjoys staring at me and hearing me talk. Don't get me wrong, he will give his input on the subject matter at hand and seldom does he bring up a topic himself. Even when he does suggest a topic, I'm usually the only one to elaborate on my response. His intellect is evident, and his sex appeal is undeniable. But was he a man of his word, I wondered. He has the same complexion as Bama, and seeing as how I met them on the same app, my expectations weren't very high for the light-skinned Greek God! Looking the way he does, I'm sure he has many options. But this conversation was going to prove my assumptions wrong.

"I don't have much time to talk right now. I called to make sure you are still able to come see me this coming week?"

"Yes, I can still come see you," I said.

The first thought I had was that flights are probably gonna be crazy expensive a week before departure for the Fourth of July weekend. I didn't voice those thoughts though.

I didn't want him to think I wasn't use to a guy spending money on me, even though I wasn't. Instead, I said, "You're going to New Mexico, right?" As if I forgot.

"Yeah! Just send me a picture of your ID and text me your email for your flight itinerary."

Wowwww, this was really happening!

"That sounds like a plan. I get off work at 7:30 a.m., and I'm about 30 minutes from the airport, so please schedule my flight after work because I might oversleep if I go home. I'll bring my stuff to work with me. Please get me a flight that gives me enough time to get to the airport."

"All right, well, you should have your email before the night is over. Have a good night, beautiful. I'll talk to you later."

I'm extremely curious to know why Jay is an online dater as fine and successful as he is. He seemed to be the male version of me. What's his story? What landed him on the app? I couldn't wait to be in his presence and ask him all these things. We haven't really spoken a whole lot in detail about why he's single because he works so much, and when we talk late at night, I'm at work. He's at work, so we have as much conversation as we possibly can, but it's been in pieces. I know I'm a good catch, and I know why I'm on this dating site. I know what has happened to me. But who left this Adonis of a man? And why did they?

On the outside, looking in, he was the type I wouldn't want to just fuck around with. He definitely exceeded my internet expectations and standards, apparently because the only other guy that I have really been entertaining online was Bama Boo, who set the bar very low, so now, I'm contemplating getting off this site, depending on what goes down with Mr. Border Patrol!

Baby, I got my email! He even sent me a text letting me know that my flight was booked and a screenshot of what time my flight left the morning after my shift. My departure was an hour and a half after I got off work; so I had just enough time to park my car at the airport, check my bags, and get on the flight. The City Girls had just put out a song about getting "fl wed out," and here I was, getting ready to live my best city--girl life!

He picked me up from the airport in his uniform, looking just like the pictures! I mean, we had FaceTime multiple times, and I knew what he looked like, but to see him in person, knowing I was about to be lying next to him, it all seemed so surreal. He had just gotten off work, and I just got off work. We are about to shower, fuck, and cuddle! I could not wait to feel his body next to me, and feel how strong he was inside of me. I barely got a nap on my hour -and-a-half flight, just off the thought of being next to him. He greeted me with a hug and took my bags as we walked to his company truck. I could tell that he was happy to see me and excited that I looked like my pictures as well. Angles can be deceiving and these days, women have become masters of illusion online. I tried to hold back my Kool Aid grin, but on the inside, I was happy as fuck.

We got back to the hotel, and as I got comfortable and took a shower, I put on something cute but not too fancy. Just a nice little red panty and a tank top. I was preparing for that scene when Melvin was bouncing around the room inside Jody's Momma. He definitely possessed the ability physically. When he came out of the bathroom with his black boxer briefs on, Miss Mocha started to tingle with anticipation of what was to come. It was the first fuck of the vacay, and I felt a little disconnected. His rod was a nice medium length. If I had to guess, I would say it was a solid 6.5 inches. He didn't even attempt to French kiss my lower lips, which was off putting, to say the least. But I was wetter than a mutha-fucker just looking at him, so we didn't need extra oral lubrication. There were some small kisses, a few ass slaps, and mediocre thrusting.

There was little passion, no sucking and slobbing, or hot and heavy gasp for air. Our hotel neighbors had no idea intercourse was taking place, and that wasn't what I signed up for. His looks had deceived me. I expected him to be able to lay pipe better than that southern nigga back in AZ. I was used to men bringing their A game the first time around. It's like they wanted to dick-ma-tize me. Maybe that was a broke nigga quality. 'Cause the type of dick I just got was like we lived in the suburbs with a nanny and were married for the past twelve fifteen years. It was nowhere near vacation dick. After he politely cleaned me off and I rolled over, I kept thinking i that if Bama Boo had his muscle mass, he would've had me sneaking in the bathroom to brag to my friends about all the things I would be willing to do to keep him around after what I had just experienced. Nobody really ever wants to admit when a man has dick-ma-tized them, but if you were a woman and you were over the age of thirty, you have done something crazy for a guy that trampled all over your values and morals —all because of that thang he knows how to slang. But this experience wasn't that at all, so I rolled over and went to sleep.

He could've just been tired since we both just got off work. He probably wanted a little taste to put him to sleep. What was quite alarming was the fact that he did not use a condom. He did not pull out. Why was he so comfortable entering me this way? This experience was not like we were meeting for the first time. He was not cautious at all. He gave me what I would call lazy -relationship dick! We needed to discuss this for sure in the morning. As I drifted to sleep, he pulled me close and wrapped his fifty-pound arm around me like all those black love couples do on the memes on Instagram. He kissed me a couple of times as if to say "I love you" and "Good night." Or maybe that's what I was fantasizing about. He told me that he had to work in the morning, which was the Fourth of July. I was disappointed because he was supposed to be off. I was leaving the day after. I brought my computer, so I had things to occupy a couple of hours of my time.

He left his debit card so I could get food and drinks at the hotel, and I could order room service or delivery while he was gone. He was chivalrous, very nice, and he seemed to be very trusting of me. I was literally living a hood novel, and somebody had to hear this! When he returned, we opted to grab a bite to eat and catch a movie at a nearby theater. We strolled around a couple of stores, and he gave me a tour of the town. I was enjoying his company, but it dawned on me that our conversation lacked depth. I didn't want to seem overly probing, especially since he wasn't asking much either. Feeling the need for a more candid discussion, I brought up the topic of our decision to engage in unprotected sex and questioned his comfort with it. We had both sized each other up based on our professions and self-care routines, assuming cleanliness regarding STDs. However, as the saying goes, assumptions makes an ass of you and me. Luckily, that wasn't the case for us. He assured me he believed I was clean, and if pregnancy were to happen and be undesired, we would handle it together. Despite his nonchalant attitude, the prospect of potential parenthood on our first meeting felt somewhat disconcerting, considering his previous marriage and two children.

After we got dinner and couldn't figure out a movie or find one nearby, we went back to the hotel and decided to try this intimacy thing again. The overall experience was subpar, definitely not up to my expectations. We cuddled a lot afterward and ordered some room service. We talked, and then he told me how he enjoyed my company, intellect, and being able to communicate with me. He explained to me how he and his ex-wife have been divorced for two years. His travels played a big part in the demise of their relationship. He went on to say that he didn't feel that he could just be with one woman for the rest of his life and that he had tried that with her, but it got boring. I couldn't believe he used that word after what I had been experiencing sexually on this trip. He wanted to try new things, so the relationship stayed fun and flirty. Apparently, she wasn't down because they're divorced now. I just listened to his explanation of events.

The next day had come, and we had slept the night away. We had more unprotected sex. Not that much more excitement; but every time he came close to me, I felt so protected, warm, and desired. I was just refl cting on why I was even out here as I sat and worked on my website, waiting for him to pick me up to take me to my flight.

He was an overall gentleman. He didn't make me feel like a hoe, like he paid to fuck me. I truly believe he enjoyed my companionship and the time we spent together, but he also seemed as though he had a problem with expressing himself freely, allowing himself to smile and laugh a lot. He reminds me of those war veterans with PTSD who have trouble expressing their inner happiness and emotions. He gives me those vibes. I'm still looking forward to talking to him, and I even would like to get to know him a little bit better, regardless of the fact that he's made it very clear what type of sexual relationship he wants. For now, I would like to be the person who catches flights and not feelings with him. So we'll see how long this continues until the next time he flies me out somewhere.

My phone rang, and I thought it was Jay telling me he was downstairs, but it wasn't. Look at who's on my line now. I guess I'm poppin' when I'm busy. Lately, he's been too distracted in his own life to make time for me. Omar was calling me. I guess he noticed he hadn't heard from me for the Fourth of July and probably wondered why I wasn't available to come to the little soirée he had at his house, or why I hadn't been on social media for him to see what I've been up to this past weekend; but I'm going to go ahead and answer it!

When life gives you lemons, find a sugar daddy
to make lemonade with.

—Unknown

Chapter

6

Sugar-Free Daddy

The beginning of what I would consider to be my hot girl summer really started in the spring of 2018, after I decided to be single and focus solely on myself after Sweetz hurt my heart. I decided it was time to get the Brazilian Butt Lift (BBL) I had wanted since I was twelve, when that procedure didn't yet exist. I was well on my way to attracting what I thought was going to be my very first sugar daddy. Young, dumb, and full of cum I was. If I only knew the power of words! Be careful what you ask for —you just might get it.

I decided to go out with a home-girl that I know from Milwaukee. She was having a lunch date with a few of her home-girls at this restaurant. I wanted to meet new people, mingle, and live what I thought was the beginning of a housewife lifestyle. You know, brunching throughout the week with mimosas before noon. LOL. I was making good money, single, with no kids. Beautiful face, a nice-sized waist, and an awesome personality. —I had no trouble attracting men from all walks of life, especially older men. But actually, keeping a man that I could grow with was a different story. At this point in my life, I was just looking for someone to love me. I wanted them to be an older man because, consciously, I thought older men had been through some things in their day; so I figured they were more mature and didn't have time for games. They wanted to be with someone that made them feel good and that they could make feel good. The man I wanted would be someone who is more financially stable and has more money than I do to be able to spoil me, take care of me, and make me feel secure and desired. That's what I wanted, but what I got was not even half of that. Anyway, I went and met up with my girl Danaya at this little sports bar. Danaya had invited two other girls who were also from Milwaukee. The vibes were cool, and the drinks did what they were supposed to do, we all had a good buzz. Danaya just had a baby, and it was time for her to attend to some mommy duties. As the crew departed from our midday gathering, the other two young ladies asked if I wanted to hang out more. We had been vibin' and sharing surface-level conversations, so I was interested in staying out a little longer.

They took me over to this house, which was about twenty-five minutes from the sports bar. I rode with them, and the entire time, all they could talk about was how big Omar's house was in this gated community and how he always came to their shop looking like a bag of money. One of the young ladies is a hairstylist, and she does the hair of the other young lady who was in the car as well. The beautician's brother also worked at the same shop and he was the barber who cut Omar's hair. That's how they met him. She elaborated to the other girl about how every time he comes to get his hair cut, he's wearing a different label from some designer. He is what we call a BON (Big Ole Nigga), which means he was large in size but not sloppy fat. Just imagine a retired football player who might have put on a few extra pounds since leaving the game. So you know he had to spend a lot of money on his clothes because of his size alone. She said he's always well-groomed and smells good too. Since they had taken notice of all of these things, I just sat quietly and soaked up all this information. Omar sounds like he could potentially be my sugar daddy! When she said he was Jamaican, I was even happier to know I was about to get some good authentic food.

When we arrived, a peanut -butter complexion man opened the door with a round face and a Boosie Badass haircut. You know, the damn near-bald fade around the bottom with the low fro at the top. He had to be every bit of 280 pounds. He reminded me of the guy from the

Bone Crusher video back in the day. He probably could've been one of their bodyguards. So, upon first sight, the element of security was there. His size alone made me feel secure in his presence, and I didn't even know his name as of yet. But you better believe my Scorpionic ass was sizing him up to see if he was worth flirting with to achieve my desired outcome. He invited us in, and I sat at the bar. His house was spacious and clean. He had nice furniture that was well-maintained for him to be a so-called bachelor. I was definitely taking notice of all of these things that were standing out to me.

He offered us some food, fixed us a plate, and started to make little sexual innuendos to the ladies who walked in after us. I could tell he was flirtatious and couldn't resist making some type of sexy, suggestive remarks. Nothing that would offend you, just enough to let you know your sexy presence is felt. The other girls were cheesing from ear to ear. I, on the other hand, played it cool the same way I did the entire ride there. I observed his personality.

He was over-the-top, loud, and slightly obnoxious. It's apparent he enjoys being the life of the party. I later found out he was a Libra, and then it all made sense! When I asked what the occasion was that called for this celebration, he told me that they were celebrating the death anniversary of one of his sons. I thought that it was amazing to see them celebrating his life instead of mourning his death. He had transitioned a few years back, so it got a little easier to celebrate. But you can tell he was still in pain while doing his best to stay optimistic. He told me the story of how his son passed away. We shared a brief moment of reciprocal empathy, then I asked if I could step outside and smoke my joint on his back patio. This was a test on my behalf. If he was going to be my little sugar daddy, I had to make sure he didn't have a problem with the fact that I smoked a little Gonja from time to time.

I no longer desired to be the perfect ideal of what every man desires. That shit has gotten me nowhere thus far. He was going to have to accept my flaws and all. I wasn't rude, standoffish, or giving a resting bitch face—none of those things. I was simply more calm, collected, and in my feminine power. He was diggin' ya girl, and I could tell because he followed me outside. On the patio, he told me more about his life and how he knows dancers, famous people, and all of these things. I told him that I was in the process of getting my house built from the ground up and that it would be ready a few months before my twenty-eighth birthday, so I wanted to celebrate with a themed party, and I would need some dancers. He said he could help with that, but I knew that was just his way of getting my number, and I didn't mind cause I was sizing him up to be my next conquest.

In retrospect, that Freudian shit was being played out with him. The boy looks to marry his mother, and the woman looks to marry her father. Not literally, not physically, but metaphorically and subconsciously. He was definitely the embodiment of my father in many ways. He was large, like my dad, in height and weight. He was over the top; he had money, I assumed, and he had multiple kids by different women. Ten kids, to be exact. Which didn't surprise me with his flirtatious ways. He made it clear that each pregnancy manifested because he doesn't believe in abortion. I heard the nurturing side of him come out as he told me about his family. Regardless of the fact he and the mothers no longer wanted to be together, he had a good relationship with all of them and was an active part in all his kids' lives, which translates into my ears that he would treat me with love. I didn't know any of these things to be facts, but I gave him the benefit of the doubt. From my observation, he was older and had made it clear that he had been through some things and that he was an illegal immigrant who got it out of the mud. You know, when you think you're Pimpin, that's usually when you get pimped. Don't get tired just yet, take this ride with me.

My first BBL surgery was not a success. Although the doctor had added some volume to my backside, there were still some visible dents in the top portion of my cheeks and on the side where my hips were supposed to reside. I was not satisfied. My clothes still didn't fit the way I wanted them to. My ass wasn't flat, but it damn sure wasn't round. I didn't desire to look like Nicki Minaj, Kim Kardashian, or any of those ladies. I simply wanted a backside like all the women in my family. Since I was eleven years old, I have been teased about being knocked kneed, bald-headed, dark skinned, and flat chested. "No ass at all," my aunt would say. My family instilled a subconscious inferiority complex about my beauty way back in the days when it wasn't cool to have a fat booty. Now every man drooled over the one thing I didn't have. We've all heard of the triple threat woman. She has brains, beauty, and booty. I said to myself, "Once you get your ass, you're gonna be the complete package! You're going to be what every man wants and desires from the inside out, and there will be no way that I wouldn't be able to attract the man that you would truly make me happy." I really did believe that in my heart! I had no idea that I was manifesting from a position of lack. I thought I needed to change something about myself physically to attract the type of man I wanted mentally, spiritually, and financially. I would soon learn that's not how manifestation works.

I found a surgeon who could deliver the results I wanted since I still lack confidence in knowing I am enough, with or without a fat ass. All of my men had cheated on me with women who were well-endowed back there. Once again, logically, it made sense to me —if I fixed this one thing about myself, there would be no way I wouldn't find Mr. Right.

The day of the trip came. My bestie (my mom) and I packed up the car and headed toward California. Less than seventy miles from my home, I was now stranded between the borders of Arizona and California. We were pulled over in this small town by a cop who claimed I was going ten miles fifteen over the speed limit. When he ran my license, he said they were suspended, which was news to me. He then elaborated that he had to impound the car until I was able to show proof of a paid parking ticket! I was devastated. We were stranded with no car and no way to get home. It was awful, and just as my world was ending, or so I thought. Here comes Mr. Omar calling, ready to come to my rescue. I told him my mom and I were headed to San Diego for the weekend, and he was just checking on me to see how things were going. I didn't tell him about the surgery, though. I had just met him and didn't feel the need to divulge those details.

When I answered, I immediately fell apart. Complete damsel in distress needing to be rescued, needing a knight with a chariot. All he could offer was comforting words, a calm tone, and a concerned demeanor. He called a couple of his homeboys to see if someone could come get us, but his attempts were futile. The fact that he wanted to be there for me in my time of need after only knowing me for a few weeks meant that he was checking off more of my sugar -daddy boxes. I took note that he desired to be my security, my savior, and my protector in a way I never had from my father. He was even willing to pay somebody to come get me. His willingness to dip into his finances so that I was no longer in the predicament that was causing me so much distress plucked the strings of my heart. My mom thinks I don't listen to her, heed her advice, or even learn from her mistakes; but she's wrong. She taught me how to bait and hook a man. She taught me how to flirt by simply being myself and not giving them too much, always leaving them wanting more. She taught me how to be soft, sweet, and submissive when needed. She showed me how to be tough, strong, and independent. Somewhere along my journey, the strength and independence had taken over, and I was struggling to be soft and submissive because I had no one to submit to who would correctly handle the role of being my caretaker. He seemed like he wanted to step up to the plate. Slowly, he was creeping into my heart. Once the crisis was resolved and my mom and I headed up the road toward California, I missed him. I wanted to be around him so that he could make me feel desired. Once I was back home, seeing him was almost an every-other-day type of thing. He started bringing me food to work, which had never happened before. It was fun to have somebody want me, but I was still just a little bit out of his reach. I wasn't sure if he was willing to be the sugar daddy that I needed, not only to give me comfort and take me places, but most importantly, was he someone who was going to spend money on me?

It took him a while—I will say maybe a month—to realize that I wasn't going to give in to his playful antics the way most women do. I think he was quite aware that I had my own money and was secure in my financial status, so he needed to show me a little bit more in order to get what he wanted from me. Some sugar from his baby. Now let me remind you that he was every bit six foot three, pushing three hundred pounds. He claimed he was 250, but I'm sure he was a good 275. Although he was tall and solid with a dad belly, appearance was less of a problem as long as he continued to dress well, smelled good, and kept me happy. The night came when I was finally able to sit comfortably without my booty pillow. I was healing quickly and feeling pretty. He decided he wanted to take me out to a club just to have fun and enjoy the atmosphere. This was the first real occasion we would be in public together besides grocery stores and errands where you could easily think he was my dad or uncle. I like being the sexy, young, hot woman on this grown-ass man's arm. I got a lot of stares at the club that night. Guys were shocked every time I would walk up to him and they saw him grab my waist. I soaked it up, it helped to boost my ego, which made me feel even more like the baddest bitch in the desert. If I only knew the wounded child inside was crying for help!

I wasn't in a rush to go home when we departed, so we headed to this late-night dinner to get some food. The assumption that I would go back to his house afterward was apparent because of how late it was. The sun was about to rise. When we arrived, there were no traces of any women's hygiene products in any of his bathrooms, so it made me think and feel like I was the only one, that I was special, and that he wanted somebody to spend his time with. Before things got intimate, we laid in bed; and he held me tightly with his strong, heavy, thick arms. He warned me that he wasn't a daddy with a long third leg the way everybody would assume. So I figured he was preparing me not to expect a snake like Sweetz had, even though they were both tall trees to climb. He didn't let me touch it as he began to arouse me. Once he became erect, I grazed my hand over it, and I was completely taken back. Imagine stacking two Vienna sausages on top of each other—that's what he was working with. The room was dark, thank goodness, so he couldn't see my reaction.

"He's your SD, girl, not your man. It doesn't matter if you never cum or feel sexually satisfied by him. That's not his main role," I told myself as I decided to let him get on top of me.

Ironically, his thrust made it pleasurable, as if he were working with a much larger penis. When he finished, I asked for him to go down on me. I wanted to have some type of release. This muthafucker had the nerve to tell me he doesn't do oral sex. I should've ran for the hills then. I've never been in a situation where a man told me oral sex was out of the question. Especially a man with half of an Oscar Meyer wiener between his... Excuse me, sir? You're not paying any of my bills y. You do little first -date type of things. Your dick isn't as big as I would like it to be, and you got the nerve to not eat pussy?

Was he really gonna become someone that I entertained, or was this going to be a one-time situation? Logically, it should have been latter, but subconsciously, I had no idea that I was falling for this man. The pillow talks we had after that first night made me feel as though I was the woman he truly wanted to be with. His story invoked my compassion for his situation being an illegal immigrant. None of this was supposed to be part of the plan. I was trying to play a role that didn't belong to me. I wasn't that cold blooded bitch that left niggas high and dry if they didn't meet all of my requirements. I got to know them. I got close to them. I felt sorry for the things that they lacked. I had empathy for the background stories and the childhood. Omar was no different, regardless of the fact that I went into this for my own selfish reasons. I was now falling into my old habit of putting their needs before my own.

The first time he called me Oprah was after he paid for me to get my hair done. I wore my natural hair whenever it wasn't braided. So I assumed it was my appearance he was teasing me about. So I asked him why he called me that. I told him I had been called that before, and I didn't think I resembled her. His response made me like him even more: "It's not your appearance i. It's the qualities and characteristics of your personality, the standards that you have for yourself. You're the total package, and you don't really need anyone." He recognized my worth. He complimented me constantly on what I had accomplished so early in life. The way I carry myself, it's like he saw all of the things in me that I wish my exes appreciated. He admired me, and when he finished with me, it was because he knew he could no longer manipulate me by saying things like I didn't need a man or why I would never be married because I didn't need a man, and men need to feel needed. Every time he would say things like that to me, it would remind me of my cousin. I desperately didn't wanna be her. I didn't want to be such an overachiever that a loving family would never come my way. It consciously perpetuated my fear of being alone, which made me cling to him more.

This is my boo now. I felt compelled to give him the relationship version of me the more he opened up to me. He told me his real name, which translated to him trusting me. I now had the ability to have him deported if I ever got mad enough. Over the next three months, I continued to ask myself what was really keeping me engaged with this man? One, knowing that he's forty years old with ten kids, two he's; an illegal immigrant; and three, he would never be able to satisfy me sexually. What possible future could I see with him? Why was I giving him more of my time, my energy, my body, and then my money!?

Now that a few months had passed and we had been spending lots of time together, I went on a trip and even left my car at his house for him to drive. I felt like I was stating my claim to this man. He dropped me off at the airport. He proceeded to drive off in my vehicle; and of course, all the while on my trip, every time I got dressed up and put on an outfit, I would send it to him. You know the type of things you do when you are in a relationship with somebody. I had created this whole fantasy in my head, thinking that I would be the exception to whatever rule he had about being in a relationship. We talked about past traumas and relationships and why they didn't work out. While I was back in Chicago visiting, during one of our conversations, I confided in him that, for a while, I lied to myself and said I didn't like flowers. It was a lie because no one had ever thought to bring me flowers, so instead of feeling unworthy to receive them, I made an excuse about them dying and not being worth buying. So you know what he did when he picked me up from the airport in my car? That's right, he had flowers! He had handpicked roses cut in water and in a vase waiting for me when I got to his home. Little things like that were what kept me wanting more from him. If hindsight was 20 /20, I would have seen he had primed and prepped me to get what he truly wanted or needed at the time from me, which was finances and coochie, smh.

I was already well aware that he used to be a big-time weed dealer back in the mid 2000's. There were photos of him hanging out with Kevin Hart before he blew up into the megastar he is today. They were all sitting in a row, like a scene out of *Scarface* with celebrities in a room. He was right in the middle, not paying much attention as the picture was being taken, giving off the vibe that it was his party. He used to flaunt his lavish lifestyle with plenty of examples like this. Now he's on the run from ICE, living a more low-key life. His freedom to move around isn't as easy as it used to be, so he's relying on others for help. I overheard a particular conversation where he was on the phone trying to arrange for a car to pick up more weed, but the folks on the other end must have wanted more money for their involvement than he had. What did I do? You guessed it, I offered to help him. The deal was that if I fronted the money for the truck and the product, I'd get a return on investment (ROI). On top of that, I wanted to ease some of the stress he faced because I thought he had been helping me with the stress in my own life. So I pulled $6,000 out of my bank account and handed it over to him. That's when everything started going downhill at a rapid pace!

He had more product than he was able to get off. Now we were Bonny and Clyde because he asked me to send some to my people up north for free, and anything over what he asked for they could keep. I'm so conditioned to being a people pleaser that I did it without hesitation 'cause it seemed as though this was the only way I was getting my money back. Two grand came back to me from my folks, and I kept it despite him insisting that he needed it. Hell, I needed it too. My house was almost done, and I knew I needed furniture. Plus I was losing confidence in him that he had the ability to get me my funds back. Two months went by as I patiently waited to receive the other four grand of my money back, which never came. Not only did it not come after those two months had passed, he stopped mentioning it as if it never existed. It was now December. We're going into the New Year. I just met this sugar free daddy back in April, and all these things had taken place. I was over it! I didn't want to be in this cycle any longer, but I also didn't wanna let go without getting my money back. I had no intentions of fucking him anymore, and I barely wanted to be his friend. I woke up one day in early January and decided it had been long enough for him to figure out how to pay me. I called his phone, and another woman answered! I was hot as a firecracker. Not because I wanted him but because he was with someone else and, in my mind, doing all the things he had done with me, with her. Honestly, none of that matters besides the fact that he didn't have my money. He should be over there milking her ass to pay me back. You already know that wasn't the case or his intention. I took everything of his that was at my house and dropped it off on his doorstep with a note that read, "I deserve better." But clearly, that lesson had not yet been learned.

Love yourself first, and everything else falls in line. You really have to love yourself to get anything done in this world.

—*Lucille Ball*

Chapter

7

International Booty

et me tell you how my bad bitch body excursion went down. This is about to be my second time going under the knife to create the look of desire I desperately felt I needed. Somehow, I convinced myself that I deserved this. I had a deep-seated desire for a booty since childhood, long before Nicki Minaj or Kim K existed. The fact that I felt something was lacking in my beauty began as early as I can remember. See, all of the women in my family have a nice bodacious booty, a small waist; are light-skinned, most have long, thick hair; and small perky titties. I, on the other hand, was the exact opposite: skinny legs, knocked knees, big breasts, no ass at all, and dark-skinned like my father. As I grew and hit puberty, my boobs grew even bigger, my thighs expanded, my hair struggled to reach the nape of my neck, and my booty was nowhere in sight. After multiple failed relationships and constantly dealing with men who would go out and cheat on me, my thought was that I had the brains, the beauty, and the personality; but I was missing the booty. My mom used to tell me how she prayed for my nose to be like hers while she was pregnant so that I didn't get my dad's "bell pepper nose," as she calls it. My response was always, "You should have prayed for my butt also."

Meanwhile, I was cursed with his flat ass and his mama's big breasts. I would like to give them both credit because they both have a great pair of legs, so I was destined to have a stride that would complement my pseudo-confidence. According to all of the wealthy men on TV these days, the bad bitches come with the full package. Lil Wayne even went so far as to say in one of his songs: "you like a bitch with no ass, you ain't got shit." What a way to kill a woman's confidence globally! You can have millions in the bank, a beautiful face, and a brain that could get them out of any situation; but if you ain't got no ass, you ain't got shit. The perception of beauty in the media has heightened my low self-esteem in this area.

Although I don't subscribe to the need to follow fashion trends or spend hundreds and hundreds of dollars on designer brands, I didn't realize part of my self-worth is tied to my beauty or what is considered to be beautiful. The first procedure happened about six months before I graduated from nursing school. I was working as a home health aide when I convinced my mom to cosign care credit so I could get a BBL as my graduation gift. She agreed because she knew how much I coveted a round backside. She even went to interview doctors with me. The doctor I chose she didn't think was the best option and urged me to continue looking. Ohh, I wish I would've listened, but I was fixated on a picture from his website that I wanted him to create for me. When I got off his table, I was not confident that he had delivered what I desired. I was barely sore, as if he had barely taken any fat from everywhere marked and paid for. My results were less than stellar, and as I began to heal, I could see as the swelling began to subside, there was barely any additional fat placed in the areas that had now sunk in. Not enough, at least, to give me the full round curvature that I wanted. I dealt with this botched job for almost two years.

Now that I was a nurse and still living in my parent's house, my savings account was swollen. During one of my shifts, my homegirl/charge nurse told me about this place that she had been following on the internet for a couple of years now. She was planning to get a mommy makeover with a BBL. It didn't quite make sense to me because she already had a big booty. She probably didn't like the way it appeared beneath her clothes, despite the fact that it appears to be in good shape.

There were hundreds of women posting before and after pictures, and I was absolutely confident in their ability to make me look exactly how I wanted to look.

The Brazilian Butt Lift (BBL) was becoming mainstream. We all knew that celebrities were going under the knife, but it was kind of hush-hush that women needed or desired to change their look to stay relevant. I had little knowledge about any of the drug or human trafficking that was going on in this town. I had a goal in mind, and I was dead set on doing it. The facility was in Tijuana, Mexico, less than five miles from the California border. The surgeon lived in Cali and drove across the border daily to his facility. I did my due diligence to make sure he was board certified. I wasn't willing to die for this ass, no matter how badly I wanted it.

You already know my mom and I were pulled over for going ten miles above the speed limit going through this small, hick town. After Omar couldn't find someone to get us, depression set in. I was sad that my dream was being put on hold, which meant I might possibly have to reschedule the procedure. My mom wanted me to be happy and finally get the look I desired. However, she tried to be the voice of reason. She said to me, "Maybe this is a sign that we shouldn't go." She was already leery about going to another country. She knew nothing about the doctor or their certification, which were all valid concerns as a parent, but she still wanted to support me. After they towed my car, we sat in the McDonald's parking lot for a ride back home to get my mom's car. Even though my sugar-free Daddy wasn't able to rescue me, it still made me feel good that he wanted to be there for me. I was almost twenty-five years old, and I couldn't remember one single time ever hearing my dad say that I was beautiful. I'm sure if I had, that would have greatly impacted this area of low self-worth.

We arrived at the hotel a little bit past midnight. I showered and mentally prepared myself to get up on this table once again. In the morning, my life was about to change. I still felt that a piece of me was missing and needed to change in order to truly be viewed as the total package that I felt I was. The owners were amazing. The husband-and-wife team expanded their bariatric center to include cosmetic surgery so that women losing weight could feel confident in their new bodies without all the extra skin. Their passion and professionalism put me and my mom at ease.

When it was time to go into the prep room, the wife walked in to greet us, and let me tell you, her body was absolutely on point, like it was a gift from the heavens. Okaaay! I mean, her waist had to be every bit of eighteen inches. She was so sweet, she even knocked off $500 because she said my current situation didn't need much work to fix. That little sprinkle of good fortune alone made up for the things leading up to our arrival. She led me to the area where I would change out of my clothes. I took a deep breath and relaxed. Before I knew it, I was on the table waiting for the spinal tap, which made me nervous. I'm a nurse, so I knew I had to sit very still as the anesthesiologist inserted the needle; otherwise, the new ass they gave me nobody would see because I would be paralyzed, bound to a wheelchair. He told me to hunch my back as he applied the cold cleansing solution to the area. It was at that moment that I internally questioned whether or not I really needed to do this. I was slightly afraid, but hell, I had done all this to get here. I might as well go through with it!

I woke up hungry and ready to eat. I was in a bed in a room with another young lady. I had dreams about my butt, and I was excited to see the results. The next morning, my mom came back to the clinic to pick me up. I was in very little pain, although it was pretty hard to sit on my butt. We spent the weekend in Mexico to allow for a few days of healing. The company sent over a nurse for three days to change my bandages and massage my body to improve drainage. This experience had trumped the first procedure tenfold. Those three days of rest and relaxation afforded me time for refl ction. I now had everything I desired physically, and I was no longer going to allow myself to engage with men who didn't meet my standards. The last time I consciously decided I was no longer entertaining men with "potential" was back in college. But now, I was a grown woman who knew what she wanted and how to recognize a man who possessed it, or so I thought. I probably should have revisited the different ways potential had manifested prior because those lessons continued to elude me.

So many of our young women today,
they're growing up without a father, but
they're still thirsty for that and
desiring positive male love.

—Hill Harper

Chapter

8

Edible Arrangements

My entire life, older men have been attracted to me. I've always been called wise beyond my years. I decided if I was going to get a sugar daddy, I needed to see if physically I could handle sleeping with one. This is the story of fulfilling my fantasy with Mr. Jones. I call him MJ for short. I remember the first time I met MJ at work. It was another day at Edible Arrangements. I had been working there part-time when I went home for summer vacation. I was now the manager, which meant on slow days, I would work alone in the shop and there would be a delivery driver for any orders that came in. I came out of the office when I heard the door ding, thinking it was a customer, but it was actually the new delivery driver. He was roughly six feet, stubby-built, caramel -complexion man with a scruffy beard and some dark lips; and he smelled like he owned the entire cologne counter in the mall. I could smell him before he even walked past me, and it was intoxicating. He definitely smells better than he looks. Don't get me wrong, he wasn't an ugly guy, but you could just tell life had thrown him some hardship. His face had those holes in his jaws that indicated he had been smoking for probably more years than I have been alive. His strut reminded me of a 1980 pimp from St. Louis, LOL. He was in his late thirties, possibly early forties, but he dressed up as if he were still in his twenties. His gym shoes were clean and relevant for the current trend, his jeans starched, and, of course, his work shirt. Overall, well groomed, yet rough around the edges. He was exactly the type of guy that I would date if he were my age.

I consider myself to be a good girl. I do what's right. I go to school, get good grades, and obey my parents; but for some reason, the rough-neck guys excite me. Yeah, the new delivery driver was cooler than a fan. We chopped it up sometimes on the nights when I closed the store down and he brought in the last delivery. He would tell me about the adventures that he experienced delivering to the suburban housewives. I like MJ. He treated me like an adult, although I was only in my sophomore year of college, and every time I came home, I was reminded how I was still a child in my mother's house. It was refreshing to have an older guy see me for the mature woman that I thought I was. We talked about life; relationships; and his daughter, who was a little bit younger than me but still around my age. I shared with him issues in my current relationship with my high school sweetheart, which is becoming more and more frustrating. We hadn't yet broken up, but we were definitely on the verge of it. I told him about all of the things that I wish I could've told my dad, but we just didn't have a relationship that deep for more reasons than one. My mom's only living brother was still in jail, so I didn't really have any uncles to confide information in, so I would tell MJ.

On days when he and I worked together, he would notice if I was having a bad day or not. By the time our shifts were over, he would ensure I went home with a smile. It seemed as though he looked forward to seeing me. When I answered the phone while he was out on deliveries, he would be happy to hear that I was there. We enjoyed each other's company and conversation. We naturally flirted a little bit unintentionally. It was just two charismatic people vibin'. I think MJ would be the perfect candidate to test my limits sexually with older men while fulfilling a fantasy of having sex at work. He smelled good and kept himself clean, he wasn't a horny old guy, and he didn't give me dirty -old -man vibes either. If he agreed to it, I knew I wouldn't kiss him because I didn't have that sort of passion for him.

There was a girl at work who definitely thought she was the shit. She had a fat bubble butt and a pretty nice face. Still, every time she came to work, all we would hear about was what one guy would do for her and how much money she expected to receive from other men. I was working two jobs and going to school. I enjoy being an independent black woman. I didn't depend on my boyfriend for anything because he didn't have shit to give. I wasn't yet privy to the understanding that when you are in a relationship, a man should provide things for you or enhance your life in some way. Now, my mom did teach me "if they're not enhancing your life, they're taking away from it." But I have never depended on a man to do anything for me financially, and this is probably due to the fact that there was never a man around who could do something for us financially on a consistent basis.

One day, big booty Judy and I were working together when MJ came to pick up a few orders. I mentioned to him that I wanted to have a bigger backside. That was the first time I had ever heard him, or any other man, tell me I was perfect just the way I was. I have always seemed to seek some type of physical validation for my appearance since elementary school.

The summer was almost over, and it was a slow day at work. MJ came in to get the last batch of deliveries for the day. It was now or never to proposition him for a good time. A big smile lit across my face. It was to the point where I would look forward to him being there just so he could give me compliments and make me feel beautiful, for us to flirt and talk a lot of shit. I guess since we were alone and there with no other witnesses, aka employees around, he decided to tell me how much he wanted to taste me and that when he got back from his last delivery, if I was willing and ready, he would make one of my fantasies come true. He was reading my mind. Sex had been a topic of discussion before, but never with each other. We discussed things that we enjoyed, and how neither of us had yet fulfilled all of our fantasies. Now, I'm not sure what type of woman he usually dates, but I'm pretty sure I was the youngest person on his belt of notches at this time.

I was fresh otherwise, but I knew if he wanted to taste me, I wanted to smell good and taste good—no muss, no fuss, none of it. So I hurried and took a hoe bath in the employee bathroom sink. I locked up the front door. I made sure that the kitchen and everything was clean and all the little pans, pots, bowls, and cutting utensils had been put away. The chocolate was still a little warm, so I grabbed a few strawberries and dipped them in there just in case he wanted to run them around my breasts and lick them off. He took my shirt off, and that's when I knew that this was really gonna happen. The smell of his cologne helped to put my mind at rest. I closed my eyes and pretended I wasn't about to fuck this man, who was twice my age. As he pulled my pants down, there was no objection or worrying. He laid me back on the cold metal table that I had just sanitized, and he began to eat me like a Thanksgiving dinner. His tongue was strong, thick, and wet. He knew right where he needed to be. Usually, I had to lift my hips and rotate Miss Mocha until she was just in the right position for my boyfriend to figure out where I needed him to start before working his way to the middle. But you see, this seasoned, salt-and -pepper beard, with dark lips and crater face of a man clearly had plenty of practice in this area. I was leaning so far back that I just decided to lay all the way down so that I could comfortably enjoy the pleasure of what he was giving me. The intensity of his suction and the moisture of his tongue had Miss Mocha's juices flowin'. I'm sure if we had more time, more space, and a comfortable place, he would've turned me around and eaten me from behind. Maybe that was too much to do on this experimental journey we were on right now. After about, I don't even know how many minutes of shaking, squirming, and moaning passed before he came up for air. He told me to get off the counter, and I proceeded to take my pants fully off because I knew what was coming next. We relocated to the office where I usually sit. Instead, he sat in the chair, so I knew he wanted to see how well my tongue game could please him. After what I had just experienced on the counter, I did my best to showcase my skills. I must have done a good job because I wasn't down there long at all. My jaws didn't even begin to ache before he was ready to feel inside of me.

When his pants came off, I wasn't disappointed in the size. He didn't look or feel old. Although the penetration felt good with my high school sweetheart, 98 percent of the time, I faked the moans and screams to expedite his climax so he could get off me. This was not the case with MJ. I couldn't care less how old he was as he bent me over the black leather chair. I'm sure he didn't think about how old I was either. I wanted him inside of me. This was no longer a tryout for the sugar -daddy experiment. This was me wanting to be pleased, finally! He went deeper as he grabbed the back of my neck. I tried my best to contain the pleasure that I felt so that it didn't moan too loud, just in case somebody came to the door or the boss decided to stop by for whatever reason.

Neither one of us had yet clocked out. We were getting paid to get laid! It was a win-win without the physiological trauma of prostitution. No pun intended. He eventually came and removed the condom. I smiled, pulled up my pants, and went to the bathroom to freshen up. I couldn't believe I just had sex at work with this older man. I was on cloud nine. I would keep this a secret because if I told anybody at the job, it would absolutely get out. The respect for each other continued moving forward, although he did call on several occasions to get me to come out to a bar to hang out with him and possibly have another experience. I respectfully declined. The majority of the time, I was usually busy and couldn't attend these events anyway. We kept it cordial for work, and we continued to flirt and play around with one another. Nothing changed between us, and nobody was the wiser. I was definitely prepared to find myself a sugar daddy when I headed back to school after the summer ended. As long as he looked good enough, smelled good, and was willing to relieve some financial stress, I was convinced I could lay with an older man for my benefit.

Oh, I know that she's disgusted,
cause she's feeling so abused. She gets tired of the
lust, but it's so hard to refuse.

–Elvis Costello

Chapter

9

Fellatio Fraud

N ow that I have gotten my older man experience under my belt, thinking that I'm clever, I went on a site called "SugarDaddy4Me. com" to put my new confidence to the test. I ended up being tricked out of some head by a man in the front seat of his truck. Now that I was back in Alabama, most of the potentials that popped up on the site were white. This man, however, was black, around my complexion, and MJ's size; so I gave him a chance. His location was about thirty minutes from my school. After we exchanged a few messages, we agreed to meet in a public place to feel each other out.

The city of Auburn is a suburban college town with a lot of cute places to shop and eat, so we met there in the parking lot of a burger joint. He was running late, so we didn't go inside to eat because he claimed he had something to do right after. Thinking back on it, this was probably part of his plan all along. I mean, he didn't pay for a damn thing on this day, but he got everything he wanted. We agreed prior to our meet-up that my allowance would be given weekly and that I would see him one or two times a week, depending on his schedule. Although we wouldn't spend much time together the first day, he agreed to give me the $300 I needed to pay my light bill. He told me to follow him to the gas station. I swore I would take this to my grave, but someone out there needs to know that they are worth so much more than what someone is willing to give you for a piece of you. What you gain is far less valuable than what you lose, both consciously and subconsciously. Your self-worth should never be for sale. I wouldn't have been a good prostitute because, even though they get paid to play, psychologically, you truly have to disconnect from your emotions to do that kind of work.

I parked my silver Malibu next to his green Ford F150, and he motioned for me to get into his vehicle. I was much more nervous this time around because, indeed, he was a stranger who could have driven off, and I would never been seen again. I took a picture of his license plate and sent it to my roommate at the time, just in case. He was heavier than my first older encounter, and I wasn't as attracted to him as I was to MJ. But his skin was clear, he smelled good, and I could see he was dressed comfortably as if he were going back home to watch some sports and eat snacks on this Sunday afternoon. I reminded myself, "As long as he was clean cut, smelled good, and had the financial means to help me, his overall physical appearance wasn't much of my concern." I wasn't looking to marry the guy, and I would hope that we wouldn't have to go into public very often anyway. So, as we chatted, he could tell I was nervous, and I smiled and pretended that I wasn't, but I was. I mean, I didn't know this guy from a can of paint, and as the conversation was winding down, he began to insinuate that he wanted to sample the experience, so I told him I was on my cycle and that that wasn't physically possible right now. I lied. He asked me to perform oral on him, and reluctantly, I agreed. I figured he wanted to get something from me since he was supposed to give me $300. I slobbed on his knob for all of five minutes and told him that's all he could get for now until we were in a more comfortable environment, plus he seemed to be in a bit of a hurry. And I was okay with the fact that he didn't want to spend too much time in this car. It was a cloudy day, and it had begun to drizzle a little bit, so I was eager to get back to school so that I didn't have to drive in the rain.

I reminded him that he agreed to give me the money for my light bill as I wiped my mouth and prayed to God that he didn't have herpes or any other STD that I couldn't get rid of. He told me he was going to run into the gas station and grab the money from the ATM. I got out of his car and started up my vehicle. He pulled off as if he were driving toward the gas station door, so I put my car in drive and went in the same direction. Before I knew it, he was speeding past the building as if he were in a NASCAR race! I couldn't believe that this nigga was trying to play me. I called his phone multiple times as I drove as fast as I could to catch him. He weaved in and out of traffic like he was running from the cops. I saw him exit, so I pressed on the gas, trying to keep up with the green truck. Now it was drizzling even harder, so I was being cautious not to get into an accident. By the time I made it to the exit, I didn't know which way to go left or right. I'm calling him and calling him, but it was apparent that I just got played by a trick! I was beyond pissed.

Why couldn't things ever go as planned? Why couldn't I be like all the other pretty little white girls who had older men hounding them down to be their sugar daddy? Here I am in school, trying to provide a better life for myself. All I wanted was a little assistance that my parents were unable to provide. Was it really too much to ask to have a man who would take care of some of my financial needs, who would protect me physically and make me feel loved and appreciated? I was already in a relationship I wasn't happy with, and now I couldn't even find a mutually beneficial arrangement with no strings attached. I was still searching for love and affection in all the wrong places.

*She goes from one addiction to another.
All are ways for her to not feel her
feelings.*

—Ellen Burstyn

Chapter

10

Me and Mary Jane

I kept my mind on my books and my high school sweetheart! I gave up on finding a sugar daddy after that day, of course. He may not be the best boyfriend, but I know he loves me. I wanted to have one of those high school sweetheart stories that resulted in marriage. So I decided to focus on my relationship. Sometimes we make our lives harder than necessary by not listening to our elders. Everyone, including MJ, told me I would outgrow my high school relationship when I went off to college; but I wasn't ready to accept that reality. We had shared so many first-time experiences that it was hard to let him go.

I'll never forget the first time I got high. It was senior ditch day, and everybody was planning to go to the lake. It was a beautiful day. The sun was out, and the breeze was nice. A perfect day to chill at the lake and act as if we were grown. My boyfriend Travelle—we call him TJ for short—decided we should ride with the crew to the beach instead of driving. All eight of us piled up in my home-girl Bubbles' truck for senior ditch day. I believe Bubbles and I were the only females in the van with six other guys. Before we could make it out of the parking lot, everyone, excluding me, pulled out their own blunt. A few guys had two. One for the ride, and one for the beach. If I wanted to partake, there was more than enough weed to go around. Thank God I was sitting in the back seat next to the window because I was fully prepared to let in some fresh air so that I could breathe. I swear, before we even made it to the first red light, I was coughing and gagging because I was breathing in nothing but marijuana. There was not a clear oxygen molecule in sight. As soon as I hit the window to get some fresh air, I was immediately scolded for letting out all of the marijuana smoke. I was then educated on what hot-boxin' was. Letting down the window was out of the question. So I tucked my nose in my shirt and tried my best to breathe in as little marijuana as possible. I've been around this group many times and never caught contact, but today was not one of those days. Sitting in this truck was basically equivalent to wearing a gas mask filled with nothing but weed smoke.

None of my friends attempted to get me to hit the rotating blunts; they all knew I didn't smoke. They didn't judge me for not smoking, and I didn't judge them for doing it. Today was a little different though. Internally, I felt a little peer pressure to partake in the senior festivities. I was the only one not smoking.

"I mean, hell, I had already decided to ditch class like the rest of them. I might as well give it a try, seeing as how I had already caught some contact by now." That was what I said to myself as I continued to cough and gag. I started to feel the effects of the marijuana, so I decided to hit the blunt. This was the beginning of a toxic habit that came along with toxic mates. Until this point, I only saw addiction as alcohol, crack cocaine, heroin …you know, cigarettes and things like that. Things that I knew would take you down a path of destruction. Things that I have seen within my own family, which prevented those that I love from being able to function without their drug of choice. In my head, weed was a different story. By now, in 2009, it was cool to smoke. The biggest pothead, Snoop Dog, was all over the TV. He is the most famous rapper who seems to live well despite his weed use. He wasn't strung out like Whitney Houston and Bobby Brown. Even my neighbors that live a few houses down on my block are smokers. Her brother smokes, and she smokes, and they are cool. Weed didn't have you walking around like a zombie and selling items out of your home to get them. So, to me, it wasn't really a drug, I rationalized. I no longer wanted to be the oddball out all the time. It could be a recreational thing that I took part in when I felt like it.

TJ wasn't the first guy that I dated who smoked. He was actually the second. I remember meeting him my first week in high school. He was in my English class, which was the last class of the day for me. My lunch period was after English, so I was free to go home after English. It was my sophomore year, and I was new to the school. The first few days, he would sit across from me, just staring. Before the first week of the sophomore year ended, he asked for my number as we left the class. "Do you even know my name?" I said. I figured he was only trying to holla at me because I was the new girl and he wanted something from me. I mean, by now, most of us were fifteen or fifteen years old, so I'm sure sex was on every young man's mind. Although he was able to tell me my name, I told him that I wasn't interested because he didn't even know me to be asking for my number.

For the rest of the year, he came to class last, with glassy eyes on the days he did come. He reminded me of one of those semi-rough necks that copied off the smart girls in school, which kept me from giving him the time of day. For two years, his flirting was consistent —I'd give him that. Every time he saw me walking down the hall, he would flash those pearly white teeth, occasionally grabbing my hand and asking me how my day was going. He was the first person ever to call me Oprah while running his fingers through my blowout. He called me Oprah because, to him, I looked sophisticated and intelligent. There was a presence about me that commanded his attention! Apparently, he was the weed king in school. I thought that was quite funny because his appearance said to me that he came from a nice home. He drove a nice car, he had nice clothes, and I highly doubt that his weed sales were providing all of this. A few of the ladies that I made acquaintances with told me that he was a star football player his freshman year before he injured his knee. Prior to him meeting me, he was one of the hot shots. Everybody who was considered a cool kid knew him, which turned me off even more. I had no desire to date an athlete because, on average, they associated with the group of guys who dated mean girls who made judgments and engaged in gossip about those of us who could not afford name brand, fly, fancy, and trendy clothing, like myself.

Although my mom was doing much better financially, I didn't feel the need to ask for things she really couldn't afford. Plus, by now, I appreciated my individuality in fashion and mindset. I didn't find any reason to mingle with the cool kids. They knew of me, and I knew of them b. But I wasn't about to hop, skip, and jump to sit with them at the lunchroom table, if you know what I mean. Even after those two years of constantly seeing him pass by in the hallway with the same emotion, the same excitement, and the same smile every time he saw me as if it were the first time, it was beginning to wear me down. He definitely made me feel desired, yet slightly out of reach. My previous relationship ended drastically and devastatingly about a year and a half prior to senior year, so my desire to be with anyone who didn't treat me or make me feel extraordinary was out of the question. I began to take notice of him more and more. I looked forward to seeing his face after each class was over. I started to take inventory of the fact that I had never seen him date anybody, ever! He still knew next to nothing about me. He knew that I was smart and that I went to class, but that was it.

I finally decided to give him my number. I will never forget the first date he took me on. It was fall, and Halloween was a few days away. I drove over to meet him at his house so I could ride with him. Before he told me where we were going, he asked me to come inside for a second. I had no idea I was about to meet his mom! She was nice, pretty, and tall like him. Their house smelled amazing, like I had just walked into Bath and Body Works. You could tell she had just woken up because she was still in her bathrobe with sleep in her voice as she greeted me and told me she had heard so much about me. She gave him money to make sure that he took me out on a nice date. She told him to be a gentleman.

When we left out the door, he told me he was taking me to Six Flags for the Fright Fest! I was ecstatic! I love roller coasters and carnival games. Six Flags was about an hour's drive from the inner city of Chicago. The last time I had been was in the summer before my freshman year, when my cousin took me after visiting Milwaukee while my mom got us a new place to live. The entire ride there, I was smiling so hard on the inside. He clearly wanted to make a great first impression on the girl he had been wanting for the past two years. This date was not cheap! The tickets to enter the park were about $40 per person, not to mention food, drinks, and gas.

The sun was setting as we walked around the amusement park, and the chilly Chicago breeze was cutting through my sky -blue sweater. He was wearing this purple -and -gold Lakers starter jacket. He saw me shivering and gave me his coat. Oh, baby, he had me! If I had any reservations about dating him, after this date, he had convinced me. When we returned to school the following Monday, it was clear things between us had changed. My home girl, whom I call Hun Bun, caught me giving TJ a peck on the lips as he walked me to my class. From that day forward, the cat was out of the bag that we were a couple.

Senior year rolled by. I didn't judge him for smoking; I just did my own thang. After senior ditch day, I didn't smoke frequently with him, but I did partake during social gatherings. It seemed to excite him, knowing that his good-girl girlfriend, whom nobody really knew, was now a smoker. It made me feel like one of the cool kids in my own way. The night I began to question why I was even smoking weed was after I had smoked beyond my limit in a room full of guys once again. I apparently OD off weed because I puked so hard as if I were drunk. I was smoking to fit in. Because everybody was so shocked that I smoked, it made me feel that much more exclusive when they saw me do it. I enjoyed seeing their reaction each time I reached for the blunts. I was the good girl who did what was right the majority of the time. Now that I did smoke, I was able to spend more time with my high school love. I no longer had to isolate myself or find something else to do when he wanted to partake with his friends. This was a horrible method to get more quality time with him, but I didn't see it that way at the time.

By the time prom rolled around, I was over the relationship. I no longer felt like his princess. I no longer felt like someone special that he desired, who was kind of out of his league. But we were deep into a relationship at this time. He had shared his past hurts, pains, and traumas; and so had I. We were bonded through our pain while trying to figure out how to make one another happy, yet failing miserably. He had become meaner and more focused on being with his friends and being fly than making me feel as special as he did the entire two years he chased me. Because he was not as focused on me, I did everything in my power to show him I was still of value just to spend more time with him, which included smoking more and more. Now it had become my own habit. Not just something I did on occasions with him and friends. Emotionally, things had gotten so bad with us that I found myself needing to smoke weed when we were together to numb the pain of feeling disconnected from my high school sweetheart. To be honest, I didn't even want to go to prom with him, but I felt like I had to.

The big day had come, and it was time to get ready for prom. My dress was custom-made. I just knew I was going to look the part of a princess, so he had no choice but to treat me as such. My mom took me to the mall to have my makeup professionally done. When she finished, I was pleased. My hair was gorgeous. My mom did her best to make sure that this was an awesome experience for me. If only the person taking me to prom cared about making me feel beautiful and desired, it would have been an experience to remember. Instead, it was a nightmare of a day that I was in a hurry to end. When he picked me up with my family, he was too busy rushing me to leave. We barely took any pictures. He was in a hurry to get to his family's house to take pictures, which lasted about an hour compared to the twenty minutes with my family. Once we got to the hotel where the prom was being hosted, his attitude didn't change. I don't remember dancing with him not once at the prom. He was more focused on how good he looked in his suit with his fedora hat. Nothing that I did was right that night. It was clear that I was no longer his trophy. I felt more like his emotional punching bag if anything. He didn't even hold the door for me as I walked into the gas station in my prom dress after we had left prom for the evening. Another guy who was coming in behind me had to hurry up and grab the door for me. It was embarrassing, and I felt lonely. But I wasn't ready yet to let him go. I wanted to make things work, even though I didn't really know where things had gone wrong. By the time I left for college, I had happily become addicted to being desired by men who thought it was cool that I smoked.

*Recognizing patterns is the single most
powerful thing that you can do
to improve your life.*

—Tony Robbins

Chapter

11

Mischievous Muslim

The relationship with my high school sweetheart had run its course. Not one time in those two years did he ever attempt to come down and visit me. Not even for homecoming, which was always during the week of my birthday. I might have been more understanding if he was in school or even working full -time, but he wasn't. He was working sporadically with his dad, doing little jobs here and there. He would make plans but not execute them at all. So after my rendezvous at Edible Arrangements, enduring the self-loathing after my fellatio fraud took place, I really began analyzing whether this relationship was worth trying to save. I wasn't getting the love and affection I wanted, and he absolutely wasn't in the financial position to relieve me of any of my school expenses not handled by my scholarship or parents. Don't get me wrong, I wasn't expecting him to take care of me as if I were his wife or something. But damn, my nigga, you can't send me $30 to get my nails done in two years! No wonder I was yearning for a sugar daddy. It was already bad enough that I had been working at Edible Arrangements since senior year, and he never thought to buy me one, just to make me feel special. Even though he definitely got one for his mom on Mother's Day and her birthday, which I probably made. All these thoughts ran through my mind as I contemplated how to break up with him. You know the saying, "I can do bad all by myself."

Another birthday went by, and there was no gift or visit. By the time Valentine's Day rolled around, I had ended it! I hadn't received a card or a bouquet of flowers—nothing to show me that he was even thinking about me while I was far away doing my best to get an education! When I finally said goodbye to that relationship, I told myself, don't get caught up in the potential of the next person I decide to give my time and attention to. Although I consciously made that decision, subconsciously, I was wounded and wanted to feel loved by someone other than my mom.

I was leaving campus and headed to the gas station to get some gas, vacuum out, and clean my car for the weekend. That's when I met the "oil man." He was dark skinned, with a slender build, and extremely charismatic. I mean, you have to be in order to be an herbal pharmacist. My roommate was riding with me at the time. Now that I had finally left my toxic relationship, I thought I was a relationship guru. Laughing but very serious (LBVS). I tried to give her advice about what I had done in my relationship when I felt I wasn't getting what I deserved, and I told her she should do the same. As we pulled up to the car wash next to the gas station and proceeded to clean out my car, the country boy continued to try to impress my roommate. He was infatuated with her! She was about 210 pounds, five foot nine with hips for days! Not much ass, but the hips gave the illusion of a juicy booty! She was probably a B-cup, to be generous. So she had a nice pear shape. We were both in the military and kept our health up. He did everything he could to flirt and get her attention; but she had eyes for this older guy with three kids, no job, and who was the suspected coke head back in their city.

I encouraged her to get the "oil boy" number. It was clear that he was the neighborhood weed man. I'm sure he had money, and he was overzealous about being her friend. Which translated into him being pretty willing to spend a couple of dollars to get her attention. She wasn't feeling it though, so I knew that I would be able to at the very least, get some free weed and hang out and, you know, just chill. We played cards a couple of times. We went over to his family shop after they closed to have a few drinks. Now we were living off campus, as we were sophomores. We didn't want to have curfews or not be able to have male company over.

I invited him and his brother over to paint! We wanted to liven up the place with a paint party! With liquor, music, and, of course, some weed. On the low, I had been coaching my roommate on how to get what she wanted from the "oil- boy," since her boyfriend wasn't able to do it. By this time, we were on a first-name basis, Mr. Oil Boy, aka Tobias and I. One day, he invited me and my roommate over to play cards again, and she came, but she didn't stay for a long time. I stayed a little bit longer than her. I really wasn't ready to go, and she was rushing home because her boyfriend had been calling her. She was leaving so that she could have a quiet environment to sit on the phone with him when he was finally available. She couldn't see his manipulation and controlling behavior. That night, Tobias and I became more cordial and cooler. Although he was not flirtatious or anything, it was safe to say that we had developed a certain degree of attraction to one another.

He invited me out to the club with him and his crew. My roomie made it very clear to him that she wasn't interested in him. She had a man, and there was nothing that he could do for her besides buy her things and give her money. She said that to him with no finesse at all. I tried to coach her to be smooth with her words so that he would want to do things for her, not for her to demand them of him, knowing that she wouldn't even give him half the attention that any man would want in order to feel obligated to do anything for a woman financially. He met me at our house as I got ready for the night. It was obvious he had a couple of drinks already, so I decided to drive just in case for whatever reason, I wanted to leave early.

The entire time at the club, he kept me close to him. He only wanted me to dance with him, and I knew he was trying to flirt and pretend as if I were his woman, but I wasn't, and I had no interest in him claiming me. The night lasted longer than I expected, and those drinks were stronger than I knew. My head was spinning. He wanted to take a picture with everybody in his crew; and when the lights flashed, I felt uneasy, as if something was about to go down. But I wanted no part in, so we left in a rush. Because I was so heavily intoxicated with my head spinning, I didn't really know where I was, so I decided to let him drive us home. We took this long back road, which ran outside the school limits. I wasn't quite sure how to get home, but I'm sure I could've found my way. But in the state that I was in, I allowed him to drive. When he finally stopped at a gas station close enough to town that I could recognize, I told him I would drive the rest of the way. His homeboys were following us back to my place so that we could all reconvene and talk about the night. Tobias asked to come in to wait for them to pull up. Apparently, they had stopped a while back to get something to eat, so they were no longer right behind us.

While we were waiting for them to come, we both laid down on the bed, drunk but still fully clothed. I had taken off most of my party accessories and shoes. Tobias laid there with everything, including the windbreaker he had on. Before I knew it, I had fallen asleep when I began to feel his arm around me. He was trying to cuddle. I pushed his arm off me and attempted to shake him to wake him up. I didn't want him to think he was about to get lucky. I was not looking to have drunken or sober sex with him. He played the drunken role and asked if he could lay there a bit longer. Since his friends still hadn't made it, I said yes.

The sun rose through my window, and I could feel he was still lying next to me. I slid from the side of the bed and checked the living room for his homeboys. Nobody was there. I peeked through the window and saw they were all sleeping in the car in my driveway. I went to wake Tobias up so he could wake up his friends and leave.

He did everything he could after that night to claim me to the entire neighborhood as his own without being my actual boyfriend. I was looking to make a little extra money. I knew hella people who smoked a lot. Most of those guys flirted with me, and I figured if I copped a pack from him, I could break it down and sell it on my own, which I did. I would call him when I needed to get a little bit more weed. He noticed that I was coming back faster than he expected. He wanted to know what my secret was. It was really just my femininity and knowing the potheads on campus. He admired my hustle, my beauty, and my tenacity. He bragged about me to his friends and his family, and when I came to his parents' shop to get an oil change, he would say t, "This is her t" or "That's the one that I was talking about," as if he had been telling his parents about me. His mom and dad were still together. He belonged to a large family. They had eight children n. None of them really seemed to be doing much with themselves. The majority of them worked at the shop, and a couple of them worked at the school that I went to. All of them smoked, drank, or both. But they seem to all love each other and have each other's backs. That was an anomaly in my neck of the woods.

Tobias's older brother, whom he brought to my paint party, seemed to be the most involved in the family business. I got to know him better because he would bring me breakfast in the morning before school on his way to the shop. Whenever the dad decides to step down, I would assume he will be the one to take over. He was nice. He was older than his brother Tobias by about ten years, so he had a more mature conversation, so we bonded intellectually. He had children and only one baby mama. He was going through some things. For some reason, people just love sharing all of their business with me. They have no shame, no guilt. Somehow I kept attracting broken individuals in need of love and attention. I never thought it was because I was broken myself.

Spring turned into fall, and now I was no longer an independent salesman. Tobias had attached himself to me. I was known by the "locals" as his lady. This was the first time I consented indirectly to be in a situationship. If you are unaware what a situationship is, that's when two people engage in intercourse regularly and spend free time together, yet neither party commits to a monogamous relationship together and it is expected that neither party gets angry if the other has interest or intercourse with someone else. However, this never works. Typically, one of the parties wants more from the arrangement. He would dish out money to me as if he were my weed pimp. He wanted my customers, so he took care of my bills and things I needed so that I didn't have to "hustle," which is how I fell into the mindset of letting him take care of things.

Things became cloudy when he introduced me to a child he said was his. The boy had his entire name but looked nothing like him. But to be fair, he really did bear an uncanny resemblance to his mother, so maybe his genes were just playing hide-and-seek. Interestingly, the strong family genes were pretty consistent and strong. Everyone in his family looked like they came from the same genetic mold. I naturally expected a hint of that resemblance in the little guy. Despite his streetwise demeanor, he seemed keen on projecting a lifestyle that may have been a tad beyond his actual situation.

One day, the house phone rang, and I picked up. It was evident that the caller hadn't anticipated a female voice on the other end. Swiftly establishing my role, I let her know that I was Tobias lady and that she had dialed into my domain. Despite her initial anger, she was insistent on talking to her Baby Daddy. Fast -forward two months, and a DNA test from Walgreens dropped the bomb—no biological ties between them and no shared offspring. It turns out that adorable JR, who's about to hit the two-year mark, wasn't biologically his. Nevertheless, Tobias chose to soldier on, continuing to raise him as his own. I couldn't help but find the whole scenario amusing. Despite being deceived for the first year and a half, Tobias was all in for a lifetime of parenting. It was an unconventional twist that, if my hypothetical son were in a similar spot, I might not necessarily recommend.

All the trips to different suburbs came to a halt for about two months. No more high-quality trees for the low. He had to see different dealers who had weed that he couldn't afford, and if he could afford it, the quality wasn't good. It wasn't enough to be able to make back anything substantial. He was damn near living in my back room now. While he was serving the bud, I was selling plates of food. I aspired to have a food truck one day, and in this type of city, it would do extremely well. Tobias worked himself into my life because I wasn't able to say no. His company and his presence gave me a sense of fulfillment, and by the time, he was living with me. He kept me high so often that my judgment was definitely clouded. I would roll a blunt the night before class, hit it before bed, tap it before and after class, and then again before I went to sleep. This was now my daily routine. My addiction to "bad boys" had now blossomed into a full-fl dged Mary Jane habit!

Part

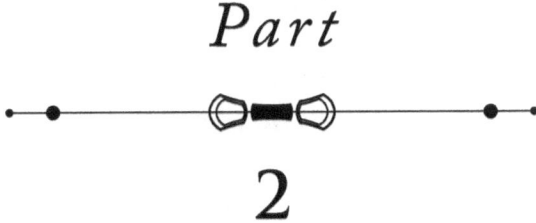

2

Root Cause of the Problem

The absence of a father's love can leave lasting wounds on a child's heart.

—Unknown

Chapter

12

Distant Daddy

I was just about seventeen when I became preoccupied with working on my daddy issues. I wasn't quite sure what that meant besides being angry at him for not being present for the majority of my childhood. One of my earliest memories of time spent with my dad was going to one of his company picnics at the beach. It was a family day, and we all drove down in his work semi-truck. My mom had my hair all pretty with nice ponytails and some awful bangs that I could not stand! My dad seemed to be happy and was always pretty pleasant and talkative around his friends and coworkers. At home, the majority of the time, he and my mom just argued, which turned into him ignoring her and spending time away from home/me. For family fun day, we spent the majority of the day at the beach. It was about a forty-five-minute drive from our home to where the picnic was happening. There was lots of good food, so of course, my dad bragged about being a chef, although he never actually finished culinary school.

A few months later, after the company picnic, Dad was on his way back home from another stint on the road. He drove trucks for JB Hunt at this time, and he did over-the-road trucking, which means he would drive from state to state and would usually be gone for one or two weeks at a time. A funny story: —if he was gone for a really long time, he would usually bring back a pet. On this occasion, my mom and I were in the living room, playing around and watching TV. Dad was in the kitchen, and he told me it was time for bed, but it was in the middle of the day, so I was a little confused. He told me to come to the bathroom, and he was gonna bathe me, and as soon as I approached the tub, I saw these large red creepy crawly animals. At the time, I didn't know that they were lobsters, but he picked me up and proceeded to pretend he was gonna put me in a tub with these weird-looking things with large claws. I screamed, and I kicked, and I screamed, and I begged him to put me down. Of course, he did as he laughed and smiled. I don't know any four-year-old that was eating lobster for dinner. Making high-quality and high-class meals made him feel as though he was one of those chefs in the restaurants downtown where everybody dressed up fancy and lifted their pinky finger whenever they drank something. But yeah, those are the two most prominent memories of my childhood with my father being in my life. He and my mom were together for about three years before I was born, and they were married for a total of seven years before they divorced. They separated when I turned four, so out of my four years of living with my father, I have two distinct happy memories of him. That alone is sad. The rest was filled with crying, yelling, and the slamming of doors. It seemed to me that my dad hated being home. He was always so much happier when he was anywhere but at home with my mom and me.

One fall night —I know it was fall because it was starting to get cold outside and the leaves were changing colors. My mom talked to my dad several times on the phone that day to see what time he would be home and how far he was from the house. He was on the road again, working. So all day, Mom and I cleaned the house. I put all of my toys away. She did my hair really pretty, she made a delicious dinner, and then together we baked him a chocolate cake. It was almost 7:30, and she called to see how close he was because it was approaching my bedtime.

We had candles on the cake, and the lights were turned down low just in case he decided to walk through the door. The table was set with his birthday meal. Mom sat beside me, and I stood on my knees in the chair next to the cake that I helped decorate. She let me blend the ingredients, and once the cake cooled, she even let me put the frosting on. It wasn't perfectly smooth, but it was made with a lot of love! 7:30 turned to 8:30. At 8:30, I told my mom that maybe he hit traffic and couldn't get to a pay phone. Every screech we heard, I just knew it was my dad, and I would run back to the table.

I was waiting to hear him put the key into the door so I could say, "Surprise, happy birthday!" But that never happened. My mom saw the disappointment in my face. She held back her tears every time somebody walked into the building, and it wasn't him. My head and eyes were heavy, so I went ahead and went to bed. In the middle of the night, closer to three in the morning, my mom didn't wake me up to sing "Happy Birthday," but I knew Daddy was home. They were so angry and upset. So I decided to sing the Barney song instead of Happy Birthday.

I love you
You love me.
We're a happy family
With a great big hug and a kiss from me to you
Won't you say, you love me too.

By the time I had finished, my parents were staring at me in disbelief. Love was what was needed at that moment. My mom, who was already crying, put me back in the bed and said that everything would be all right.

The next day, my mom took me to the park at the corner of our block, and we played and laughed. We didn't discuss anything that happened the night before. I'm not sure if she thought I was too young to understand, or maybe she just wanted to make me happy so that I could forget about the sadness that she saw in my eyes the night prior.

Time is an allusion, especially to a toddler. It would seem like only a few short weeks after Dad's birthday that my mom was on the phone ordering a U-Haul and packing up boxes, and of course, Dad was on the road again. The doorbell rang. All of my clothes, stuffed animals, the kitchen dishes, and anything that could break were wrapped in paper and put in boxes that were sealed and labeled. And from the conversations my mom had with her sisters, the relationship between her and my dad was finally over. Although I love both of my parents, I was excited to be leaving. This house was filled with so much pain. I'm not sure if Dad just enjoyed working a lot or if he stayed over the road to avoid being at home. What I do know is that nine times out of ten, whenever he was home, the energy in the house was tense. Mom was either sad, angry, or a combination of both. Dad was in, and then he was out. He was there, and then he wasn't. I didn't understand why we couldn't be like the family on *Family Matters*, a popular TV show that my mom and I often watch together. The mom and dad were home every day; the mom would cook, clean, and make sure the kids were nicely dressed; dinner was on the table; and the father would come home from work every day, interact with his family, and show love to his wife and kids, cracked jokes, smiled, and be happy, but that was not my reality.

I really didn't know where my dad was. We had moved three times in the past five years. Somehow, no matter where we went, my dad found a way to get in contact with us. It was hard to track him down or to keep a phone number where we could reach him. He would always tell me how much he missed and loved me and that he'd be coming to see me soon. Soon was never a definite date. I would sit by the window waiting to see him walk up, and it never happened. My mom scolded him and told him never to tell me that he was coming to see me again and not show up. If he wasn't sure that he was going to make it, just call and talk to me, not promise me things that he couldn't follow through with because she had to watch the disappointment on my face every time, I sat by the window waiting for him to pick me up. The same sadness and disappointment she saw on my face as I sat in that chair, waiting to say "Happy birthday" and have cake.

After that argument, I didn't hear from him for what seemed to be an eternity. Year nine turned into year ten. By now, my mom and I were living back at my grandmother's house. My papa had moved out; and it was just me, my cousin, my mom, and her boyfriend (Tony). Before I had the ability to reach my dad anytime I wanted, he stopped by and apologized for not being there for me over the years and said that he wanted to make it right. He said he would come to pick me up every other weekend so we could spend time with each other. I wanted to get to know him so he could learn more about me and the young lady that

I had grown to be. I was excited to get closer. I finally had a number that I could call him on that actually worked. It rang each time, and if he didn't answer, somebody did and would say they would have him call me as soon as he got there.

The first weekend that my dad promised to pick me up and he actually showed up was it fall time. He had a nice pair of blue jeans on with a suede-looking jacket. He always had a big smile on his face and a toothpick in his mouth. He had a gray Oldsmobile car that smelled like cigarettes and the new car air freshener. The new car air freshener needed to be replaced in order to drown out the cigarette smell. He always pinched my cheek and talked to me as if I were still four years old. I reminded him that I was no longer a little baby. I have grown a lot, and I have my own opinions and different taste buds. On the car ride to his new place, I wondered if he had been living less than twenty minutes away from me this entire time.

Meeting my dad's new girlfriend, Brandy, went well. She was a relatively attractive woman, a little lighter than my mom. When I got to her house, I saw how easily, at home, my dad fit in with her family. How happy and pleasant he was! How much he smiled and how happy he seemed to be. I couldn't help but wonder why he couldn't be that way at home with me and my mom. On the weekends, when I visit my dad, we always stop at Rainbow.

Although it wasn't Macy's or Nike or a luxury type of brand, it was still a step up from having to wear clothes that came from Family Dollar that my mom would buy. I had the chance to experience things at Brandy's house with my dad that I never had a chance to experience at home, primarily because there was no money for those things. Since her daughter was old enough to go to the nail salon to get her eyebrows waxed, I went with them on one occasion and got my eyebrows done. My mom saw them and was furious. When my dad would drop me off at home, he would always give me what he called pocket money, enough to last me throughout the week if I bought a couple of bags of chips or if there was little food in the house and I wanted to get a couple of wings from Harold's Chicken with some French fries. I could do that if I didn't spend it all in one day. So I did my best to make sure that I stretched that $20. I made the mistake of telling my mom that my dad gave me money for my pocket, and when she found out how much, she would conveniently borrow it from time to time, and often, I never got it back. I stopped telling her that I got anything. Anything that I bought with the money my dad gave me, I ate outside of the home, or I didn't let her see me bring it into the home.

Things were getting worse financially at home, and money was very low. My mom was stressed and crying, just sad. I knew that things were pretty rough for us when the lights were shut off multiple times. The water was shut off before in the middle of winter, and they were even coming to shut off the gas. But some of the local addicts had a key to the switch, so in the middle of the night, they would drill a hole in the ground and cut the gas back on so that we could stay warm. On this particular weekend, my dad told me that he wasn't coming to pick me up, that he and Brandy had broken up, and that when he settled into his new place, he would be coming to get me. Well, that weekend turned into about three weekends. Before I knew it, my mom was asking me how I felt about moving with my dad. She told me she needed to go into treatment and get herself together, and she wanted to know how I felt about staying with my father. For the few consistent months that my dad did pick me up when he lived with Miss Brandy, things were pretty good. He was happy, and I actually felt loved. I know I didn't know him very well, but based on my mindset and what he had shown in those few months, I figured we would get close very quickly. I've always wanted to know my father. Things like what makes him laugh and his favorite color. I would love to know anything about his side of my family, his parents, whether or not he had any sisters. I knew of only one brother. I didn't even know my dad's middle name until I turned twenty six. So yeah, I agreed to move in with my dad, to the new place that he had found. According to my mom, where she dropped me off was two blocks away from the apartment that we lived in when she brought me home from the hospital. I thought at that moment, wow, what a coincidence! She said that the area wasn't the best, but it's a relatively quiet neighborhood to me.

We stayed in the basement-floor apartment, which had two bedrooms, a living room, and a kitchen. The bathroom was close to the entrance. My room was right off the front living area. I had a dresser in my room, as well as some toys and clothes that I had brought from my mom's house. I slept on a pallet on the floor almost from the time that I moved in until we moved out. Eventually, we got a couch for the living room, and that became one of the places I slept most nights. Unlike my mom's house, there were no rats or roaches. Everything worked, and it stayed relatively clean. After about two months of living in this basement-floor apartment, I started to notice my dad would come home later and later. We had a house phone at the time, and he would typically call to check in on me and see how I was doing. When he wasn't at home, I would spend most of my time in his room watching his TV, which had cable. When he was home, I would mostly stay in my room or the front room. Things had started to change. I think we stayed in that apartment for less than six months before we moved again.

I was reintroduced to the woman that my dad cheated on my mother with, which was the ultimate straw that ended their marriage. I wasn't aware of this at the time, but my mother told me that I was the one who told her that Daddy took me to see Miss Lauryn. Apparently, my mom knew exactly who Lauryn was. Now, my dad has a baby with Miss Lauryn. Sometimes, Miss Lauryn would come over to the basement apartment to check on me when my dad wasn't at home. She would make food that resembled something like my mom would make: homemade food with love. Something that made me feel warm and comforted. She wasn't the most attractive woman my dad had been with, but she was a good person. She walked a little funny. She talked a little funny. She had these wide hips and a small little head. I was about to turn twelve in two months when my dad told me we would be moving again.

I remember him fixing me a flank steak and eggs for my birthday brunch. There was no cake, no ice cream, and no cupcake. I got a happy birthday hug and a kiss, and I was fine with that, I guess. It was absolutely more than I had gotten from him on so many birthdays before this one. This was also the first birthday I did not hear from my mom. If she was in treatment, they should at least allow her time to call her daughter on her birthday. The call never came, and I was devastated! It was the first time in my entire life that I had not heard from my mom on my birthday.

Food was starting to get short around the house again. It was becoming increasingly similar to living with my mother, minus the affection. I was still sleeping on the floor with no air mattress. Lauryn told my dad that there was a studio apartment available in the building that she lived in since she knew we needed a place to stay. When we finally got there, we were less than five minutes away from my mom's older sister's apartment. The one that we had previously stayed with for a few months when my mom and dad first split. I was excited about the move because I knew I would be staying in the same building with my little brother. Although I had two older siblings that I knew of, I was raised as an only child because I never saw them.

This place, by far, was the worst. People were hanging around on the corner. We parked my dad's gray Oldsmobile in the back alleyway, where all of the other tenants parked their cars. When we walked through the front door, it reminded me of something off New Jack City: how the hallways reeked of urine, cigarettes, and another unidentifiable smell. Winos and crack heads were standing around the steps. Lauryn and her kids stayed on the second floor. We moved in on the fourth floor. When we opened the door, it was all one area. I guess that's what studio meant. There was a full-size fridge next to the stove, a tiny kitchen sink, and a 3-eye stove. All we had room for was to do the dishes. This place reminded me of something out of an Iceberg Slim book. After we got settled in and all the boxes were unloaded, Lauryn told me she would bring Lil Randy upstairs to meet us. Why would my dad allow himself to have another child in the seven years he's been distant from me since he and my mom broke up? I wonder why he was back dating the lady who broke up his marriage between him and my mom. I began to draw conclusions about why we were now in the hood-hood when, less than a year ago, I was visiting him with Miss Brandy. Maybe she found out he was creeping with Miss Lauryn again. Maybe that's what caused their separation.

In the last nine months that I have been living with my dad, I still know next to nothing about him. He didn't talk about having any siblings. He didn't tell me where he had been all these years or why he wasn't in my life. He didn't tell me about his childhood or going to high school. I didn't even know my dad's middle name, but from what I can see, he loved women. He didn't seem to ever have just one at a time. So I'm sure there were some overlapping of women in his life. I didn't know if he liked sports. The only thing that I knew was that he drove a truck, which he had been doing the majority of his life. He was from Kansas City, Kansas. He never talked about how he met my mother. I barely remember him asking me if I needed help with my homework. But I'm starting to see that maybe he just didn't know how to be a dad. Despite the financial hardships my mom and I faced—lights being cut off, water getting disconnected—I always knew she loved me.

She made it a point to tell me she loved me. She hugged me and gave me kisses at night. Even if she had to hand wash my school pants, she would do so that I would have clean clothes to wear. Now I had to fend for myself. My dad went to work before the sun rose. He would wake me up while getting dressed at five in the morning, which was just around the time that I needed to get up and start getting ready for school. The school bus came and picked me up a few blocks away from home, so I had to be out of the house at a certain time to get there. Not only was I responsible for washing my own clothes the majority of the time, but I would also have to wash my dad's clothes. On the weekend, he would give me money to go to the laundry mat. He would drop me off and sometimes start the loads, but never stay there with me to finish them. After laundry, I would cook my meals. He was spending more and more time away from the house, but the money wasn't matching his efforts. I got used to sleeping in his bed, so I didn't have to make a pallet on the floor at night. Apparently, the mice that lived in the building were going inside the apartments to stay warm because they were popping up left and right in our unit.

I started to suspect that my dad had a drug problem. He was exhibiting all of the signs and behaviors of someone on drugs. He was never home and never had any money when he did come home, even though he claimed he was working. He was on edge and angry often. He would lash out and yell at me for just asking a simple question. The day that I got confirmation that my dad was on drugs, it was about eight or nine at night. The news was on, and I was sitting on the floor watching TV. I had no idea what he was talking about when he said that he left a small straw in the bathroom, and it wasn't there anymore.

I hadn't moved anything, but this question also confirmed his drug of choice. I knew that the only ones needing a small straw were heroin and cocaine addicts. I'd seen my dad's head nodding off as he watched the news, absentmindedly picking at the hairs on his face. That's when I started thinking it must've been heroin. It was at this point when I began hoping my mom would come and pick me up. Regardless of the tough living conditions, what I craved was love and nurturing. I yearned for a hug from my dad and to hear that I was beautiful and that everything would be all right. But those words never came.

I was looking forward to enjoying the time we spent together, but instead, I actually felt like a burden. He had never truly been responsible for taking care of someone other than himself. He was failing miserably at both. Winter had turned into spring, and summer vacation was almost right around the corner. I was going to the eighth grade next year. I was so excited to still have good grades despite the many transitions I've had since I left mom's house. I always wanted to make my mom proud. She had been in her treatment program for a while now, and they finally gave her day passes so she could come out for a few hours and visit me. She saw where we were staying, and she knew it wasn't in a good neighborhood. She had to kiss me and tell me how much she loved and missed me and that she was getting herself together. I didn't tell her about his late nights, drug abuse, or his temper. I only wanted her to focus on getting better so I could get out of there. I was tired of him screaming and shouting. I made sure to ask her how long I would be staying with him and when she'd be coming back to get me. She said this program had another step where she could make sure she was strong and ready to stay clean. The next step in the program would also help her get a job. I was excited for my mom! She looks better than she had in a long time! She had weight on her. Her hair had even started to grow. She is the most beautiful woman I know.

About a month before school was scheduled to start back after summer break, my dad sat me down and told me that, financially, things were very tight and that he would more than likely be going to live on one of his friends' couches for a while. Uncle Benni, who was Uncle Pucci's brother, said there was no place for him to bring his daughter. He contacted my aunt, who lives a few minutes away, to see if she could take me for a few months until my mom got out of treatment. Little did I know my Cinderella story was about to get worse. He was about to drop me off n a hell that I had not yet experienced.

While I was living in hell, becoming a real-life version of Cinderella, my dad was staying with his brother in his three-bedroom apartment in the middle of one of the south-side projects. He continued to pick me up every now and again for a weekend visit. It wasn't as consistent as when he lived with Miss Brandy. Maybe once a month, I would see him, and then that came to a halt. It was my final year in elementary school, and the guy I was dating at the time was a freshman in high school. He wanted to take me to his first homecoming game. He picked me up from Dad's new residence during one of the last weekends I stayed over there.

The house was crowded. He had two daughters around my age, so we played hard whenever I came over. I was no longer oblivious to his struggles. Not once did he even apologize for not being in a position to be a better father to me, which left me to wonder why my life was so hard. Why did he seem to be so unhappy? According to my mom, she started out doing drugs recreationally because they didn't know the harmful side effects of them. One day, she looked up, and she had a full-blown habit that was hard to break, especially because she was depressed. She was going through a lot with losing her sister and her mother. She was sad, so she was trying to cope with that sadness with drugs. But what was my dad suppressing? What had him depressed and trying to escape? People have a hard time getting over their addiction because they're suppressing a part of themselves that they don't want to feel, and they don't know how to cope with it. But we never had that conversation.

The next time I heard from my dad again after going to homecoming from his place about four months had passed. It was almost time for my eighth-grade graduation, and I didn't think my dad was going to be around. He did manage to make it to my graduation. He called my name as I walked across the stage, and I nearly broke down inside with excitement! For the past two years, I had bounced from place to place, but as I walked across the stage, that was the first time I actually felt like I had a dad who loved me. He had finally made me a priority despite whatever he was dealing with! That version of him was short -lived, and he almost immediately disappeared for the next two years.

My mom, who was doing well, had gotten a job, and we were living on the outskirts of Chicago in a city called Riverdale. Somehow, someway, my dad found a way to get in touch with my mom two years after graduation. Hurricane Katrina had just hit New Orleans, and he was starting a new job down there and needed a place to crash for a couple of days before he hit the road. I hugged him, but I was reluctant and cold. By this time, I was fifteen, and I had a mind of my own. I figured it was time I told him exactly how I felt about all his disappearing acts through the years. I wanted answers as to why he kept dipping in and not being present for years at a time. Popping back up like everything is okay. I was no longer willing to give him an excuse for his drug addiction or an excuse for him to run away from being a father. Simply picking up the phone and calling to say, "I love you," "I miss you," and "I hope you're doing well," was that too much to ask? He missed so many birthdays that it was ridiculous, as if he didn't remember the day that I came into this world. It was heartbreaking knowing your father knows where you are, what city you live in, and even what school you go to, yet makes no attempt to see you. He doesn't go the extra mile to show his love.

No matter if he never had a dime in his pocket to give me, emotional and mental support would've been more than enough, which I wrote it in a letter, and I gave it to him before he left to go to New Orleans. I was hoping with the deepest part of me that my letter would touch his heart in such a way, even if it were anger, that it would make him angry enough to make a change to be better and to do better.

Now that he was living in New Orleans, I could call him, and he would actually answer. He would even send me money sometimes. I was happy to have communication with my dad, although it still wasn't the father-daughter dynamic that I always sought after. Just knowing that he was okay and doing well, working, and providing for himself made me happy. Although he didn't make it to my high school graduation, when it was time for me to graduate college, he actually made it. It felt so good to have people there who loved me because the rest of my family on my mom's side didn't even attempt to come. To cover up the pain of not having your loved ones celebrate major accomplishments, I told myself that those who were there were supposed to be there. He pulled up to the small town on the street where I live in a semitruck, looking like he was damn near 300 hundred pounds. As he walked up to my apartment, he was chewing on a toothpick per usual. He bought cupcakes for the after party. He smiled and told me how happy and proud he was of me at the celebration after graduation. We all went to a steakhouse and had a nice dinner. As I sat there and refl cted on how far I had come, a few tears dropped.

Not much changed after graduating. He still kept in contact. I found myself giving my dad more advice than I received. I tried to help him improve his health and convince him to stop smoking cigarettes so that he could live longer and hopefully have more time to spend together. By the time I entered my mid 20's, I only expected him to be who he'd always been. I had very little faith in ever being a daddy's girl. All the mistakes I made with men that he could have helped me with, time had passed. I saw more flaws that probably would have prevented me from taking the advice anyway.

I figured I was on my own now with this healing journey. I had corrected the generational curse of poverty. Particularly the stability of having a home. My root chakra was vibrating low due to the instability of going from house to house. So what did I do? I built my first home from the ground up. I picked every door knob, every light fixture, and every addition that was now in this home. It was truly my own. Not only had I graduated with a degree in biology, I then went on to get a nursing degree. I wasn't a disappointment; however, I was unfulfilled. My dad and I were still in pretty consistent contact. I wanted to be there for him. I still wanted to hear something from my dad to make up for all the love and missed time. I needed an explanation; I wanted to know why and it wasn't until I started analyzing the types of men that I had attracted to my life that I realized I was still searching for the love my father never gave me.

There will be so many times you feel like you failed. But in the eyes, ears, and mind of your child, you are a super mom.

—Stephanie Precourt

Chapter

13

Mother Nature

The love of a mother is unmatched. What they say is true: You only get one mother. Regardless of her struggles, I knew I was absolutely angry at my absent father, but a part of me wondered if I resented my mom for choosing such an irresponsible person to have a child with. She was thirty-one when she had me, not a young, naïve teenager. Didn't she know what a good man was by then?! She was the youngest of eight children born to my grandmother. She watched her mother struggle to raise children after moving from Mississippi to Chicago. My mom watched as her older siblings took part in gang violence, street life, prostitution, drug use, teenage pregnancy, running away from home, and even dropping out of school. She vowed to be better since she knew what not to do. She was determined not to become one of the many stereotypes that plagued our family.

Growing up, she had a big Afro that she rocked. Brains, beauty, and booty —my mom had it all. She was probably about 110 pounds until she got pregnant with me. With a small waist and a nice little bubble butt, my mama was the original bad bitch. She had class and swag, and she had a mouth on her that commanded respect. My mom was a hustler too. She worked a part time job while in high school and even hustled a little bit of weed on the side. English was her favorite subject in school; —that's probably where I get my way with words. It didn't surprise me that she was able to use her mouthpiece to sell salt to a snail. Charismatic, for sure—all the attributes you would expect from a Taurus. She was very open with me and honest about how she grew up: seeing her brother being murdered, the pain that her mother went through when her older sister ran away from home, and even the stress she endured when another sister had a baby at fourteen years old. My mama was determined to make something of herself.

Right around the age I am now; twenty-eight, she met the man who would become my dad. When I asked how she and my dad met, the story went something like this. About two blocks over, maybe about three blocks over from my grandma's house, one of her good friends at the time had a homeboy who was a hotshot drug dealer and truck driver. He saw my mom around the way and wanted to be introduced. She declined and said she had better things going on.

One day, he spotted her at the local park getting some exercise in, and he figured the best way to convince her to go out with him was to jog around the park with her. After she finished her laps and he was panting hard right behind her, she agreed to go out with him. I'm assuming subconsciously her biological clock was ticking, and although she had a comfortable life at home with her mother and was making good money, having a family of her own crossed her mind.

They moved in together, and the apartment was made at home. Not too long after that, she found out she was pregnant with me, and my grandmother convinced her to have me because my mom didn't really envision herself having kids. She knew she needed to have a skill and make money, and she had always been into the retail and cosmetic industry. She made herself feel and look beautiful from the inside out, and she wanted to recreate that for others. She enrolled in cosmetology school and graduated valedictorian of her class. Now, with me on the way, she took clients at home to make extra money.

I remember at the same picnic I told you about with my dad, I didn't tell you guys that my mom insisted I have bangs on my head. All my pleading to not have those bangs fell on deaf ears. They made me look funny after a day at the beach. They got wet and shriveled up.

They were hideous. So when we got back from the beach the next day, I cut my bangs off and hid the hair behind the garbage can. I didn't think she was gonna be that upset. My dad came home from work, and he was furious. That's when I got a whooping, after he found the hair behind the garbage. Somehow, my mom was the one that gave me the whopping. My dad scolded her for allowing something like this to happen while he was away at work. Of course, there was lots of yelling and screaming that night.

Many nights have passed the same way. As you know, eventually, they decided to call it quits. One day, boxes were being packed, and the movers loaded them into the truck. My dad wasn't there to help us, but I remember the phone ringing. The last few boxes were unloaded, and it was him. He must've said something awful that upset my mother. The cry she let out was painful, and I have no idea what he said to her. It was then that it occurred to me that we weren't just moving to a different place. We were moving to a place that no longer included Daddy.

Now that I was privy to what divorce looked like, I kept hearing my mom and aunt say that word over and over again. I figured that must be what they were talking about when it came to my mommy and daddy not living in the same house anymore. Now, we were actually living in the house with my aunt, her youngest daughter, and her grandchild was on the way. It was different and uncomfortable in our new environment. I couldn't play too loud. I couldn't move too fast, and I couldn't drink juice in different rooms. I had to be on my P's and Q's all the time as a four-year -old. There was a lot of arguing with my mom and her sister. They didn't always see eye to eye. On the early -morning walks to the bus stop, my mom would tell me that it was me and her against the world. U, usually, with this same cracky, squeaky voice that people have when they're holding back tears and trying to be strong. She promised me she was going to get on her feet and get us our own place so that I could be a kid and have fun and not be yelled at for damn near anything.

I knew my mom didn't wanna live with my aunt, but she had very few options and next to no money. I was going to this day care in this lady's house while my mom went to work. She was an older lady with very little patience. None of it made sense because she was watching kids below the age of five. We weren't yet ready to get our own place, but mom got out of her sister's place with the quickness. We went from a middle-class neighborhood to a trap house. We were now living with her sister who has a son a few years older than me. I was just excited to be around another kid for a change. But little did I know the horrors that awaited me there. It was a much more loving environment, with not as much yelling between the sisters. A lot of laughter found its way to the house, even though we were poorer than before. I was in pre-K now and going to an actual facility for school instead of an angry lady's house. I remember the first time I came home to no hot water. My mom and my aunt made a game out of bath time that night, so it was not so bad. We still had food to eat, and we were living in an even bigger house than the one we had just come from. But it definitely wasn't as nice. The furniture wasn't new, and I wasn't scared the majority of the time to play around the house. I was still blissfully unaware of what my financial troubles were. My basic needs of food, clothing, and shelter were being met. Stability, not so much, but my mother did her best to make sure I had a routine wherever we landed.

My aunt's husband yelled a lot though. He was angry, frustrated, and short-tempered most of the time. He reminded me a lot of my dad. One day, after learning about the life cycle of a chicken, I came home from school, got three or four eggs out of the fridge, and squatted down over them. I was behind a table so I could be inconspicuous. Uncle Hank saw me and was pissed off. He couldn't believe I would do something so stupid and wasteful and said that if I had broken one of those eggs, we would no longer be able to eat it. That was the first time he had yelled at me. My feelings were hurt! I did my best to stay out of his way after that.

Months and months passed, and my mom got a new boyfriend who came to stay with us. He helped her clear out the attic and make it homey. Tommy was nice; he drove trucks like my dad, but he was always friendly and happy and smiled a lot. Just a few months after he stayed with us in the attic, we were finally preparing to move into our own place. These were the longest two years of my life since moving from the home I once knew with my dad. That would soon be a distant memory as I eagerly packed my toys to get ready for our new home. My mom's boyfriend, Tommy, was coming with us. I like it when he's around; he makes everything feel balanced. Sometimes, when emotions get out of hand, he always seems to be cool and level headed and knows the right words to say. He was the total opposite of my dad. He treated me as if I were one of his own children. He was loving and funny, yet stern with me when he needed to be.

Our new place was nice and clean. It was ten times better than where we had just come from. The floor didn't squeak when you walked on it. The water coming out of the pipes was always warm. The paint was new, and the hallway was clean. Less than six months after we moved out of my aunt's house, she transitioned. It was sad. My cousin came to live with us. My mom wasn't going to let her husband raise her sister's son. My cousin Jason was like a true big brother. He explained death in a way that didn't make me feel so sad. We all grieved for months and did our best to continue with life.

Life was getting better for a change. Stacey, my mom, was working downtown for this fancy, hotshot white lawyer. Jason and I would go to Mom's job sometimes when she had to work overtime. The office was huge. It was filled with all different types of offices, decorated in all types of ways. We would try to imagine what they did in those offices during normal business hours. Some people had big balls made of rubber bands on their desks. There were candy land-themed offices. Basketball, White Sox, all different types of themed offices—we will run around going through the cabinets in the break rooms to see what they left behind to eat. Some areas on the floor had so many different office areas we could get a whole meal by the end of Mom's shift.

Tommy was still driving trucks, so we went from having no money to having extra funds. We would go places and do things. We had nice clothes, a lot of food on the table, and love. Just as soon as I was getting excited about having the necessities, everything suddenly changed again. My mom was becoming short -tempered and angry. Now she was sleeping a lot. I didn't know that this was what depression looked like. My sixth birthday came and went, and I was starting to notice a pattern around the house. What was once a loving environment turned into doors slamming, and and name -calling. After all the loud screaming, Tommy would storm out for a couple of hours, come back, and then they would have make-up sex.

Stacey was doing her best not to display her dysfunctional relationship in front of the children she was raising. She did her best to be a good role model and example for doing the right thing. Despite the fact that she wasn't making all the right choices, she tried her best, and we saw that. I guess that is why the nice lady who managed our building let us stay there for so long. Mom was barely home; we assumed she was doing overtime but barely had any money to show for it. We were now being threatened with an eviction. Jason said that was when the sheriffs put you out on the street. That's exactly what happened. I experienced my first eviction. This time, there was no U-Haul truck to take things to a storage facility. We packed our clothes in a few boxes and got on the bus. We headed to Big Mama's house.

After Big Momma passed, her husband, who is an alcoholic, my paw paw, took over the house. He rented out the basement to a stripper. She had two daughters, and they stayed in the basement as well. It was partly finished downstairs. There was a shower, running water, and a toilet; but it was not aesthetically pleasing. It could definitely use some updating. They would cook on a hot plate on top of the washer and dryer. The funny part about this is the stripper tenant and my mom are both named Stacey. But this Stacey was very voluptuous; s. She was high yellow with dark hair. I guess that's what a stripper was supposed to look like in the early 90's. Although there were three rooms upstairs, my paw paw only occupied one room. My mom, Jason, and I were forced to occupy one room as well. My paw paw was a mean drunk who loved some Barry White. I imagine that on the days I would catch him with his Smirnoff vodka in one hand and Barry White blasting in the kitchen, maybe he was missing my grandma. Sometimes, when he got too drunk, he would make us stay in the room. He would go downstairs and turn off the lights, like physically turning off the circuit breaker in that area of the house upstairs where we needed light. He acted as if we were not descendants of the woman who purchased this home. Whether she was still in existence or not, we should at least be treated as if we were welcomed on the premises. But wait there more! We would have to sneak downstairs and turn the lights on. Feeling like a burden was becoming normal in other people's spaces. Sometimes we would come home in the middle of the day, and we would be locked out of the house. Paw Paw would put the deadbolt lock on, which we didn't have the key to. This happened so frequently that we started jumping in and out of the first-story bedroom window we slept in to get in and out of the house.

This went on for months! It was so embarrassing. We literally had to jump in and out of a bedroom window to access the premises on which we claim to live. We had little money to contribute and few resources, which gave us very few options. So the treatment that we got, we had to endure it. Grandma's house was a blast from the past, to say the least. It. I needed some major renovations aesthetically and some renovations done structurally. My big mama moved up here from Mississippi to create a better life. After moving out of the Robert Taylor projects, she purchased this home. Her very own version of *A Raisin in the Sun*, so to speak. She ran a candy store in her front room. Her blue recliner was nestled after the front door and before you got to the candy store. All the options were laid out across the dining -room table. A partition of beads separated the recliner, the front door, and the candy store. The porch was small and had a couple of holes in different steps that sometimes squeaked when you walked up and down it. The pipes would get clogged. There were a lot of other maintenance issues that needed to be addressed. My mom found out that Paw Paw was behind on the taxes for the house. She mustered up the resources to clear the taxes and informed him he was no longer going to treat us like shit while we stayed there. The stripper tenant had to go because our family was going to inhabit the entire house. She made plans to renovate the basement, which was going to be for me and Jason. My mom had big plans and high hopes. Stacey and Paw Paw got into a huge argument that night, and little did she know it was going to be her last argument with him.

In addition to my paw paw being an alcoholic, he also had diabetes. Since we've been living back in Big Momma's house, he has had two seizures because he forgets to eat after excessive drinking. Because he has spent most of his day either sleeping off the liquor or throwing up, so he stayed dehydrated. We had come to learn a lot about how to manage his health. Now that he was having an active seizure on the kitchen floor, we hurried to get him a piece of candy, but that wasn't helping. His eyes began to roll in the back of his head. My mama said that was the first time she had seen him do that. I rushed out of the house to the payphone down the street and called 911. They picked him up and took him away, but he would not return home with us. The doctor said his brain was fried from all the electrical activity during his seizure. Paw Paw was laid to rest. We did our best to help my mom clean the house to make it our own.

Tommy finally moved in with us. I'm not sure where he's been living all these months since we were evicted from the last apartment. Now that my mom had a house, the memories of her mother being there made it extra special for her. We cleaned out most of the furniture that was left behind. The 1970's home decor needed to be updated. We looked all over the south-side for furniture. My mom finally settled on a beige carpet with black and gold chairs. Black -and -gold tables with glass tops. Not only did I start to feel like I had a home. It's starting to look more like home as well. She began remodeling the basement, putting up a wall around the shower. We no longer had to jump in and out of the window to enter the house. I have my own room now that was decorated with a pink wall left over from Big Momma, a full-size bed, and a dresser. All the other things seem to be off to a good start with the house, and life is starting to balance out. Before things could get too good, arguments between my mom and her guy became more frequent again. He would leave for longer periods of time before returning after an argument. I enjoyed having Tommy in our lives, it felt more stable. Honestly, I was afraid that if he left, life would be hard again. As he stormed out of my mom's room and walked through the front door, slamming it behind him, I ran right behind him to plead my case and beg him to stay. That was pretty much the last I saw Tommy. He would come to the house every now and again just to say hi to Jason and me. He would even take us to get Subway sandwiches during his drive-byes.

My mama would get excited every time he stopped by. She still cared for him. I know it, and I'm sure she didn't want him to leave. The pattern of loss was deeply ingrained in me. As soon as the door started slamming, the voices were yelling, the money stopped flowing, I knew hard times and heartache were right around the corner. It was also an indication that the man of the house would soon be departing from our lives. My mom said a man was supposed to be the protector and provider in the house. With Tommy around, typically, the basic needs were met, and even some wants. I hated to see him go.

Unconsciously, I was learning not to fully depend on a man because when things get heated, they can leave at the drop of a dime! I didn't know about compromise or all the intricate details that went into a successful relationship, but what I did know was that when things got tough between my mom and any man, including my dad, it was always the man who left us to fend for ourselves. I believe my mom wanted to be submissive, loved, and protected by the men she chose. But there was something that seemed to go wrong every time. My mom was the only constant in my life. I didn't know whether she was the main problem as to why these men kept leaving our lives or if she contributed to the problem, but one thing was for sure: I never felt abandoned by her. I never questioned her love for me. She made me feel seen and loved. Men, on the other hand, no matter if you bake them cakes for their birthday, cook their food, wash their clothes, keep a clean house, and have sex with them, they will still leave. Consciously, I was yearning for the love of a father while simultaneously subconsciously learning not to trust and depend on them!

Intentionally, we are not taught what the subconscious mind is and how it works. If they taught us that in schools, the propaganda, political atrocities, and demonizing stereotypes would no longer work to control the masses of people, melanated especially. The subconscious mind stores and categorizes everything in your environment, including the things you are not consciously aware of. The feelings I was developing about men were being stored and attached to my conscious beliefs of the same situation that I was aware of. So, while my mom was teaching me to expect a man to love, provide for, and protect me (consciously), the environment I was being raised in showed me that the men who came into my life couldn't be trusted to fully provide for me e. Even if they did love me, there would be fighting and arguing often, and once they decided to leave, I would be left out in the cold to protect myself! Whew! Talk about a catch -22.

It wasn't until my world was blown wide open one day in the basement with my cousin that my childhood struggles made more sense. I was almost ten, and my cousin Jason had just turned thirteen.

We knew how to keep ourselves alive, but I still wanted to know where my mom was. It was almost midnight going into the next day, and she still wasn't home. There was no food or hot meal on the table, and she wasn't there to tuck me into bed that night. Jason asked me where I thought my mom was and why she wasn't there. I didn't really have an answer. He told me that my mom was on drugs and that's why she's never here and that's why we never have any money. I immediately broke down and started crying. He went on to explain that every guy that my mom has dealt with probably has used drugs too, which is why they would fight and argue often. See, he knew his mom was on drugs. I speculate that he had seen her do it before because he was way too knowledgeable about how it all worked. He showed me things around the house that aided them in being able to consume the drugs. I will never forget when he pointed out the ChoyBoy, a Brillo pad used to scrape pots and pans. He told me that they broke off a piece of that and stuffed it in their crack pipe to secure the drug as they smoked it. "This is why the ChoyBoy is always missing." I had so many questions for him. I was overwhelmed with emotions. I didn't know if I should ask my mom about her addiction. I wasn't sure if I would get in trouble, but I needed to hear it from her. I decided to wait until after my tenth birthday, which was right around the corner. Tommy came over to celebrate me turning ten. He even brought cupcakes, chips, and drinks. A few kids from the neighborhood came over to dance, play games, and sing "Happy Birthday."

My birthday passed, and the weather started changing. The Chicago snow was coming. I suspected my mom got a new boo because the same guy comes over a few times a week, and he and my mom always go to the basement for hours. Vergil, the computer man, always had a bag on his shoulder, glasses on his face when he worked, and semiprofessional business clothes on. By springtime, my mom decided she was ready for a new relationship, so he moved in. Come to find out, my cousin Jason was friends with Vergil's son. They went to the same school that was in the neighborhood.

Vergil's ex-wife and kids lived right around the corner from us. I assumed they were divorced because he had been living with us for almost a month now. Little did I know this was going to be one of the most subconsciously damaging relationships I would ever witness. The lessons I learned from watching my mom continue on with this relationship for nearly seven years were by far one of the worst things she did as a mother raising a daughter. What was even worse was, this one never left. She couldn't seem to get rid of the most toxic individual even if she tried. I don't know how my mom viewed it, but his not leaving subconsciously made me think Vergil really cared about us, even if his overall actions didn't display that.

I was getting older now, and I had questions. We have been in Grandma's house for a couple of years, and we have been through harsh winters and long summers, from having money to not having it and then having even less money. By the time I reached eleven, I finally got the courage to ask my mom if she was on drugs. She broke down; looked me in my face; and told me the cold, hard truth. She promised me she was working on getting herself together and this would no longer be her reality soon. She apologized for all I had experienced since she left my father. It has been almost six years now, going on seven. In that time, two men have come and gone in and out of our lives. She apologized for not having money, being taken over by her sickness, and being overcome by sadness and shame. She told me she was going to do better. She was getting a job, and Vergil had a part-time job, so that's how we kept money in the house. She reiterated to me that a man should make sure you always have things like eggs, milk, bread, and meat in the fridge at all times; and she was sorry she had allowed me to go hungry. Her version of what to expect from a man providing for the house had been reduced to the bare necessities because, at this time, she was in such a low place mentally and emotionally. All she could expect from a man financially came from a mindset of lack. What my mother didn't know in that talk was that she was planting a seed that would manifest in my own relationships moving forward.

I could feel the sadness and shame in her voice, and I knew that everything she said had come from a loving place. She didn't want to be on drugs, and she didn't want to take money out of her child's mouth to feed her habit. She was so overwhelmed with sadness, grief, and shame for what her life had become that she had been dealing with the pain in a very unhealthy way. We hugged and cried. I then went on to ask if Vergil was on the same drugs she used. I think she didn't want my perception of him to be tainted by the reality of me knowing the truth. So she lied and told me no. That's when I told her about what happened. Vergil's son Buddah teased me and Jason in front of all of my friends on the block by saying that one of the biggest crackheads on the south-side was living in my house. Immediately, I thought he was talking about my mom. I got defensive until he said, "Tell him to put that in his pipe and smoke it." That was confirmation that he was talking about his dad and not my mom. Her response was that Buddah was mad that his parents had split and wanted to make me feel bad for them being together. Maybe she was hoping that soon she and Vergil would be clean and everything she told me would be true. But it wasn't; and it seemed like every year, around the winter, money would be especially low, food was always low, and yelling was always going on in the house.

A little bit after Easter, Vergil informed us that there was a church that was right across the street from his old home, which he once shared with his ex-wife, and they gave out food and boxes of clothing to those who needed them. It was one box per family, and only people who needed to know knew. The later you would line up, the less chance you had to get a box. First come, first served, until supplies ran out. Canned goods, sweets, and boxed dinners. So we would go up there individually at different times and pretend to be living in different households. They didn't ask for your ID or anything of that nature, and we were too young to have one anyway. Jason and I would say my mom is sleeping or something like that if they asked where our parents were. As always, if we could carry it, they would give it to us. Every Saturday, we would go and get those boxes when they gave them out, and some weeks when they didn't have boxes to give out, those would be some long weeks. They would give us desserts, bread, pastries, and canned food. Sometimes the cake was the last thing we had to eat until the next Saturday, so breakfast consisted of cake, lunch, and anything else we could get our hands on. This went on for a few months. I was happy that my dad had semi resurfaced around this time because he gave me pocket money, which helped bridge the hunger gap. I made the mistake of saying something about the pocket money to Stacey one day and it was taken from me, so I kept it a secret between my dad and me.

Things had been bad for a while now. The only time I seemed to have anything to myself was when I visited my dad on the weekend. It was a much-needed escape from everything I was dealing with on a day-to-day basis. I made sure not to miss any school because if I did, that would be a day of uncertainty as far as meals were concerned. November had rode around again, and Thanksgiving was in a few days. The house was more quiet than normal. The house wasn't giving off holiday season vibes at all. The energy of the house wasn't happy, void of any cheerful emotion.

On days like this, the sun would rise and set, and Stacey and Vergil would only get out of bed to use the bathroom. Vergil was down on his luck he slept just as long as my mom did. Nobody really wanted to get up and face the fact that there was nothing to eat especially on the holiday made to feast, Thanksgiving.

We still had things in the fridge from last week's donation, and I was determined to make a meal. Because it was around the holiday season, they put things like stovetop stuffing, cranberry sauce, macaroni, and cheese all into the box. I'm pretty sure I got my love of cooking from my dad, although my mom is not shy to a good home-cooked southern style meal. I just don't think she enjoys doing it the way my father does. I watch cooking shows on TV with the little white housewives making all the cute little appetizers to take to the neighbor's feast. And I could all but smell it through the television! The thyme, rosemary, nutmeg, and cinnamon. —OMG! We had all these spices in our pantry. So I took what we had and added what I learned; and then, in a little less than four hours, I prepared an entire Thanksgiving meal. We didn't have a turkey, but we did have a chicken. I defrosted it, oiled it, seasoned it up, and baked that sucka at 350 for 1 1/2 two and a half hours, and it came out perfect! The Stove-Top stuffing didn't taste like Big Momma's dressing, of course, but I did the best I could with what I had. My mom had all of Grandma's pretty fine white china, so I cleared off the table in the dining room and set everything up so nicely like the ladies on TV. Then I went and woke my mother up and told her I was having Thanksgiving dinner. She was more than shocked. She was overwhelmed with an array of emotions at that moment, I was sure. She was happy. She was sad that she hadn't done it for me. She was grateful for the beautiful presentation and the love that went into making everything. She was shocked that I was able to do such an elaborate feast on my own. I'm sure she was disappointed that we didn't do it together, and that I have even grown and matured enough to be able to do it on my own, right underneath her nose. She sat down, we said grace, and we began to eat and enjoy quality time. The happiness that I brought to my mom's face, I hadn't seen in a while. It was beginning to be very few and far between when she smiled.

My mother could no longer disguise that her drug abuse was out of control and had definitely not ended. There was drug paraphernalia all over the house. They would stash things in different hidden spots, just in case one of us kids got into one of the other spots. It was not as though we walked around the house looking for it, but it would come up in some of the oddest places. Food was always in scarcity, I reckon, because food stamps would be sold for cash and used for things other than food. Water and gas got cut off every few months, so I knew how to handle it depending on the season.

The summer before my twelfth birthday, I was happy to know that I was joining Jason in Wisconsin to visit our cousins. He had moved there when he graduated from elementary school. He was living with another one of our aunts, the one who had the baby at fourteen. Yeah, her. On different occasions when we visited for the summer, she would take us out to eat sometimes. We would go out for pizza and wings. Our favorite spot was Buffalo Wild Wings (BW3)! I couldn't wait to hear how it had been since he moved. I assumed life was better now that he was no longer subjected to the daily poverty struggles he was use to in our house. Every time we visited our cousins, we would typically do things like go to the park, bowling, or the movies. Life was much more interesting when there was money to do things. I was counting down the days until summer vacation.

One night, while I was waiting for my mom to get home from the gas station after the food stamps hit the card at midnight, I prayed so hard to God to heal my mama from drugs so she could be happy and healthy again and so we wouldn't have to suffer anymore. I asked God to heal her heart so that she wouldn't be sad. To remove the taste of drugs from her mouth. I knew that it was gonna happen, but I just didn't know when. I knew that night I needed to pray and ask for my mom to return to me much better than she had been. So far, I have endured seven years of mental, physical, and emotional trauma. I prayed hard that I wouldn't have to go through another seven years of figuring out from one day to the next if she would be alive, if I would have food or a place to stay, or if I was around people who loved me. As I began to drift off to sleep, she came in to give me some of the snacks that she had gotten from the gas station now that the food stamps were on. A Mr. Goodbar, some Flaming Hot Cheetos, and a pickle were some of my favorites to take to school for lunch. She even had two pieces of chicken and some fries from our favorite spot, Harolds. Even though it was well past midnight, I was happy to have the chicken wings and french fries. I had been snacking on potato chips and saltine crackers all day because we didn't have any real food to eat. I wondered why my mom no longer required Vergil to ensure that there was milk, meat, eggs, cheese, and bread in the fridge, like she said every man should.

It wasn't until I began the journey of retracing my childhood to discover the subconscious programming that was running my attempts at finding a spouse that I realized that my standards and expectations for what I should expect from a man were very low. Having a protector and a provider was never my reality, at least not from a man. My mom protected me and did her best to provide for me, even in the worst of circumstances. But every man she had came and went, and during the duration of their stay, only partial needs were met. Consistency was never the case. Financial support was severely lacking, and emotional support was nonexistent. On the other hand, fighting, yelling, and screaming were in abundance. It has taken me almost two decades to realize that my mom has severely misrepresented her worth and value to these men. Her self-worth was so low due to shame and the bad choices that had impacted her life so drastically, which added to the shame. All the while, my subconscious was storing all this information from my environment.

Summer break was over, and the seventh grade school year had begun. Only a few weeks had passed when my mom came into my room and told me she needed to go to treatment to get herself well. I wasn't aware at the time, but the house was under foreclosure, and we would soon be evicted again. All I knew was that God was answering the prayer I put out a few months ago. That's when she asked me if I wanted to go stay with my dad. I jumped at the chance to finally build a relationship with him, but we now know how that turned out.

The happy family is a myth for many.

—Carolyn Spring

Chapter

14

No Church in a While

I finally found a venue for my party, so the invitations will go out soon. I don't expect my family to come and celebrate with me. From my vantage point, they were still operating from their shadow themselves. My courage, confidence, and persistence offended the parts of them that they never explored. Meanwhile, I was chasing my dreams, hoping not to become stuck like them. My family sees each other as competition. Whether it is subconsciously or consciously, I don't really know. Have you ever heard the saying, "They wish you well, just not better than them?" That's exactly how the maternal side of my family always made me feel. This didn't really become apparent until after my mom got on her feet and stayed on her feet. All while she was suffering from her addiction, they showed pity on me and my cousin Jason by buying little trinkets here and there. They would pick us up for weekends occasionally, and even summer vacations, so we could spend time with other family members. That didn't stop me from hearing the whispers about how bad my mom looked and how she let Big Momma's house get taken. All of the bad things that were going on in our lives seemed to always be the topic of family tea. Not once did I ever hear them congratulate her for the success of pulling herself up by her bootstraps and staying up without mentioning her past in the same sentence. You know how people give you a backhand compliment. It's like they must acknowledge the obvious success, but in order to not feel small in comparison, they throw shade. Not only had she stayed up, she was thriving and even surpassing many of those who had such an easy time with looking down on her from their castle while she was in the trenches.

They would say things like, "Stacey looks soooo good now that she's not on drugs," as if the "on drugs" part of the statement was really necessary. They loved to say how far she's come and how proud they are of her, but not without mentioning how much she's overcome in the same sentence. Guess what, they do the same thing to me. They may never openly admit it, but they aren't truly happy with the progress they have made in their lives. Compared to where we started and where we are now versus where they were when we were in a horrible state and where they are now, we have succeeded leaps and bounds while their progress has been slow, minimal, or nonexistent.

Initially, when my dad dropped me off at my aunt's house, I felt like I was on an episode of the *Jeffersons*. "Moving up to the east side to a deluxe apartment in the sky." I was no longer walking up three flights of stairs with piss-stained carpet with addicts slumped on the side of the building or living in a building attached to a liquor store.

My aunt stayed in a beautiful apartment which, in all honesty, was less than a ten-minute walk from where my father and I were currently staying. Just a few blocks down was a totally different world. This building had glass doors, a clean parking garage, and a parking lot home to cars that didn't look like they belonged in a tow lot or a junkyard. A doorman greeted you when you walked through the glass door, only after being buzzed in by the tenants themselves.

There was a speaker system: you had to dial a number that rang a phone to the apartment that you were trying to gain access to. Once you were buzzed in, the doorman had you sign in and show identification. I felt protected instantly. We took the elevator up to the eleventh floor. I had not been in a building that tall since going to my mom's job when she worked for the lawyer a few years back. The elevator didn't squeak, and it was clean and a smooth ride. If this building was a refl ction of the tenants that inhabited it, I was about to enter into a home that would make me feel safe and loved.

This was the same aunt my mom and I stayed with for a few months after my mom and dad first got divorced. Since then we would only see her once or twice a year for Thanksgiving or Christmas when she picked me and Jason up and sometimes my mom so that we could be around family and have a nice meal. I didn't know much about her, but from the looks of things, life was about to get much easier. Her one-bedroom apartment was clean. It smelled good, and there was art on the walls and statues in the hallway that led to a small kitchen on the left. It had a high bar counter top with a few bar stools along the edge. There was no kitchen table or real dining room area. She didn't need it; it was just her. The kitchen flowed into the living room space, where more artistic, crafty furniture was neatly arranged. The couch was beige, the coffee table had a white base with a glass top. The wall behind the couch had glass mirror panels so you could see the refl ction of the entire apartment when facing it. There was a lot of natural lighting. On the wall across from the panel mirrors was a love seat. It was beautiful. I quietly sat on the love seat, patiently waiting to hear the discussion that my dad was about to have with my aunt.

My dad hadn't exactly told me why we were there, only that he needed some help with me. Since she lived so close, I assumed that's why he was asking for her help. He gave her some sob story about how the job he had been working ended and that he needed to take another job that would cause him to go on the road. Since my mom was still in treatment, he couldn't leave me at home alone for extended periods of time. I knew it was bullshit he was selling, but I didn't care. I was onboard for getting out of the rat-infested, drug infested, urine-smelling apartment building that we stayed in.

I was tired of being verbally and mentally abused and scolded for no reason, all because he couldn't find the tools, he needed to get high. He was trying to save face as to why he needed to dump his responsibility off on my aunt. I knew he was going to live with his so-called brother because we were being evicted from our apartment. Honestly, I didn't care what version of the story he was telling her. I was hoping she was buying it so she would agree to let me stay for a little while until my mom got out of treatment. She agreed. She hugged me and told me that she loved me and that in the next two weeks, I'd be moving in and we could start getting my life back to normal. Once again, I had no idea what was in store for me.

Moving day came; and all I had were two bags of clothes, a few personal items, and my school books. All of which was able to neatly fit in the closet in the hallway. My aunt, Diane, was strict. After I unpacked, she sat me down to give me the rules of her house. I couldn't be on the phone after 9:00 p.m. and had to set my own alarm to get up for school. She showed me where I had to walk to catch the school bus. She explained to me that it was my responsibility to be there on time and that she didn't own a car and wouldn't be able to drive me. The bus stop was about three blocks away. Seeing how it was a fairly decent neighborhood, I wasn't afraid to walk by myself. I won't lie; it would have felt good if at least she went with me for the first couple of days just to give me moral support. You know, to reinforce that she was there for me and not immediately start treating me like I was old enough to take care of myself. She showed me where all the towels were, where we kept the dirty clothes, and what chores I would be responsible for.

Because it was a one-bedroom, I slept on a blow-up mattress in the living room. I wasn't allowed to sleep on her couch. If I chose not to blow up my bed, I had to sleep on a pallet of blankets on the floor. I had two house keys. One that got me into the building, and one that got me into the apartment. She showed me where the storage facilities were in the apartment buildings basement. So once I unpacked all of my clothes, the extra things that I didn't need on a daily basis were put into the storage locker.

About a month into my stay, it was clear to me just exactly who I was living with. My aunt, Diane, is a functioning alcoholic. She went to work and maintained her bills, I assumed, because we always had heat, water, and electricity. But on most days, whether she worked or she didn't, she consumed at least a bottle of wine, if not two. Sometimes, she would buy a box of wine that would last her about three days. She also had a temper, so I did my best to make sure my chores were done every day before she got home from work. Diane barely cooked, and there was almost never any food in the house. Iceberg lettuce and fried chicken wings from the grocery store up the street were typically what we ate on Fridays. Noodles, eggs, and anything else that I could afford for myself were what I ate after school.

I had been living with Aunt Diane for about two months when I heard her on the phone with my mom, discussing how she needed food stamps for me. My mom had applied for them and was going to send the card in the mail so my aunt had food to feed me. That was a part of her frustration, now having to spend her own money more than what she normally would have to feed Stacey's child. Of course, she looked down on my mama because she was now in a position in her life where other people had to take care of her responsibilities (i.e., me, due to my mother's indulgence in drugs). I wonder if my mom was privy to the fact that her sister was every bit of an addict as my mother was. The only difference was that my mom had gotten to a point where she couldn't function without it or take care of herself financially.

One Christmas, four years prior, Diane came to Big Momma's house to pick Jason and me up for dinner at her house. She pulled me to the side and asked me if I ever thought about calling the police on my mother when I knew she was in her bedroom getting high. I told her I had never thought of that. She explained to me that when people have a drug problem, sometimes the only way to help them is for them to go to jail. She said that it might be the only way she gets clean. I couldn't believe what I was hearing. I'm sure her anger and frustration from my mom being in the position that she was in led her to think that jail might be the best option for her. But she never thought to ask or even extend a helping hand in any other way than random acts of kindness on holidays. Maybe she didn't think about what my mother going to prison would do to me mentally and emotionally.

The very next day, after asking me that awful question, we went to church with her; and I witnessed her praise the Lord harder than I had ever seen before. I guess that's what they call catching the Holy Ghost. She told me to pray for my mother. I prayed, and I cried, and I asked God to give Stacey strength. When she dropped us off at home later that Sunday night, I hoped she had prayed just as hard for my mother.

Now that I was living with her, I was able to see her get high off alcohol a couple of times per week, slurring her words so badly that I would get in trouble for not understanding what she was asking of me. All the things that she said and did to my mother came flashing back with anger whenever she would yell at me while drunk. I never saw my mom get high or ever really noticed when she was high. But since alcohol was legal, I had to witness my aunt drink in excess frequently. One weekend night, she woke me up in the middle of the night, accusing me of drinking one of her Jamaica Me Happy Seagram's wine coolers. I had drunk it. I wanted to see what it tasted like. There were six other coolers in the fridge just like it, so the fact that she noticed just one missing after being hung over from the night before was a clear indication of her addiction to alcohol. That same night, I cried myself back to sleep. Wishing, praying, and hoping that my mom would be home soon so I never had to live with anyone else ever again. All I could think about was how this was the same woman who had called the Department of Children and Family Services (DCFS) on my mother, trying some way to get us taken away from her. I guess this was her solution to getting Jason and me out of my mother's custody since she couldn't call the police to arrest my mom as she was getting high. After our conversation, after having Christmas dinner, I think she knew that I would never call the police on my mother, so the next best option in her mind was to call DCFS on us. The DCFS lady was so impressed by how well we were taken care of, how clean the house was, and how happy and healthy the children seemed to be that she went against the policy and told Stacey that it was her own sister that had called and reported her. All of these memories continued to flashback as I laid on the full-size blow-up mattress.

I was thinking about how I was now forced to live with a hypocrite and an alcoholic who hadn't made me feel very welcomed at all up until this point. I was more like Florence, the maid from the Jeffersons without the pay, than a child. Now that she was getting food stamps for me, we had more food in the fridge, but it was really only things that she liked. Cheese, salad, bread, and olive oil. She would buy frozen meat like pot roast, chicken wings, and other things you can make a meal out of to stretch the food. I know what it's like to have food stamps, and the amount of food coming into the house could not have possibly been her spending all of the money to purchase food for the house. By the time we reached the third week of the month, I was back to eating noodles, boiled eggs, and saltine crackers again. One day, her daughter picked us up so that we could go grocery shopping, and that's when I found out that the food stamps were being split between two households. She would give some to her daughter, who lived in the same building with her granddaughter, to help them out. Some nights, when my cousin would make tacos or chili, she would bring us food. I was a child, so who was I to complain about how she spent the food stamps, as long as I didn't have to go hungry.

When the food stamps came the following month, I asked if I could buy lunch, meat, and food that I can make to eat before she got home because I would go hours without eating anything between school and her getting home from work. Most nights she was either too exhausted from work or too drunk to make a meal, so I got really acquainted with iceberg lettuce. All I wanted were a few things I liked and could make while I was home alone for several hours, and you know what happened? I was scolded, and I was told that I was ungrateful in the middle of the grocery store. So that was the last time I opened my mouth up about that.

Now that my mom was out of the detox center, we were able to talk on the phone more frequently. She had made it to a recovery home where she would still be monitored but had more freedom to get approved for weekend passes and search for jobs. I was very excited about the progress she had been making. She had been clean for almost six months now, which is the longest I've known her to be clean since knowing that she was even addicted to anything.

One night after the third grocery -store run, where I was denied anything I possibly wanted, I cried and called my mom once Diane went to sleep. I told my mom exactly what had been going on. Up to this point, I had kept my living conditions secret since leaving her because I didn't want her to worry or stress. I only wanted her to focus on getting well so we could be reunited as soon as possible.

Although I was now in a more structurally secure environment, but mentally and emotionally, it wasn't too much of a difference between living with my dad and living with my aunt Diane. Every weekend, I had to wash her clothes, my clothes, and even her granddaughter's clothes. Sometimes I even had to pick her up from her school down the street from our building. Although I felt like I was doing my part to help out around the house in an attempt to make life easier for me being there, it never seemed to be enough. I now had to wash the dishes, clean the windows and the entire mirror wall, vacuum dust, and make sure that the glass doors to the hallway closet stayed clean. I had to clean the entire apartment, excluding her room. Since she wasn't willing to buy any quick food like sandwiches, lunch meat, and TV dinners; and most nights I had to cook dinner. I learned very quickly not to fry any chicken in her house because she despises the smell of fried foods, so I guess that was the reason why she always bought chicken from the grocery store instead of actually frying it at home.

I did my best to stay on my P's and Q's so I wouldn't upset her. She never said it, but I absolutely felt like I was a guest in the house instead of her niece. All the kids at my school would brag about how much they got for allowance and would invite me out to the movies, bowling, and other preteen activities on the weekend. Most of the time, I was stuck babysitting, so the option to go wasn't there. On the rare occasion that I was free on the weekend, I had no money to go to these places, so I decided to ask for an allowance for my chores. After scolding me and calling her eldest daughter to tell her that I had the audacity to ask for an allowance as if her providing a roof over my head wasn't good enough, her daughter must have said something to convince her that I deserved an allowance. I was about to be twelve years old, and I needed to feel a sense of pride for the work that I did and for keeping good grades. The very next day, after asking for an allowance, Diane told me I would get five dollars a week for my chores. Although I felt as if I had won that battle, $5 a week meant it would take me a month to have enough money to buy bus fare to get to the movie theater, with just enough money to buy a movie ticket, popcorn, and a drink. I took what she offered! It was better than nothing.

I told my mom all of these things, hoping it would speed up the process of her coming to get me. I told her that I felt like Florence from the *Jeffersons*. I told her about how I was forced to babysit my cousins and how no one ever did my hair. No one ever asked me if I needed help with my homework. They just assumed that I knew how to do it.

I felt like I was a burden. Despite the fact I was getting five dollars a week for allowance now, if I bought a pizza puff and fries twice during the week to hold me over until dinner, if dinner was ever made, those five dollars would be gone. So my mom told me the next time she gets drunk and passes out to take the card with the food stamps on it out of her purse and hide it to get some groceries I wanted and store them in the storage. I wasn't sure about that because if she ever went down to the storage room, she would see it, and I would have no explanation. But little did I know that the circumstances of my living situation were about to be the beginning of me becoming an entrepreneur.

I did what my mom told me and stole the food stamp card out of her purse one night, but I had a different plan. Since I had at least four hours of being alone at home before anybody got there. On a day that I knew I didn't have to pick up my younger cousin from school, I didn't get on the school bus that took me home. I stayed after school, and I used my allowance for bus transportation so that I could ride down to the candy store that was about twenty blocks from my school. I only had to take one bus to get there. This was the same candy store my grandma used to take us to when she stocked up on the goodies she sold out of her living room. When I got there, there was a box of flaming hot Cheetos that everybody loved to bring for lunch. Well, for those who brought lunch. And being in the seventh grade, everybody I knew liked those chips. One box had fifty bags in there, and I knew that I could sell them for $.50 each, which would yield me a $25 profit. But where was I going to hide this box of chips? Well, I planned to take all the chips out of the box, put them in a book bag, store them in my locker, and sell them to the other kids as we passed between classes. And that was exactly what I did. But it didn't stop there! I figured if they wanted something salty, they would also want something sweet! I couldn't hide or carry a case of pop or juice, so I decided to make brownies.

I had baked a box of brownies once before at home. It was one of the few things she had in her cabinet that she never made. I took a few of those brownies to school for a few of my friends, and everybody loved them. They were soft and moist, with just enough flake on the top crust. The best part was that I could get two boxes of brownies for just under three dollars. If I sold them for $.50 each, and each box made about twelve brownies, that was another twelve bucks I could make from two boxes of brownies. Two boxes of brownies were something I could afford to buy with my allowance, which wouldn't raise any red flags as to the missing food stamp card.

When I got home that day on the CTA (Chicago Transit Authority) bus with my big box of chips, I hurried up and stashed it in the storage until I left for school the next day. Since no one ever walked me to my bus stop, I had time to leave early and pack the chips into a separate book bag I could take to school without anybody being the wiser. I made my two boxes of brownies and sliced them up evenly, and the next day, I was in business selling chips and brownies to my fellow classmates just so that I could make some money to buy me lunch after school! In retrospect, the Divine Creator of all that is was showing me how to turn lemons into lemonade, a skill many people lack. I wasn't going to complain about my situation and not attempt to fix it! I was a hustler by nature, and since I wasn't being properly nurtured, I took matters into my own hands. After purchasing these items, I cleverly discovered the missing EBT card under some paperwork on her office desk, as if she had just misplaced it rather than trying to slip it back into her purse, knowing that she would notice. It worked! And for the next few months, I would stock up on chips and brownies and sell them to my classmates.

I was now in eighth grade, and picture day was approaching. My mom promised me it was close to us being reunited again. She was now working at the swap meet on the weekend, and she got me some cute outfits for my eighth-grade picture day. And to my surprise, I actually had to ask my cousin who stayed downstairs, who at the time was a licensed and practicing cosmetologist, if she would make my hair pretty for picture day. I guess they assumed I would do it myself, as I had been doing since I moved in. But I wanted it to look nice, fancy, and professional. The night before picture day, she did my hair, and I tried very hard to sleep pretty and not mess it up.

Now that my mom was working, she would give me money, so I didn't have to hustle. But I enjoyed being an entrepreneur. It made me feel good at school that people knew my name and wanted something that I had. I was never particularly lame, but I kept to myself the majority of the time. I had too much shit going on in my head to be the socialite that I could've been. You see, being let down by my dad and other men along my journey, they were not the only people who let me down. My family dropped the ball in that area as well. I seemed to be a burden everywhere I went, even though I required very little. No one had to do my hair; and after a while, they didn't have to cook for me, feed me, or even help me with my homework. The most I required at this point was shelter. That was the one thing I didn't know how to provide for myself yet. I became an independent woman before I became a teenager. I did my best not to think of those things.

I never gave up hope that my family would show me an ounce of love and admiration when I graduated with my first degree in biology from the illustrious Tuskegee University, but I was reminded of how little support I had from my family. Although I had a full-ride scholarship for the four years that I spent there not one person ever asked if I needed a box of cereal or a pack of noodles or if all of my books were covered. I was surrounded by people the same age as me from all walks of life. Some more fortunate, some less fortunate, from every part of the United States you could think of, and even those worse off than me had somebody who would send them care packages. I saw my classmates carrying big boxes from back home filled with foods that they liked. My roommates would get regular Skype calls from parents, aunts, and cousins to check up on their first year of transitioning into college life. As for me, the only person who did that for me was my mom. She made sure she handled anything my scholarship didn't cover. Don't get the wrong impression that I was ungrateful to have a supportive mom, and I hope she knows how much I appreciate her always being in my corner. But to know the same family members who saw the progression and elevation of your life despite the multiple challenges and hardships that you went through without becoming a product of your environment, I thought that they would be happier for my success. Hell, my mother was not the only person I would have liked to talk to about challenges and things I was experiencing in school. But that wasn't my reality.

When it was time for me to graduate, I invited everyone I knew in my family. Every single one of them had a reason as to why they couldndespite the multiple challenges and hardships that you went through without becoming a prnowing that my school was twelve hours away, even if a few of them rented a car, they could've driven three hours a piece, shared at a hotel, or anything of the sort to be there to congratulate me and support me on my accomplishments. One thing my mom always said was that actions speak louder than words. When Stacey promised me she was done with drugs, I believed her because her actions backed it up. So when my family members called to say how proud they were of me, I politely thanked them and swallowed their words with a lump of salt fuck a grain. As my only living uncle would say, "They were giving lip service love," the type of love that was offered without any action backing it up. The type of love that was convenient for them via the phone. I didn't know it then, but the chip on my shoulder was building for all the people who have watched me struggle throughout my mom's addiction, who watched and participated in me being shuffled from house to house while she got herself together. All of the family members who talked bad about my mom's predicament before turning her life around and me excelling past all of their expectations showed me that all that hard work was worth just a phone call. I wasn't buying it!

Now here I am, months before my celebration of life party, and I'm contemplating whether or not I should even extend the invitation to those same family members. Not only did they not make it to my first graduation, which was within driving distance if they really wanted to show up and celebrate my accomplishments, but when it was time for me to graduate with my second degree, Stacey told me not to invite them to that graduation. If they couldn't even rent a car to drive, why would they plan ahead to take off work and spend money to fly to a graduation. Even she knew that was unrealistic for our family, and I'm sure she didn't want to see the sadness fill my face when nobody showed up. Instead, she decided I should create a GoFundMe account for my graduation vacation. One of her coworker's daughters had just moved across the country from the East Coast to the West Coast, and many of their family members wouldn't be able to make it to her graduation either. So her mother created an account so that those who wanted to support her but couldn't be there in person could give a donation so that the graduate would be able to have a nice, enjoyable vacation after graduation. We both thought that was a genius idea. This was convenient, and they could give as much as they could afford. So I sent out a text message that said; "Family and friends, it's that time again! I will be graduating from nursing school, and although your presence is preferred if you're not able to make it, I would greatly appreciate it if you made a donation to my go-fund me account for my graduation vacation!" Oh boy, why did I do that!?

When I sent the message to my aunt Diane, we had been texting back and forth because she wanted to know if there were some deals that I could find her on hotels. Her best friend was paying for them to go on a trip to New York, which just so happened to be the same weekend as my graduation. I told her that I would help her out and that I would find some good deals for her and send them to her the next day. I followed by saying that I hoped she enjoyed her trip, and since she couldn't make it to my graduation, would she be willing to make a donation to my graduation fund? Her response was, "Honey, I'm too broke to pay attention." When I tell you the anger, frustration, and everything else inside me, the unresolved hatred that I had for the way she treated me while living in her house, to the mean cruel things she said to me, and the way she treated my mother during her darkness by calling DCFS on her, all came rushing back to my consciousness. That one statement was the trigger that caused me to verbally release all of the emotions I had suppressed all these years. I couldn't believe she had the audacity to tell me that she wasn't going to make a donation to my graduation fund. A fund that I felt was a very noble and worthy cause. She might as well have said, "PJ, I don't give a fuck about your second graduation. I didn't come to the first one, and I'm not supporting this one." Before I finished typing back my response to that message, she followed up by saying, "I feel that GoFundMe accounts should only be used in dire situations like when somebody dies unexpectedly and they have no money to cover the funeral."

Whew, if I had a mirror to my face as I read her text, I'm sure my face would have been as red as the Chicago Bulls mascot. The Taurus horns of my mother grew with each word that I read. I wanted to rip her a new asshole so eloquently, so I responded by saying, "No problem, Aunty. I hope you enjoy your trip. You are entitled to your opinion of what the GoFundMe platform should be used for. However, it clearly states on the website the different purposes the platform can be and should be used for, such as fundraising for businesses, school projects, and a host of other reasons. Furthermore, if I ever were in a dire situation, I would never expect my family to come through for me. We barely come together and help support one another during times of tragedy now, so I guess it was foolish on my part to expect my family to want to participate in celebrating the accomplishments of someone else." Well, I guess that struck a nerve! Instead of responding to me, which I'm glad she did not, she called up her eldest daughter to tell her what I had said and how she felt disrespected by me. The next thing I knew, my cousin was sending me text messages so long that you had to tap on the message in order for the entire message to appear as if nobody knew how to pick up the phone. If only I still had those messages, I would quote them right now for you. I was told that I was worse than a man panhandling on the street for chump change because I was doing it from the comfort of my own home via the Internet. Asking for donations from someone who doesn't owe me anything. She went on to say that if anyone owed anybody, it was me who owed my aunt for everything that she did for me the year and a half that I lived with her while my mom was getting her life together and that she's a retired woman, and whatever she chooses to do with her time, it's her business. I had no business trying to make her feel bad for not coming to my graduation, which is exactly the opposite of what I was trying to do.

My cousin and I continued our tongue-lashing battle via text message. After about three messages were sent back and forth, I decided to be the bigger person, despite being the youngest, and told her she could call me like a grown-ass woman if she had anything more to say to me. I said what I meant, and not only am I not taking it back, I should've said more. But because I knew that asking for a graduation donation wasn't the atrocity they were making it out to be, I'm keeping it moving, and she can keep whatever dollars she doesn't even have to pay attention to and save it for a rainy day! Because I dono pay attent Not only was I hurt that my own aunt could say such things to me, but for her daughter, the one person in our family who had made an honest living, was beautiful, charismatic, and seemed to have it all besides a man, of course, to further tear me down with her words was devastating. I had admired her while growing up, and subconsciously, I'm sure I wanted to be like her in some ways. And what did she do? She took everything she knew about my past about me living with her mom, and instead of being happy and proud that I turned out to be the type of woman that I am, she used it to degrade me by saying I was worse than someone begging on the side of the street asking for change. All of this was because I was simply asking my family to donate to me. I graduated from college not for the first time but for the second time! *What the fuck is wrong with ya'll!?* I thought. The only person in my maternal family who made a donation to my graduation fund was Jason, the cousin whom I was raised with. So I guess they were all in agreement that a GoFundMe was not appropriate for a graduation!

Everyone's opinions circulated around about how they felt like I shouldn't have created the account and I shouldn't have asked Diane to donate. It was said that anyone who wanted to donate would have without me asking. This conversation was the reason I didn't speak to them for three years.

After burying the hatchet, I tried to reason with the thought that maybe even they didn't know why they didn't want to make a donation. I assumed it was an unconscious envy that prevented them from wanting to celebrate me. I tried to have empathy for them because, in the two and a half years since graduating and working as a nurse, I had built a house from the ground up. I bought a car that was paid off in less than a year and a half, and now I was planning a grand celebration to acknowledge all of my accomplishments. Majority of those relatives who chose not to participate in either graduation were still working at the same job, making the same money, renting the same apartments, or even worse off than they were three years prior. So maybe it was hard for them to be happy for someone else who was excelling, when their life was very much stagnant. This is what I told myself to justify their actions being so sour toward me when all I ever wanted was their approval and admiration. The backstory was necessary to explain why I was so surprised by Diane's response when I asked for a graduation donation.

Somehow, I still wanted them to show me that they were proud of me for succeeding the right way and not succumbing to my environment by becoming a statistic. The more generational curses I broke, the less they cared. We already know they congratulated me with their words, but their actions did not match. I was even made to feel like I shouldn't expect anything more than what was being given. No wonder why I was turning to men, searching for love in the lowest of places. I expected so little from men. What most would call the basics of relationships always seemed large to me because I wasn't getting any unconditional love and support from the people I thought were supposed to love me. My family!

Love is but the discovery of ourselves in others,
and the delight in the recognition.

—Alexander Smith

Chapter

15

Government Cheese

After searching for the answers to my pain and suffering genuinely for over three years now, and with the new information that I am gaining on my spiritual journey, the answers were finally starting to unfold. The God within helped me to realize that what I was calling love was really a manifestation of my insecurities and unresolved childhood trauma. I had mistaken and confused codependency for security and loyalty. While looking back on my life, I was subconsciously groomed at an early age to attract struggle love. Struggle love comes in the form of a relationship where some of your standards are lowered to hold on to companionship in order to not be alone or to supplement the love and compassion you lack internally. Typically, it involves you having to constantly prove your worth and value to an individual, hoping that their actions will reflect how much their mouth says they love and respect you. My dad didn't have much, but when he did come around, the twos and fews he was able to provide were a big deal, while my mama struggled to hold it all together. Anything more than the basic necessities of life I began to view as being "treated well," so it was no surprise my first love, the man I chose to give my virginity to, lived in the projects who also had drug -addicted parents. This was the beginning of me learning how to bond with people who have similar trauma as me. This would be my first trauma bonding friendship turned relationship.

I met Randall at a house party while I was living with Diane. A girl from school who stayed about fifteen minutes from me threw a party for her birthday. Of course, there were people from our school that I knew, but then there were also about five other dudes who appeared to be older than us that we didn't know who didn't attend our school, and Randall was one of them. Apparently, one of the guys he came with was dating one of the girls at her party. I wasn't paying him any attention at all. He was not the most attractive guy to look at. He was big and burly, and he had to be clinically overweight. His face had more acne than I had ever seen before. But he seemed to have a lot of confidence. He was dancing with other girls at the party, cracking jokes, and just being overall outgoing! The birthday girl was trying to hook him up with another girl from our school who was what most would call an outcast. She was just as big as him, just as tall as him, super shy, and insecure about her appearance. It didn't seem like it was a good fit personality-wise, but who was I to judge. Being the sociable person I am, I went up to the crowd of boys I didnas dancing with other girls at the party, cracking jokes, and just being overall outgoing! The birthday girl was trying to hook him up with another girl from our school who was what most would calt we planned with different groups of kids at the school. At one of those events, Randall asked for my number. He wanted some advice on the girl that he was now dating from the party. I agreed and gave him my number. He said he didn't want to let her down, but he wasn't really feeling her vibe, and he didn't have anyone else he could really ask who knew her well. His charisma, confidence, and listening ear, during a time when I felt very much alone in Diane's house was comforting. I still viewed him as a friend, and we didn't cross any lines by even engaging in the thought of dating. Even though his current girlfriend wasn't exactly my friend, we rode the school bus together every day, we had a few classes together, and if anyone tried to bully her and I was around, I would come to her defense. I knew that she was a nice girl, but she had a hard time standing up for herself. We bonded because she knew that I had a good heart and I didn't judge her.

I accepted her for exactly who she was, which was the very trait that was attracting her boyfriend, Randall, to me. For about two months, I would give him relationship advice and tell her little tips and tricks on how to loosen up a little around him so that, hopefully, they wouldn't break up.

Now that she had a boyfriend, she had a different glow on her face and a different stride in her step. Regardless of how she looked or how he looked, he made her feel good, and I wanted that for her. I was not a magician, so I couldn't force him to stay with her. After a few dates, during which her mother attended with them, he was done trying to get to know her. He didn't feel it was worth the hassle. As soon as their relationship ended, he began calling me more. The more he shared with me, and the more comfortable he made me feel to be able to share everything that was going on in my world, the more I became attracted to his heart and caring nature. His lack of physical appeal no longer mattered to me. We were dating for about six months before I was scheduled to move out of Diane's house. Stacey had to leave the halfway house because they only allowed the recovering addicts a certain time to be able to get on their feet, find a job, and find a place to stay. Although my mom was working part-time on the weekends, she had not yet saved up enough money to be able to afford her own place. So when the phone call came, she told me that she was moving into a shelter for a few months to save up a little more money in order to get an apartment for us. I begged her to take me with her! I cried my heart and soul out on that phone and told her that I would rather live with her in a cardboard box than stay at my aunt's house a day longer than I had to! And I meant every word. I didn't mind going from living like the Jeffersons to being in a shelter with her. At least then, I would have peace of mind.

The shelter that we were moving into was divided into two layers. Only men were on the first and second floors, and the women and children were forced to sleep in the basement. The men's shelter had doors, bunk beds, and windows in each room. The basement, where the women and children, stayed reminded me more of what the general population of the county jail looked like on TV. It was one big open space with bunk beds lined up, and there was a security officer who stayed there twenty-four hours a day to make sure that everything was coordinated and nothing was stolen. The few semiprivate rooms that had no doors resembled a janitor's closest in size. There were two twin beds on each side, with no door, and it was reserved on a first -come, first- serve basis for women who had multiple children. We didn't qualify for those first -come, first -serve semiprivate areas where you could at least hang up a sheet to gain some privacy. We had to sleep in the bunk beds in Gen Pop every night. To make matters worse, not only were we sleeping in the basement in an open room with multiple bunk beds; but in order to gain access to the shelter, we had to go to the alley of the church that was riddled with piss, broken bottles, crack pipes, mice, stray dogs, and cats. We had to line up and wait outside until the doors opened to get in. On the other hand, the men had an entrance on the street side, where they walked up steps through a glass door of the same church to get to their sleeping quarters. Never made a lot of sense to me why they didn't swap out the areas that they kept for women and children with the men area. All of this was irrelevant to me; I was just glad to be out of my aunt's house!

The first night that we slept in the shelter, I could see the sadness in Stacy's eyes. Intuitively, I knew she was disappointed that her life's choices led her down a path that led her to bring her child to such a place. I did my best to comfort her because I knew that we would get through it together and come out of this situation stronger and better people than we were before. Since I was living in the shelter now and I was less than six months from graduating eighth grade, my mom didn't see the need to inform the school of our living situation just to get me on the bus route for that area. I'm sure a little shame had to do with that. According to the rules of the shelter, we had to be out at a certain time anyway. Waking up, getting ready for school, and taking public transportation for me to get to school and for my mom to go look for more permanent work was a lot easier for us. Every day, Stacey and I got dressed and rode the same bus until we made it to the train station. Then we rode the same train until I got off to go to school, and she would ride the train downtown to look for work. I would stay after school as long as I could, and we would meet back at the shelter at a given time every single day. This was our routine. Of course, I told my new boyfriend all of this; so he immediately asked his grandma, who he lived with, if I could come over after school until it was time for me to meet my mom back at the shelter. He cared for me and my safety, and it allowed us to spend more time together. I also told Randall that some guys at school were picking on me because I didn't want to date them. They would tease me about my appearance, talking about how long my nose was and how flat my booty was. One of the guys even called me a bitch and said that I wore "cheap" clothes. He was furious that his confidant, and now girlfriend, was being treated this way.

After only a few months of dating this guy who was a year older than me and in high school, he came up to my school with a few of the same guys from the party I met him at, and he started a riot about little ole me by punching the lights out of every boy that I told him had been giving me a hard time! That was the first time any man had come to my defense. Having him in my life made me feel safe. He had already shown me that he cared for my well-being and was willing to fight to defend my honor. He gave me more attention and affection than I had ever had.

Since Randall was a year older than me, he was able to get a summer job. I had graduated from eighth grade, and summer had already begun. Now that school was out, there was no place for me to go in the morning when my mom went job hunting or to the swap meet to work on weekends. Once again, he came to my rescue and asked his grandma if I could come over on the days I had nowhere to go. By now, I had been spending so much time in their house that she figured it was time she met my mom. And when my mom found out that he lived in the projects, she was not at all pleased. She grew up in the projects that were once directly across the street from the elementary school that I had just graduated from. The horror stories and life experiences she went through living in those projects, I'm sure, left a scar on her that might not ever heal completely. But when she met his family, his grandma, auntie, sisters, and brothers, she was comfortable knowing that I was in good hands. They were a loving family! Slightly ratchet definitely loud, with some anger issues, but they loved each other. They kept a clean home and made sure the kids were raised with manners. They were not the average project family demographic, so my mom trusted me to be there and that they would look after me as one of their own. Although my choice of a boyfriend was questioned upon my mom's first seeing him, she understood why I grew to like him so much. He was caring and gentle, patient, and protective over me and she genuinely knew it. So that's where I went most mornings while we lived in the shelter, not to my aunt Diane's or her eldest daughter's house who I had the text message war with years later, who ironically lived less than five blocks from Randall. I honestly wanted to distance myself from my family because they never really made me feel like family. Randall's family welcomed me with open arms. They didn't judge me or make me feel bad about my circumstances. They took me in, fed me, and treated me as if I was one of their own.

My fourteenth birthday was approaching, and the more time we spent together in his home, the more pressure I felt to grow up. My mom always expressed to me that it was better to wait until I knew a man loved me before I gave up my virginity than just to have sex because people I knew may have been doing it. She didn't preach to me about the waiting for marriage thing. I think that's because her first marriage with my father was an epic failure. Therefore, she impressed upon me that the most important thing to consider before I lay down with any man was that they respected, valued, and loved me. Even though I wasn't completely ready to have sex, we were doing some pretty mannish things for our age: fingering me on the train, sucking on my breast, and I will never forget the first time he put his tongue on me between my legs. After I got home that night, well, to the shelter, of course, I had a feeling that I had never experienced before. I wasn't ready for penetration, but if he was willing to put his tongue game to work like that, it was definitely starting to pique my interest what he could do with the rest of me.

Summer was over now, and I had spent the last part of the summer at my cousin's house in Milwaukee, which was an hour and a half drive from Chicago. My mom didn't want to continue to burden Randall's family with watching me every single day now that she was working full-time Monday through Friday for an insurance company and getting her hustle on during the weekends at the swap meet. So she asked my cousin if I could come up there for the rest of the summer. When I left for that trip, Stacey promised me that by the time I returned, we would have our own place. Since our little naughty rendezvous was cut short, Randall and I kept in touch via the telephone while I was gone.

It was now October, and I had moved out of the city. We weren't seeing each other as often, but we were still very much committed to our young puppy-love relationship. I went to visit him one weekend, and now he was living with his grandfather. He was no longer in the projects at his grandmother's house, with no door to his room. He had moved because his granddad's house was much closer to the high school he went to. Lucky for us, his granddad was hardly ever at home. Because he knew I wanted my first time to be special and memorable, he planned this nice romantic, straight out of a Hallmark movie scene for me, and by the time I got off two trains and a bus to get to him, he had the room smelling amazing with real fresh red rose petals all on the floor and bed. Candles were lit even though it was the middle of the day. It was more about the vibe he wanted to create. He wanted me to see how much he cared for me and how special I was to him. I felt like a princess.

I felt loved, I felt seen, and I felt as though he knew exactly what I needed before I said it or knew what I needed myself. The setting was right. The person was right. On October 24, 2004, I decided to give him my virginity as well as my heart. See, he had already pulled at my heartstrings when he literally fought for my respect eight months prior. But this was a deeper level of love that I was feeling for him. It was the moment when I knew that sex would forever be more than just a physical action for me; it had to be tied to something that was more meaningful or special. More deeply connected to my heart than just to please my fl sh. It was the perfect first-time experience, one that I will never forget. He made me feel that he didn't want anything from me except my time, affection, and attention. I don't remember ever having to go into my pocket and pay for anything. It's not like I had any money anyway, or even a way to make any money now that I wasn't hustling in school. He seems to be exactly what my mom hoped I would look for in a man. Someone who would love me, cherish me, provide and protect me. Although we were in our early teens, we had been through and seen more than most thirty-year-olds had at their age. And if you asked us, we knew what love was, and we absolutely loved each other.

Now I know I had grown from dating men who didn't live in the projects or have terrible skin, but they damn sure seemed to always need a little bit of something from me. Not Randall. He never seems to get enough of me! He worshiped me and the ground I walked on. I'll be completely honest: The way he made me feel is what I look for now in the men I choose to date. Most of them have their own place and clear skin these days, but they never worshiped me, and no matter how many times I've tried to get them to catch on to the fact of how I wanted to be treated was how I treated them, that also never happened. The impression that he made on me and the type of love he displayed to me at such an early age definitely created some strong feelings that were now tied to how my ideal man would make me feel.

Consequently, my subconscious had also recorded the fact that the man who brought me the deepest level of happiness and love I had ever felt, also came from poverty and grew up in chaos. So, although, consciously, after growing up more and deciding what I did and did not want from a man, subconsciously, I was programmed to attract a project type of man. Someone, in some way, I felt I needed to fix or accept less than what I truly desired, as long as they were able to give me a piece of love I still wasn't getting from my own father! Whew, child, those were some strong feelings that I needed to let go of. I had to start with forgiving myself for the choices I couldn't change from the past. Then I had to make sure not to repeat those choices in my romantic selections by reprogramming myself, which apparently required me to re-analyze the past on different or what appeared to be different relationships but weren't very diffe ent at all.

Financial instability was the hallmark of most of the men that came into my life. I was attracting people who needed me in this way; so hopefully subconsciously, and sometimes consciously, I thought that if I could be the person who helps them out of a jam, doesn't judge or criticize them and their current situation, then they would love me and never want to leave the person who held them down the way Randall did me while I was at my lowest point! Most of my exes would describe me as a ride -or -die girlfriend, and I was tired of dying. I rode hard for these men in many ways, LOL! But for myself and what I needed, I always sacrificed that for the sake of others, which my mother ingrained in me.

Before I ever knew of all the sacrifices she made for the men in her life, she would tell me countless stories of her mother's sacrifices to ensure her kids were safe and had a good home. To most, that might sound admirable, but when you constantly hear about all the sacrifices made so that you have a safe, loving upbringing, it makes you feel as though they're doing something more than what was expected of a parent. Not to mention my mom being the youngest of my grandmother's eight children, she told me on numerous occasions how she would help her older siblings get off drugs and help with their children. She would go see about one of her sisters or brothers to make sure everything was okay when my grandmother's health didn't allow her to do so herself. So self-sacrifice for those you love has always been imprinted in my head as being honorable and something that is morally right. Now that my awareness is starting to narrow in on the root cause of the problem of multiple failed relationships, I was searching for the solution.

I began to cry and feel all of the suppressed emotions I was now giving permission to be felt. I commanded my body to be released from the pain and trauma. I was ready to call back my energy. The problem is that I didn't know how or have the confidence that I could do it myself. Meanwhile, I'm planning this huge party for my last year in my 20's, the big twenty-nine! Yes, twenty-nine not thirty. I was excited to have a party, even though I had not yet reached the thirty milestones most people celebrate. I didn't want to wait for the marking of a new decade to throw this elaborate celebration because I was celebrating more than just my birth. I had overcome many generational curses up to this point. I was not a teenage mom; and I had not one, but two, bachelor's degrees. I was now a homeowner, which I built from the ground up, with five bedrooms and two and a half baths, which is just shy of 3,000 square feet. I would never have to worry about living in a shelter again. I wasn't a convicted criminal like other members of my family, despite the fact that I sold a little weed back in college. My car was bought and paid for in full in less than two years. For the most part, my root chakra was balanced. If only I could heal the wounds from my daddy issues, I wouldn't be repeating the same mistakes with these men. I knew the things I had accomplished at such an early age, even with multiple odds stacked against me, deserved to be acknowledged, regardless of whether I had totally healed.

Psychological invalidation is one of the most lethal forms of emotional abuse. It kills confidence, creativity, and individuality.

—Madhu Menon

Chapter

16

Subliminal Summers

W hen I departed for Milwaukee for a few months, Stacey said to me, "My Precious Jewel, I promise by the time you come back, we will be at our new home with a fresh start." She loves to call me by my first and middle name when she's making a point. I remember how excited I was to see my cousins. It was finally the escape I needed after two long years of hell while being away from my mom. I was ready to feel some love without all the pain. Life has taken so many turns for the worse, and I wasn't even fourteen yet. But this summer, I was ready to be a kid again. Little did I know that more life lessons were in store. My mom's youngest niece, Tiffany, came to pick me up and I will be staying with her for the summer. I admired my cousin Tiffany. She was the first successful entrepreneur in the family and the youngest. At twenty-five, she was what I considered to be the celebrity of the family. She was married to her high school sweetheart, and they had two kids. She and her husband, Lawrence, each had their own vehicle. They owned the house that they lived in. He had a good job, and she was running a successful business out of her home. From the outside looking in, they had everything that I wanted. She was my inspiration and living proof that regardless of the circumstances you come from, you can make something of yourself and live a nice, happy, healthy life. She seems to be living the life of my dreams.

Her older sister Tammy also lived in Milwaukee. Tammy lived a life more familiar to me. She was a single parent of three, although she was currently married. The rumor around the family was that Tammy's husband had a drug problem. She had food stamps, which meant her fridge stayed full of food. She was more laid-back, she was more on the chunkier side, she wasn't the perfect image of what everyone considered to be a bad bitch. On occasion, I would go over to her house to play with her children and my cousins that I was currently living with for the summer would all go over there. Never once did I hear Tammy tease me about how skinny my legs were or the fact that I didn't have big boobs for a soon to be fourteen-year-old. She just treated me like another kid. Being at her house was fun! When I was there, we played outside until the street lights came on. She lived in the ghetto part of town. The neighborhood was always loud; sirens were a part of the background ambiance. But everybody on the block looked out for each other. When the street lights came on, we had to be in front of the house, and when it was time to come in for the night, we still didnore fve to go to bed. We could play in my cousins' rooms as long as we kept it down. There was less structure at Tammy's house, but I definitely felt more loved there. Their oldest brother, Andrae, was barely around. He was probably too busy pimpin', so I didn't expect to see much of him during my visit. Although nobody ever talked about it, we all knew that's what he did for money. He never had a real job; but he stayed with a woman on his arms, always wearing fly clothing and gold chains, and driving fancy cars! He had the look for sure. Occasionally, he would stop by my cousin Tiffany's house to shoot the shit. I got to see three different ways of living while I was there. Tiffany's house was more like the suburban moving on up in life middle -class household. Her husband was very much into the church, so he made sure we said our grace before every meal. We sat at the table only to eat and washed our dishes afterward. We said our prayers before we went to sleep at night. When the sun rose and Tiffany's business was in full effect, we had to play quietly with the other children. Since I was the oldest child in the house, I was able to help with snack time and put up the books while everyone else took a nap. I never got to see where my cousin Andrae stayed. He was just one of those people you saw passing through. He lived the type of life my mom warned me about. The fast life! It seemed glamorous, he appeared to be fly and cool, but what Stacey always said was, "When you live by the gun, you die by the gun." Not to say he was going around shooting anybody, but I guess that was just a way of saying that the way that you live and the lifestyle that you lead will ultimately be the way you die. I could tell his lifestyle wasn't on the up and up.

I love my family, don't get me wrong! Even though I hoped this vacation would allow me to be a kid again, what actually happened was preparing me more for adulthood. This summer, I was introduced to different lifestyles. The Divine wanted me to see multiple ways the average adult lives based on the choices that they made. Instead of judging them the way so many members of my family had judged my mother, I decided to take the Scorpionic route and observe them, and hopefully extract all the good I saw and leave behind the bad.

As the weeks passed, I found myself having more empathy for Tammy! She never seemed to really lose her cool, but you could tell she was stressed out. She reminded me a lot of my mom. I was about four years older than her oldest child, maybe three, I'm not certain. But what I did know was that although she put on a brave face and held down her household as any mother would, she seemed sad and lonely. Although she had a man in her life, he was doing next to nothing to keep the house running smoothly. He was more of a liability than an asset. My prayer for Tammy that summer was that she would find someone who would love, provide for, and protect her and her kids. So me being the adult child that I was, I offered more assistance to her than I did Tiffany. If Tammy was going to the laundromat, I offered to help her instead of staying with the other kids playing. When she was in the kitchen cooking, I asked if she needed any help, which often times she rejected.

Occasionally, she would send me to the grocery store a few blocks over for something she needed for the meal. Like I said, she reminded me of my mother, so I wanted to do my very best not to cause more anxiety and more stress. I always wondered if the rumors were really true about her husband, because whenever I saw him, he seemed happy and in a good mood. He didn't seem like what your average drug user would look like. And since I have been around multiple, at least four by this time, I expected him to look more like them. I spent as much of my summer vacation at Tammy's house as I could. Being there, I felt more like a kid. I didn't have to worry about whether or not I cleaned up behind someone else, and I didn't have to babysit my younger cousins like I did at Tiffany's house. Most importantly, I felt more loved by Tammy. She didn't make me feel like a burden or remind me subliminally that I was there to give Stacey some time to get her shit together.

Although Tiffany's house was beautiful; and always stayed clean; was in a nice, quiet, peaceful neighborhood, the energy in her house was tense. It's something going on there. She would argue with her husband from time to time, storm out of the house, and be gone for hours as if I wasn't even there. I mean, I know I could play with my cousins, but it's one thing to leave your children with their dad, but I didn't know him at all. This summer was the first time I had met him, but since I was often left to be with him and my younger cousins, we got to know each other pretty quickly. His religious lifestyle, praying and listening to gospel music every time we got in the car, was totally outside of my comfort zone. He did make sure that we had a good time though. We went bowling, we went out for pizza. He did the most he could to make sure that our summer vacation was fun. I didn't really feel the love between the two of them that I had expected from what appeared to be the modern-day Huxtables' household.

The one thing I hated about being at Tiffany's house was I had to go shopping with her and her kids. I think on three different occasions, we went shopping for clothes so that she could get ready for back to school for her kids. We would go to places like Target or Kmart, different places like that, and she would spend hundreds of dollars on them as if they were supposed to have a new outfit for every day of the school year. Each trip, not once did she ever ask if I wanted anything, needed anything, or saw anything that I liked. That really made me feel low. She knew the circumstances of my living situation, she knew we had been living in a shelter. The only reason I was even at her house was so my mom had time to find us a place to live. Tiffany had a thriving business and a husband who also had a good job, and not once did she think to buy me just a few outfits so that when I returned to school, especially now that I was going to be a freshman in high school that I would have some nice clothes to start off the school year with. Now, I know I'm not her responsibility. I know she's not obligated to buy me anything. I'm pretty sure she felt by just coming to get me for the summer that she was doing her part and helping my mother. But just imagine how a child would feel having to watch everyone around them get new clothes, shoes, and toys and nothing was being bought for them. This further added to my little orphan Annie's feeling. It made me feel like just by having me there, her charity was done. Now, remember this is the one I called the celebrity of the family, the one that I looked up to and wanted to be like. The feeling she gave me reminded me a lot of what I experienced at Diane's house.

For once, I was staying with someone who didn't need a few extra dollars. She flaunted that she had money to spare. I just assumed she would throw a couple of dollars my way. I didn't get any allowance or money for watching her kids or helping around the house with her business, and truthfully, I didn't expect it. By this time, I was well aware that when my family did something to help out my mother by taking care of me in any way, that was all that was gonna happen. Most kids I knew got $10 to 20 a month for an allowance, but I would be happy to get just a few outfits. Really, all I wanted was for someone in my family to say, "You're an awesome kid! You've been through a lot in your young life, let me do something a little something extra special so that you know how proud I am of you and all you have accomplished despite the odds being stacked against you." I wanted to be seen. I wanted validation from the people I looked up to and loved. Since I had to grow up so fast, everybody looked at me as a little adult instead of a thirteen-year-old child who needed love and compassion.

Summer was practically over, and my mom called Tiffany to tell her she could bring me home any day. She had finally found a place, and she was getting settled in. School was scheduled to start in about two weeks, so my cousin told me that before she took me home, they were planning a big trip with all the cousins. Tiffany, her two kids, Tammy, her three kids, Andre and his son, Jason, and I were all going to Six

Flags Amusement park. It was going to be like one big family day. This amusement park was halfway between Milwaukee and Chicago, so after we left the amusement park, the plan was to just keep driving and drop me off t home.

This family day was the most fun I had all summer! We got there supper early so that we had more than enough time to get on any ride we wanted to. Since the park had just opened, the lines were short. I like to try the daredevil rides. The rides had big, long, steep drops. The ones that went up really high and twisted and turned, and those lines were really long, so we only got to go on a few of them. Although we were having fun at the amusement park, I consciously made sure not to ask for anything unless it was offered to me. No snacks, treats, toys, nothing as long as it was offered to me. When we pulled up to the park, everybody was supposed to have a Pepsi can, which cut $20 off of the ticket price. I didn't have a Pepsi can. I didn't know I was supposed to have a Pepsi can. I thought the adults were going to handle that part, and the first thing Tiffany said when she realized I was the only one with no can was, "Damn, I'm already paying for everybody's ticket why don't you have a can? You're old enough to know you're supposed to have a can." Maybe I was just too excited about the day that I forgot to bring my can. Either way, that statement made me feel like I couldn't ask for anything extra. She had already mentioned how much she was spending on the tickets. I didn't want to be a financial burden anymore, which started by not having my can. Her kids got cotton candy and dip and dots ice cream, and Tammy and Andre's kids got slushy and chips. So I did my best to stare off and look at other rides I wanted to get on until someone asked me if I wanted anything. The first person to ask me if I wanted anything was my cousin Andrae. So I took the opportunity and got some nachos.

As we walked up to get the nachos, I walked fast ahead of everyone else because I was hungry. My cousins Andrae and Tiffany took that opportunity to tease me by saying I walk like a duck. They went on to say I was knocking knee, with no backside. They got a good laugh at the expense of my thirteen-year-old feelings. I pretended to laugh it off and told them I didn't walk like a duck and some other smart comment that a kid can make without getting in trouble. Emotionally, I was sensitive. I'm sure they meant no harm, but it seemed like I was always the butt of the jokes. Having big breasts, no butt, even though I was only thirteen, was brought up on more than one occasion this summer. All the women in my family have some type of backside, especially my cousin Tiffany. Hers was really wide and round. Tammy, on the other hand, didn't have too much. Some hips, thighs, and definitely a gut. But for some reason, my imperfections were constantly being pointed out. I was the darkest person on my maternal side of the family. Everybody else was lighter than I was. Their hair was longer than mine, and they made sure that they pointed it out so that I knew I was different. I ate nachos in silence and didn't say too much for the majority of the day. I just rode the rides, screamed, and hollered as the rides twisted and turned! I kept it moving, so I could mentally enjoy the rest of the day.

I was super excited to get back home to my mom and to finally see where we would be living. So I tried not to let any of their antics get me down. On the car ride home, we listen to the jams of the late nineties and early two thousands. We laughed about all of the rides and funny stunts we pulled at the park. The energy was light, and love seemed to be in the air. Or at least what I knew love to be. As I drifted off to sleep, I could hear the grown-ups talk just below the music. They were anxious to see what type of place my mom had secured for us. In my opinion, it wasn't because they were so interested in our well-being, but rather to judge if Stacey was actually drug-free or not. I could care less; I knew she was clean. I had no worries as to where we were living as long as we weren't back at the shelter.

As we pulled up to the three-story apartment building, the neighborhood looked quiet, filled with homes like the ones in Tiffany's neighborhood. In fact, we lived in the only apartment building on the block. We were about fifteen minutes outside the city, so I expected not to know anyone. Stacey was so excited for me to return home that she was standing outside waiting as the car pulled up. She gave her niece and nephew hugs and love before they headed back to Milwaukee. She was excited to show me the new two-bedroom apartment. She had my room set up. There was a bed and a dresser in there already. In the living room was a black cloth futon. The kitchen was open. You can still smell the fresh coat of paint in the apartment. There were two doors. One that led to the front door where we had to be buzzed in, sort of reminded me of my Aunt Diane's place, but there was no fancy doorman or anything. Then there was a second door right next to it that led downstairs to the parking lot and the laundry room.

It was perfect! Two bedrooms, one for her, one for me, and a nice open living room area with a decent-sized kitchen. We would be able to prepare meals together. There wasn't a TV in there yet, but that didn't matter. We had a dining room table to eat at, and we had a shower curtain and bathroom decorations. My mom didn't yet have a bed for her room, but she did have a blow-up mattress. She made sure that I came home to a place that felt like home, so she got my room together first. I gave her the biggest hug that I could possibly give her and told her how much I missed her and how beautiful the place looked. We were both happy to be reunited with each other, and as we sat on the floor in the middle of the walkway, we just hugged each other and shared a heartfelt cry! It was one of those cries that didn't need any words. You knew exactly what the other person was feeling. This was definitely a fresh start! Everything that we have been through over the past three years was hard. It took us away from each other multiple times. It had shuffled me to different homes where I wasn't treated with the type of love she gave me. She went through her own struggle with being homeless, while fighting to get herself off drugs. I'm sure for those years that she couldn't hold it together enough to keep us in the same home, she probably felt like a failure. But now life is on the right track again. My mom promised me in the moment as she held me, and we cried that she would never let anything take her away from me again. And she was done with that phase of her life. This apartment was symbolic of that promise. She had been doing everything that she said she would do, so I truly believed her when she said this was our new beginning!

Co-dependency is using a relationship to fill a bottomless void due to not feeling whole and loved as an individual.
It's not the need to be loved that's the issue, it's the inability to love one's self that causes the dysfunction.

—Graham R White

Chapter

17

New Hebrews

The guest list for my ultimate celebration of life extravaganza was in the works and almost complete. I wrote down anyone I knew and had kept in some form of contact with. I wanted this mansion to be packed. I wanted to feel like everyone in the room loved and admired me in some way or another for my confidence, determination, and the success that I had achieved. My mom's ex--boyfriend's son was now a hotshot lawyer in the Big Apple, and he so happened to come across my timeline on Instagram as I was writing my list. So I sent him a message inviting him. If anyone knew what it felt like to overcome hardships in order to create a life that you love, it would be him. His dad, Vergil, was one of the biggest lessons and challenges for my mom. He intensified her struggle with addiction for years, and little did I know now that when she was clean, he would challenge her strengths to stay clean. I, on the other hand, if I hadn't learned what codependency was yet, I was about to have it ingrained in me for the next few years.

The first week in our new apartment was basically spent sharing quality time with my mom. We cooked together. We would go to places like the Goodwill and look for pictures to hang on the walls. We would stay up late and talk about any and everything that was on my mind. Her new job at the insurance company started next week. She had convinced her manager to give her a week off so that she could move into this new apartment and get everything settled before I started back to school. She was excited to have a normal corporate job where she could dress up in her fancy professional clothes with nude stockings and shoes that click-clacked to the pattern of her stride. I was just as excited for her. I was even more excited to be living what I considered a normal life, not living in survival mode. I didn't have to worry if the lights were going to get cut off or if we would have hot water to take a bath. We didn't have much food in the fridge, but I didn't have to worry about whether I was going to eat from one day to the next or if I would have to survive off chips. I no longer had to bake brownies or sell things at school to make money, just to have cash to eat. I didn't have to jump out of a two-story window to get in and out of the apartment; I had a key. I finally felt normal.

My new reality was shattered about a week into my first semester as a freshman in high school. Stacey told me that her boyfriend, Vergil, who she was with prior to our initial separation, was going to be moving in with us. I was angry and afraid for her. I was angry because she said that this was a fresh start, and up until now, she hadn't even mentioned him. I assumed that she was done with him. The last time I saw him was just before I left for Milwaukee a few months prior. On occasions, he would walk us to the shelter's door at night to ensure we were safe. I came to find out he was staying in the same shelter during the time we were there. Stacey never spoke of him as if they were still together.

It appeared to me that they were just two people who cared about each other, but we're now on different paths. The fact that she was letting me know that he was moving in clearly indicated they were still in a full-blown relationship. Although I knew she was clean, I had no faith in him. To be honest, I knew she deserved better. He wasn't the most attractive person, and he wasn't ugly either. Stacey, on the other hand, was gorgeous! She took care of herself much better now. She had nice, clear, even skin tone and sculpted muscular legs. I would say she was a solid B cup with a plump, juicy booty. Her stomach gave no indication that she had ever had a child. Just an overall nice physique. I'm sure there were many men at her new job who would be falling over their feet to get a chance to be with her. So why would she be going back to him? Why was she bringing him back into our lives? Was he even sober? If so, for how long?

I refl cted on the first day I met Vergil. We were still living in Big Momma's house. He was known as the neighborhood computer repair guy. My cousin Jason, who was still living with us at the time, knew his son. The same son who was now a corporate lawyer in New York City. They were around the same age. For a while, I didn't know that he was living in our basement. When I would go downstairs to wash clothes, he would be there. If I couldn't find my mom for hours at a time, all I had to do was check the basement, and there she would be, laid up with Vergil. After his presence was known, life wasn't as hard as it had been, with my mom struggling to provide on her own. He gave my mom money to keep food in the house once our food stamps had run out. He seems to still be working because I would see him come over with his computer bag around four thirty to five 7 o'clock every day for about a month. Sometimes he would bring computers to our house that he had to finish working on. He would even spend time teaching Jason and me about computers. He taught us how to play games on the computer. This was the early 2000s, so not everyone had a computer in their home.

After about three months of seeing Vergil consistently come over after work, Stacey made it quite clear that she had let him move in. Jason confirmed to Vergil's son that he was living with us full -time. He didn't hesitate to let us know that his dad was one of the biggest drug users on the block. It didn't take long for that reality to become quite apparent in our household. The honeymoon phase of Stacey and Vergil had come and gone quickly, and now money was becoming more scarce. I saw him leave to go to work less and less. I was in denial at this time that my mom was on drugs. But even that perception didn't last for too long. Money was so nonexistent at times that we would have to eat things like white rice and peas as a complete meal.

A year after he entered our lives, my mom was full-blown hooked on him and crack. No job, no car. Sometimes, no hot water and no house phone. No cable. Literally, the bare minimum. He was no longer the man who came in and saved the day, provided us with food, and helped out with bills, which contributed to our shelter. He was now the biggest liability, and even though my mom had been on drugs up until this point, when he entered our lives, our living situation was never this bad for this long. She always managed to hold down some type of employment. We always had some type of food to eat each night. I never saw her as small as she was or as stressed as she was. Even her hair had started to fall out. I knew she was stressed, and he didn't seem to provide any relief. During the years that he had been living with us, our lives completely turned upside down. The only thing that he had left to offer was to introduce us to the Hebrew Israelite's faith.

He would have my mom pray with him and read the Bible as if anything in that book was gonna save us from being on the streets or hungry. Well, I came to find out it did sort of save us. He had been a part of this church for a long time. He did computer work and IT work for the church. Now that the internet was a very popular piece of technology, he hooked up the church to the internet for live broadcasts, which brought in some revenue. Now that he was participating in the church again, he was at least clear-headed enough most Saturdays to ensure my mom and I attended church with him. Every couple of months, they seemed to always have some type of feast, so at least we ate well, and because they knew he was down on his luck, we would always go home with pans of food. My mom seemed happier to have what somewhat felt like a family life. She had a man who was taking on the role of trying to be a provider. He tried to show her a better way of living and even introduced her to a different form of Christianity that he professes to be the real form that we should be living by. Although my mom had given up pork in her early twenties, Vergil was the first person to let us know all the things that we currently consumed that contained pork. Our diets slowly begin to change according to the dietary laws The Israel of God taught about. I think I had to be ten going on eleven at the time when church was becoming a part of my weekly routine. It kind of felt good to have somewhere to belong to.

By the time their relationship was two years, in, our life had completely fallen apart. So much so that I had to go live with my dad. I wasn't aware that the house was going into foreclosure and that we had to be out immediately. All I knew was that our living circumstances had gotten so bad that she could no longer fix the situation on her own.

For the next year and a half, I shuffled between my dad and my aunt, and while that was happening, my mom told me that they were living in abandoned buildings. So, once again, why was she allowing him to be a part of our fresh start? Why had she not let that chapter of her life close? When she told me that he was moving in, those were some of the exact questions I asked her. I reminded her of all of the hardships we went through with him being in our lives. She explained how he never left her in her time of need. When they had to leave Big Momma's house, his parents offered him a way out. But instead, he rode the bus with my mom to the treatment center when she finally decided enough was enough. Subconsciously, she felt like she owed him and wanted to help him get on his feet. She loved him and wanted to believe he was ready for a change.

When he first moved back with us, I'll be honest, I was irritated and annoyed just by the sight of him. His laugh irritated me. The little nickname he called me annoyed me. I put on my bravest face and my fakest smile to get through the disappointment I felt from him being there.

Over the next six months, my mom worked overtime to get ahead, and he did not get one job. He had a few computer clients, but which it barely made a dent in the bills with the income he could contribute. I could tell my mom was becoming more frustrated, irritable, and short-tempered. I'm sure she was wondering why the fuck he just couldn't get his ass up and get a regular job and fix computers on the side. If she wasn't, I damn sure was thinking it! Stacey would go to work Monday through Friday and most Saturdays as well. So by the time Sunday came, she didn't have much energy to spend time, laugh, play, or have fun with me. She was smoking more cigarettes a day than I had ever seen, and I wished like hell that she would stop. Those things smell horrible, and they were bad for you, and I knew that her increase in intake was due to the stress that she wasn't able to express because her boyfriend wasn't holding up his end of the deal.

The icing on the cake of this uncomfortable situation was when I watched my mom put his needs before hers and mine. We hadn't even been living in our new apartment a year before his sons moved in. I was unaware of the exact circumstances going on with their mom at the time, which led to them coming to stay with us. It was never fully explained either. I guess that was outside of the parameters of a child's place. All I knew was my mom was about to take on two more mouths to feed because their dad was bringing in next to nothing because he didn't have a regular job. He, at least, had food stamps. So maybe he was going to put them on his food stamp case to ensure that we had enough food in the house. But this entire situation made me even more furious with him and with my mom too, if I'm being honest. We were barely making ends meet now, so why in the fuck would she allow his children to move in with us. Vergil wasn't holding his weight, and he wasn't paying half of the rent. Hell, I don't know if he ever paid any bills, and if he did, it wasn't nearly enough. Yet Stacey sacrificed her comfort and mine all in the name of love.

By the time they moved in, Vergil still had no job. This was yet another real-time lesson in learning to put the needs of others ahead of myself and against my better judgment. He started to come home later and later, selling the story that he was out looking for jobs or had a client that took a long time to complete. Three months after his sons moved in, his addiction secret slipped out. He came home so late without a single phone call throughout the day to let my mom know that whatever project he was working on was taking a long time. So she knew it wasn't a computer job that kept them out. She knew what he was up to. That night they argued for a very long time.

Over the next six months, he disappeared multiple times. And now that my mom had a car, he would disappear with that. It was beginning to happen so frequently that his son told my mom that when this type of thing happened when he was living with them and their mom that he would go up to the train station and solicit himself as a taxi and take people to their destinations for a little bit of nothing to fuel his drug habit. So my mom asked one of the neighbors to take her up to the train station so that she could sit and scope out whether or not he was actually trying to solicit customers in her car. Lo and behold, each and every time she went up to that station, she found him in her car. Somehow or another, she forgave him and brought him back to our house.

On one occasion, it was raining, and she went up to the train station, but she didn't see him. That was the first time Vergil stayed gone an entire day. All the children in the house were old enough to know exactly what was happening, and he couldn't lie out of this one. The shame on his face each time he returned was pitiful. He didn't know what to say to us besides he was sorry. By the third time that he had stolen my mom's car and went out on a drug binge, I was starting to get nervous that all the stress would cause her to relapse. After that last disappearance, when he stayed gone an entire day, Stacey demanded that Vergil go to rehab, or he would have to leave her home. I was happy that she was finally stepping up and demanding that he get himself together instead of making excuses as to why he had taken a turn down this path in the first place. For all I know, he had never gotten clean and had just been able to hide it pretty well.

With all of the tension brewing in my home, it was easy to fall into the hands of my very own bad boy. His name was Little Man, and I kept him a secret for about five months. It was eating me up inside because I didn't want to cause my mom any more stress than she was already going through. So I asked my mom for permission to date him.

Four months after my sixteenth birthday, the unthinkable happened, which I thought would have absolutely been the final straw to break up the relationship between my mom and Vergil. I spent the day with my mom. It was a Saturday, and she decided to work some overtime. She told me to meet her downtown at her job, and we would have lunch. After lunch, we would spend some time together and hang out for a little while. She planned to show me around downtown in the different buildings and places where she used to work. We rode the Metra train since we no longer lived in the city. The Metra was a train that took us from our home into the city and downtown. When we got back from our mother -daughter day, which was absolutely needed, we found that the car that she had just bought me for my sixteenth birthday was not parked in the lot. For a second, we thought it might be stolen, so Stacey asked the neighbor who lived upstairs if he had seen a tow truck or if he knew what happened to the car. He hadn't seen any tow truck and hadn't heard anybody break into the car. Immediately, we knew exactly where it was and who had it. We waited until later that evening and drove up to the train station that we had been to so many times before.

There he was like clockwork, soliciting rides to junkies or whoever would give him the time of day to be their cabbie for a few dollars.

We pulled up on the side of him, and my mom jumped out furious, horns raging. She demanded he get out of my car, which, instead of smelling like the peach air freshener that I hung on the rear-view mirror, smelled like cigarettes and alcohol. Why she let him ride back in the car with her, I have no idea. I would've left him right where he stood, looking stupid, confused, and high as he was.

The next day, when I woke up, my mom had already left for work. Her car was parked at the Metra station a few blocks up the road, and my keys were now in my room because he couldn't be trusted. This temporary solution to the bigger issue further solidified in my subconscious that when a woman loves a man, no matter how toxic his presence is in her life, she should try everything humanly possible to fix him and hold on to the relationship rather than walking away and starting over. Consciously, I knew I never wanted to be with a man I could not trust. I thought I was learning from the mistakes my mom had made. However, I wasn't yet privy to how the brain truly works and the enormous role the subconscious had on the reality I would magnetize to myself!

When I finally came out of my room, it was just him and me in the house. With tears in his eyes, he apologized for taking my car. He told me he knew what he did was wrong and it would never happen again. Surprisingly, I actually felt empathy for him despite never wanting him there to begin with. The thing about addiction is that if the root causes aren't addressed, anything could trigger the need to escape reality. After he took my car, my mom finally sat me down and apologized for allowing him to continue to be a part of our lives. She confessed that she wasn't being a good example for allowing the wrong type of man to influence my perspective on what love looks like. She promised me she was going to make him leave. All I wanted was to see her happy with someone who deserved her loyalty.

By now, Stacey had over three years of sobriety under her belt, and she desperately wanted to save the man she loved, who was there for her in her time of need. Witnessing the toxicity of this relationship and hearing the explanation as to why my mom allowed it to continue for so long had permanently ingrained in me to put the needs of others ahead of my own. Especially if choosing to do what's best for me would cause the other party to leave my life. The fear of abandonment, self-sacrifice, and sabotage was now intertwined with the meaning of love. Little did I know I was getting ready to repeat my mom's entire relationship in my very own teenage way. Talk about the power of the subconscious mind, huh?

You will continue to repeat the mistakes of your parents, until you realize that the broken parts in you are a reflection of the unhealed traumas in them.

—TaRah Tales

Chapter

18

Baby Momma Drama

T he suburbs were finally starting to feel like home. I had made a few friends, so I didn't feel the need to rush to the city every weekend. My current boyfriend, Randall, who no longer lived in the projects and was now staying at his grandpa's house even further from the city, was growing increasingly annoying and jealous for no reason. He felt that if I wasn't coming to the city to spend time with him, I should be at home on the phone with him all day. His controlling ways were too much to handle. We would argue just as much as Stacey and Vergil, which was a clear indication this relationship had become toxic. Our conversations got shorter, as did my patience. But in a time when the tension was high in my home, he was the only source of male attention that made me feel special and loved. I wasn't ready to give that up yet. That was until one day, my home-girl, who stayed down the street, said her boyfriend had a friend who needed a friend.

Ebony was what you would consider the light-skinned, pretty ghetto girl, even though she stayed in the suburbs. She had nice long black hair that touched her bra strap, a nice smile, and dimples that were deep as fuck on both sides. In my family, she would be considered "the pretty girl." She stayed two blocks down in a house with pretty much her entire family. Her mom, stepdad, aunt and her daughter, grandma, and her younger siblings all shared a home. It was like meeting a black Mexican family. Until this point, I had never known multiple generations of black people to stay in one home and actually get along. Even though she had a two-parent household and her mother and stepfather were still together, they were ratchet as fuck. They smoked weed openly before it was even legal. They drank coolers and different forms of alcohol on the regular. But every time I visited her, the house seemed peaceful. There wasn't all the yelling and arguing I was used to in my home, although they did talk loudly naturally. The house seemed to be filled with love. Most days, Ebony's grandmother kept a hot meal on the stove. On days when her grandma didn't cook, another adult in the house would share that responsibility. I'm sure they had their own levels of dysfunction, but from what I can see, they took care of one another and had each other's back. It was much different than my nuclear family dynamic. Their way of living was something I had never experienced before in my family, so it was refreshing to have her as a friend and to be around the ratchet love that was her family. I even found out she's a Scorpio, just like me. We vibe pretty well. We rode the same bus to school before I had a car to drive, and we even had English class together.

She had been living in that neighborhood a lot longer than I had, so she knew basically everybody. It was nice to have her as a new friend, someone to hang out with and show me who to stay away from and what blocks had crazy activities going on. Even though our birthdays were less than two weeks apart, she had a lot more freedom than I did, so I kind of viewed her as being someone who was more responsible. Not exactly like a big sister, but like an older cousin whose house you spent the night over when you knew you wanted to do something that your parents wouldn't allow you to do. Like having a boyfriend that was two years older than you come over to visit. Ebony's boyfriend wanted to come over with his friend to meet me. There were so many people in her household that she didn't really want us to all be over there, which made sense since we would have absolutely zero privacy. Not to mention, her mom considers herself to be such a cool mom, and she would probably be up in our faces asking me, her daughter, and the guys all types of uncomfortable questions. I started to get the feeling that Ebony was a little ashamed of the ratchetness that was her parents. Especially her mom. She seemed to drink a little more often than Ebony liked, and when she did drink, that tongue was loose and loud. She said anything that came to her mind and projected it as if speaking into a microphone. Now that Vergil was in rehab, I told her we could possibly have the meet and greet at my house because my mom visited him one day during the week at a certain time, and we would have about two hours when no one was in my house.

Ebony came over; and she called her boyfriend from my house phone, gave him my address, and told him what bell to ring when they were downstairs. I was kind of nervous, but the risk of possibly getting caught added to the excitement I felt. When the bell rang, this tall, slim, dark-skinned boy came walking up the stairs first. He had on all black with a thick gold cross chain hanging around his neck. His hair was cut low, and I caught a glimpse of his bright white teeth as he smiled as he walked toward the door. I had gathered all of this before he had even stepped into my house, but I had no idea that that was her man. The frumpy dressed, saggy pants, hunched over, dark-skinned guy that followed him was the one that I was supposed to be talking to. He wasn't as neatly groomed, and his skin definitely wasn't as clear as his friend's. He didn't have acne or anything, but he had scattered black spots. It was like he had chickenpox and scratched his face so badly that the scars had barely healed. He had a hat turned backward on his head, possibly to conceal the fact that he didn't have a haircut. He was grungy looking, to say the least, and about three inches shorter than his friend. I definitely did my best not to act as if I wasn't disappointed that he was the one coming to meet me and not his friend.

By the time they got to my house, we had less than an hour before I knew my mom would return; and I kept checking my bedroom window, which overlooked the parking lot, to see if her car had pulled up because they would have to rush out the front door as she would be coming in through the back. As soon as I saw the lights flash on my bedroom window, I knew that it was her, and I hurried them out to the door. I told him it was nice to meet him even though I wasn't too pleased with his appearance. He did have a semi-cool conversation, and I gave him my phone number and told him that we should keep in touch.

Since my mom was dealing with her own male struggles, it was easy for me to hide a new male interest, especially since he was a few years older, and his outer appearance alluded to the fact he was what they would call a bad boy. For all she knew, me and my project boo Randall was still going strong. She did notice that we weren't fighting on the phone as much, and occasionally, he would take the Metra train from the west side to the suburbs to see me. As the weeks passed after our first meeting, Little Man and I continued to build a relationship through conversation. The way my mom found out that this wasn't the type of guy she wanted me to be entertaining came about approximately three weeks after Vergil came home from treatment.

I was honest with Stacey, I told her that I wanted to date someone different and that my relationship with Randall had run its course. The new guy I was interested in didn't go to my school, but I went to school with his sister. One day, the phone rang right around the time that he would typically call me when my mom would go to visit Vergil at the treatment center. But now he was home. My intuition told me to answer the phone, but I didn't feel like running into the living room. Vergil answered, and the call was coming from a juvenile detention center, the prompt. They asked if we would accept the call. Of course, he hung up the phone, did not accept the call, and proceeded to go into the room to tell my mom what he had just heard. Moments later, I was now on the defense having to explain to my mom that Little Man was a good guy and why I wanted to date him. He made me feel special; he was kind and understanding; and he had gotten into a little bit of trouble, which was a complete misunderstanding. The story he told me was that he was across the street visiting his homeboy, playing video games until about midnight when he fell asleep and his father came home and saw Little Man in the house and called the police.

Being young and naive I believed him, not even giving it a second thought that his friend's father wouldn't have called the police, instead it would have made more sense for him to simply tell him to go home. My mom wasn't completely convinced that the situation went down the way I described. But I told her that he was going to be released next week and that they weren't keeping him because he was a bad kid but more so because he had nobody to claim him when the police picked him up. His grandma was elderly, his mom was ripping and running the streets because she was on drugs, and he never knew his dad, and if he had known his dad, he hadn't seen him in decades. The man that his mother was currently dating was, of course, her partner in crime and drugs. So he pretty much had to fend for himself.

We had a lot of similarities in our upbringing, which caused us to trauma bond unconsciously. The more company he kept me, the more attention he showed me. While my mom was going through her own relationship battles, the more I was willing to fight to keep him in my life. He had not yet done anything to me up until this point, so I took the opportunity to remind Stacey that if she hadn't rescued my cousin Jason when her sister died, she used to always say that he possibly would've turned up in juvie or worse. I was using that analogy to pull on her heartstrings so that she would consent to me being with this guy who had a run-in with the law. I believe she trusted in the guidance that she had instilled in me to know right from wrong. So she gave me her blessing to date him, but if anything else like this was to ever happen again, she promised me it would be over.

My sweet sixteen was right around the corner, and it was the first time that I was ever able to throw an over-the-top birthday party. We had invitations with my face on them, there was a dress code, and I even had a playlist of my favorite jams recorded on a CD to give the guests as party favors. My mom even rented a hall to host the party! It was going to be the best party any teen could dream of. It really was a sweet sixteen celebration. That was the day that I got my very first car. It was an all-white 2006 Impala with a sunroof and cream-cloth interior. She was beautiful. I was so excited that I started crying when I realized that I was driving home from my birthday party in my very own vehicle. The same vehicle that would later be stolen by Vergil on one of his many drug binges.

Life was good for me. I was an honor roll student, worked a part-time job at the grocery store across the street from our apartment, and now I had my very own vehicle. Now me and Little Man could go on dates and actually stay out a little longer because I no longer had to take public transportation. I remember the first time we ever went to Portillo's. It was a burger spot I was introduced to by my older cousin when I was living with my aunt Diane. I considered it to be fancy. The burgers were like six dollars each. They were thick, and you watched them make it in front of you. You could see through into the kitchen. This was no McDonald's burger, so I wanted to show him that I had a little class and that I knew a little something. So I suggested we have a Portillo's date. When we got there, he kept asking me what I thought he should get. So I said, "Check out the menu w. What do you like?" The look on his face was confusion, as if the menu was in French. As I waited for him to decide, he confessed to me that he was illiterate and that he couldn't read the menu. I didn't completely believe him at first. We had been too many places before, and he had ordered things off the menu. But then again, these were places in our neighborhood that he had probably been to hundreds of times, and maybe he just memorized the menu items he liked. Maybe he wasn't actually reading them at all. I didn't want to make him feel bad at that moment by laughing or calling him crazy or anything like that in case he really was telling the truth. I actually felt sympathy for him. I never knew anybody who didn't know how to read. A lot of people in my life have their own issues and struggles, but the fundamentals of reading weren't one of them. I ordered both of us a charbroiled cheeseburger, a large fry with cheese sauce, and two medium drinks; and we sat down to eat.

I did my best not to ask too many questions about what he had just told me, but there were soooo many questions floating around in my head as we ate. Like how did he make it this far in life without knowing how to read? Did he not know how to read at all, or he couldn't read as well as he should at his age? I came to find out his reading and comprehension level was less than that of a third grader. He really couldn't read at all. After dropping out of school many years ago and not being challenged to read on a daily basis, I'm sure, as they say, "If you don't use it, you lose it." I felt bad for him, and I immediately went into savior mode in my mind, as I have seen my mom do time and time again with her men. See, I was good in school. Learning came easy for me. Stacey always made education a priority, so I knew that I had the ability to help him learn to read if he really wanted to. Consciously, I told myself that his childhood was the reason he had slipped through the educational cracks and that if only he had one parent who cared enough to make sure he was learning in school, this would not have happened to him. It never occurred to me that maybe I wanted to fix him more than he wanted to fix himself.

After school, I researched adult literacy programs in the area. Even before he enrolled in one of the programs, I suggested that we go to the library, and I would get books that even a fourth or fifth grader should be able to read to try to help him learn words and how to sound out the syllables to form a word. I'm sure his pride/ego was being tested every time I sat down beside him and tried to help him learn to read. Eventually, he did enroll in the literacy program, so now he didn't have to feel embarrassed to show me how little he actually knew. I was now expressing the same behaviors my mom exhibited with Vergil. I stuck beside my man, not realizing that his confession should have been my clue to exit stage left. I didn't need to try to build up, fix, or teach this guy how to read. I should have been seeking to date someone who intellectually was on my level, if not above. At the time, I couldn't see the correlation between what my mom was doing, dating someone beneath her standards, and what I was doing now. I only viewed Vergil as being beneath Stacey because of his drug addiction and lack of employment. I now understand its levels to this game of life, and no matter how the imbalance shows up, as Stacey would frequently say, "If they aren't adding to your life, PJ, they are taking away from it."

I started leaving for school early so that I could pick him up and drop him off at school and still make it to my first class on time. Some days, he wouldn't go at all, and I couldn't understand why. On the days he didn't go to school, I would suggest that he and I go to the library so I could help him study for the GED, but it seemed that I wanted him to learn to read more than he did.

I was now a sophomore, and I had transferred to a different school, so I drove every day to school. By now, Vergil had been out of treatment for a few months and supposedly looking for work, so I basically had the house to myself for about two hours before his kids got there after school. One day, Vergil came home early and almost caught Little Man and I having sex. I was terrified. I didn't know how I was going to sneak him out of the small apartment without being seen. I had to pretend like I was there alone, but I'm sure he suspected that someone else was there with me, but since he didn't see it, he couldn't prove it.

The day my life changed forever was a rainy Tuesday, and I decided to skip school and be with my boo. I picked Little Man up, and we went to his homeboy's house, who had to be at least twice his age. I would say he was every bit of thirty-five, thirty-eight. I was confused as to how and why an eighteen-year-old would know or even be friends with someone this old. I was still oblivious to the fact my boyfriend was a drug dealer. I suspected he hid that from his goodie-two--shoes girlfriend because of what I had expressed to him regarding my own parents' addiction and how it had severely affected me. I was sitting on the front couch with the girlfriend of the thirty- something-year-old who complimented me over and over again on my beauty. She told me that my skin was beautiful and glowing and asked me a lot of questions about our relationship and how long we had been together. She even asked me if we were planning to have kids, and I knew then she had no clue that I was only sixteen because kids were the furthest thing from my mind. My response was a swift no; even though my cycle was a little late, it should be coming any day now. She offered to give me one of her pregnancy test just to see. I told her I didn't need it because we always wore condoms. But she insisted; she said my skin was radiant like that of a pregnant person.

Just for shits and giggles and to get her to stop asking me about my sex life, I went ahead and peed on the stick. In the three minutes it took to get the results, she continued to tell me why she was convinced that I was pregnant. When three minutes passed and the word "Pregnant" appeared on the clear-blue screen, my heart sank to the bottom of my stomach. I couldn't believe it! We always wore condoms. When her guy and Little Man came out of the back, discussing whatever business they had, she was the first to tell him congratulations. He could see that I looked nervous, confused, and sad all at the same time. I was pregnant, and I knew I didn't want to be. Little man, on the other hand, was ecstatic. He smiled from ear to ear and couldn't wait to tell anybody he knew that we were having a baby. I tried to get him to understand that we weren't ready to be parents. Just a few months earlier, I found out he was illiterate. He had no job, no car, no place for us all to live; but somehow he thought he was ready for a baby. I knew I wasn't ready. I lived with my mom, I had a part-time job, I was making good grades at school, and I was planning to go to college. I had my whole future ahead of me, and this was not part of my plan. Hell, I looked at him as being a baby, at least intellectually.

This was not at all what I wanted. I didn't know how to tell my mom, so for the next three weeks, it was the biggest kept secret I had ever held on to. Because he was running around the whole neighborhood telling all the friends he had that we had a baby on the way, his ex fuck buddy got wind of the news. Her name was Destiny, which was the same girl that he had sneaked off to see the night that he went to juvie. It wasn't his homeboy's father who caught him in his house after midnight; it was Destiny's mother who caught him having sex with her fifteen-year--old daughter that landed him in the juvenile detention center, which, of course, made more sense.

When she found out I was pregnant, I immediately started getting calls to my phone from anonymous numbers asking if I knew that Little Man already had a child by her and that he hadn't been to see his daughter since she was born. He denied being a father. He claimed they only had sex that one time and that he used a condom. Since I grew up without a dad, who still hadn't been in my life since he dropped me off at my aunt's, I insisted that he at least go see the baby just to make sure.

Every day before school, he would wake up early to make me breakfast instead of going to his literacy class. I figured he must've dropped out by now. He would bring the breakfast down to the car, and we would share a meal. He said he was feeding the people he loved. All this extra attention that I was getting because I was pregnant and the fact that he hadn't tried to deny being the father of my child made me feel even more special to the point that I had completely forgotten about his illiteracy. All I knew was unlike my father, he wasn't abandoning me or our child for his own selfish reasons. This just made me love him even more.

During one of the many days I decided to ditch school now that it was only my mom and me at the house, another prank call came in from his ex. I was tired of being harassed for doing nothing to her. I knew nothing about her, and I had no problems with her, but the things that she said I know came out of anger because he was catering to me and accepting and acknowledging our child and he wasn't doing the same for her. So when I hung up the phone, I demanded we go over there and settle this once and for all. He had been treating me like a pregnant princess, and even though I knew he had been drinking, I gave him the keys and told him to drive. The illusion of love will have you making awful choices. In some ways, just being around him and listening to how he defended me on the phone to this girl made me feel protected, despite the fact that I knew it was dangerous to drink and drive. He was angry, and he wasn't thinking straight, and he definitely wasn't driving straight. He was speeding and was damn near running red lights. He started to scare me. He was going so fast down the main street, swerving almost into another lane, that I grabbed the wheel and shifted. His equilibrium, being impaired at the time, wasn't able to recover from me grabbing the wheel. Before I knew it, the car was perpendicular to oncoming traffic. I was in the passenger seat, and all I saw was bright lights flash before me as my new white Impala was T-boned by oncoming traffic. It was a good thing I didn't have on my seat belt because I wouldn't have made it out alive to tell the story.

The car was totaled. The door was smashed in so far that you couldn't even open the glove compartment. When I came to, I was being pulled out of the back window by the fire department. The next thing I remember was waking up in the hospital with several nurses inserting a Foley catheter into me and asking me questions as I drifted in and out of consciousness. One of the male nurses asked me if I was pregnant. I lied and said no. After they tested my urine, probably to see if we were intoxicated, he came back and congratulated me and informed me that I was pregnant. There was no need to congratulate me; that was not something I wanted to celebrate. I could barely stay awake long enough to answer the questions they had for me, and as soon as I drifted back off to sleep, the sound of my mother's heels resounded loudly in my eardrums. I didn't have to open my eyes to know her stride in the way her shoes sounded when she walked across the room. She rushed to my side; and all I could hear was pain, sadness, and fear in her voice. She was beyond scared for me but was happy that I was safe and alive with barely any scratches after seeing the car and me lying in a neck brace as the staff waited the results of the x-rays.

Shortly after Stacey arrived at the bedside, the same male nurse asked me if I had given my mom the good news. Being a medical professional now, I know that he was way out of line, and he should've never said anything like that. But you know what they say, "God works in mysterious ways." Apparently, the universe ushered in that nurse so that my little secret could be exposed. My mom insisted that he tell her what he was referring to, and he explained to her that he couldn't violate HIPPA unless I agreed to share my medical information with my mom. He then exited the room. I did my best to pretend to drift back to sleep, but Stacey wasn't having it! She nudged me and continued to ask me what was the good news until I broke down and told her I was pregnant! Instantly, my mother began to weep, and Little Man heard my mother crying on the other side of the emergency room curtain that separated his bed from mine. In his drunken ignorance, he yelled out, "How are my babies?" The bull inside my mother raged from the other side of the room as she warned him to stay away from her "Precious Jewel." She went on to tell him that he would never see me again!

I had to take two weeks off from school due to the bad condition my body was in. I went into shock, probably in order to save the baby because there was nothing wrong with me besides a few scrapes on my head from where the glass had got into my scalp. Everything hurt. I could barely move. I slept day and night. About a week after the car accident, my mom came into my room and wanted to talk about the baby. She felt like an abortion was the best option for me in this situation. She reiterated to me how I had my whole life ahead of me and that I didn't need to throw it away to be with a man who could not provide for me or his child. And as much as I hate to admit it, I knew she was right, but just two weeks earlier, Little Man had convinced me to agree to keep it. Because I thought I loved him, I didn't wanna let him down.

My mom was answering all phone calls while I recovered. She made it very clear to him not to call me ever again, and if he did that, she would call the police on him herself. He was sneaky and had his sister call me. Whenever she heard a girl's voice, she didn't get too skeptical or asked too many questions about who they were or why they were calling me. He would relay messages through her and ask questions through her. The day I came back from getting the abortion, I lied to him, saying that the baby had died in the crash because I knew how badly he wanted to have a baby with me. Honestly, I was relieved to have gotten the abortion. I knew that he wouldn't be the type of parent that I wanted for my child. He didn't even know that I had taken advantage of his illiteracy just two weeks prior to the car crash.

He had gone to pick the baby up to bring her over to his sister to see if his sister agreed that the baby resembled him. The baby was so young it was hard to tell. I lied to him and told him that we could take her to the clinic and get a paternity test and that my health insurance would cover it. I had no idea how a paternity test went besides the few things that I saw on Maury. When we pulled up to the clinic where my primary care provider practiced, I went inside and asked them if I could have a few mouth swabs and a jar for a science project that I was doing. It was an odd request, but they obliged. The materials I asked for didn't need a prescription. I could have gone to any CVS and got the things I was asking for, but getting it from the clinic was free and added to the illusion that we were actually getting a real paternity test.

I gathered the items, t. They even gave me a bag to put it in, and I headed back to the car. I opened the sterile swabs and proceeded to swab his cheek vigorously and put it into the container. I then swabbed the baby's cheeks and put it into a separate container. I then went back into the clinic, and I continued to carry out this lie as if I were dropping off the sample to the doctor. I told him that the results would be ready in two weeks, which meant that I had two weeks to look up paternity tests and how to make them look legitimate. I fabricated a negative paternity for the baby he claimed wasn't his. I didn't want to share the father of my unborn child with anyone else. I wanted to continue to have all of his time and attention to be focused on me. I knew that because he couldn't read, he would ask me to read the results to him. Never did I once consider that if this was indeed his child and I gave him this false test, the beautiful, sweet, innocent baby would go without a father just as I had.

I had to make the results look real because when he showed them to the mother or anyone else, I was sure they could read. There was a chart that showed the specimen collected had a zero percent chance of being related to the dad in question. I read a lot of terms that he probably didn't know the meaning of, and this is why his ex fuck buddy was calling and harassing me because she knew who she had slept with and she knew that he was the father of her child. Now, not only was he denying being the father, but she claimed he was using a fake paternity test I created as proof that her daughter was not his. I guess the car accident was my karma because I was denying this child the possibility to have her father in her life simply because I was being selfish and didn't want to share a man that I should have gotten rid of anyway.

Never did I expect to be anyone's baby momma, and I'm sure this is the first time I ever truly let my mom down! Once the appointment was over, I spent a few more days at home, and we swore to keep this between us. I was like the golden child in the family until this point. My grades were good, I respected my elders, and I did as I was told. Honestly, I didn't understand how I got pregnant in the first place until he told me he did it on purpose because he wanted me to carry on his seed that. Then it all made sense.

Soon after the abortion, Stacey ran to put me on birth control. I never wanted to feel like creating or choosing when to create life was out of my control ever again. I was in control of the guys I chose to date, who I wanted to allow to enter Miss Mocha, and who I chose to procreate with. After taking the Depo shot and absolutely hating the side effects those chemicals had on my body, I settled on a ten-year non hormonal implant that would protect me all the way until I turned twenty-nine. All through college and every man who entered my temple after Little Man, the one thing I was no longer concerned with was getting pregnant against my consent. I guess that was one lesson I learned from that horrendous situation.

As you have read in previous chapters, I did repeat the same mistake of choosing and accepting less than I deserve time and time again after him. However, that was due to the fact I was unaware that I had been subconsciously conditioned to expect the bare minimum all throughout my formative years. By the time I was a teen, I was programmed to attract everything I consciously said I didn't want. Even worse, it was embedded in me to try to fix the men I came across, and if that didn't work, I tried to manipulate them with what I thought was love with the hopes that they would feel compelled to change if they wanted to show how much they loved me. It was abundantly clear to me now that what I unconsciously expected and what I was attracting and allowing was keeping me unhappy. I was the common denominator in all of these scenarios, and I was not about to spend another decade making the same mistakes.

Part

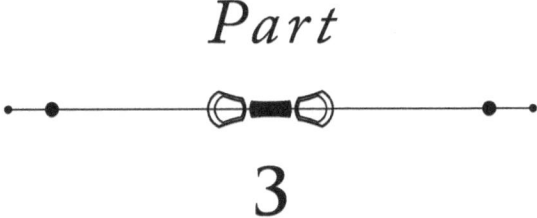

3

Boundaries and Elevated Expectations

Love yourself enough to set boundaries.
Your time and energy is precious.
You get to choose how you use it. You teach
people how to treat you by deciding
what you will and won't accept.

—Ann Taylor

Chapter

19

What's Blood Got to Do with It

My study of astrology, numerology and metaphysics, in general, has been the main theme of this twenty-eighth year of my life as I approach my first Saturn return in the year 29. The planet Saturn takes approximately twenty-eight to thirty years to orbit the sun and return to the exact position it was in at the time you were born. It makes complete sense that I felt compelled to step out of my comfort zone and cross the threshold to the next phase of life this entire year. Astrology teaches that Saturn governs wisdom and growth and is the planet that imposes karma in order to highlight patterns in action or behavior so that you may learn the lessons presented in the given scenario. Saturn is also known to create delays and rewards the perseverance on the other side of those delays.

The planning of my celebration of life embodied the aspects of myself I had ignored while trying to win the devotion and admiration of the men I've encountered throughout my journey thus far. This party was about me, for me, and to acknowledge all parts of me. I was ready to showcase a hidden fantasy of performing in a seductive setting in my true Scorpio form, in addition to finally celebrating myself and my accomplishments instead of waiting and waiting for others to acknowledge me for all of my efforts. The theme of my party was burlesque. This was to acknowledge my sensuality unrelated to my connection to any man. I had recently watched Spike Lee's *She's Gotta Have It* series on Netflix, which gave me the idea to invite all of my old boyfriends to my party just to see how many would show up. The main character, Nola, invited all the men she was currently sleeping with to Thanksgiving dinner as a way to lay everything out on the table. She no longer desired to hide the fact that she freely enjoyed the company of multiple men, and since she had not committed exclusively to any one of them, why should she continue to hide the fact that neither of them was the only one!? Man, that was a bold way to assert herself and claim her power as the goddess she knew she was, and I was ready to step into that energy. Although I was currently single and had relinquished my Bama Boo from enjoying the pleasures of me, I knew that every male I had ever entertained, if given the opportunity, would trip over their feet to get a second chance. Yeah, I wanted all that lustful, admirable energy in the building to elevate my confidence when I performed! I even put my pride aside and decided to invite my maternal family despite the fact they have not shown up to celebrate with me since I graduated high school. I wasn't sure why I wanted to give them one last chance to be a part of something that mattered to me, but I guess I decided that even if they didn't come, it wouldn't make a difference anyway.

The house was gorgeous! It was actually on the market for $3.8 million. The owners were a nice middle-aged white couple who built the house a few years ago. The husband was an architect, and the wife stayed home and took care of the kids, but they no longer felt the need to have such a big space. The wife said she was tired of cleaning it. So they put it on the market, but until they sold it, they had it on a few short-term rental sites like Airbnb and VRBO, which is where I found them. The house was ducked off into the hills of one of the many Arizona mountains that surrounded the valley. You had to travel up a one-way dirt road that went for about a mile just to get there. The ceilings were about twenty feet high and had three different levels. The main floor, the second floor, and the basement. There was a lot of natural lighting from large windows and doors. The decor was lavish and accommodating. On the first level, a huge foyer opened up into the living room and the kitchen. To the kitchen's right was a formal dining area with a table long enough to seat twelve people. They had one of those chef kitchens and stoves that had like ten eyes on it. You know, the Viking stove with triple ovens. The massive island had multiple warming drawers to keep food warm while you waited to entertain your guess. You can sit about eight people on the island comfortably. There were two different dishwashers and two different sinks. Each bedroom in the house was its own suite with walk-in closets and attached bathrooms. The living area was wide open with a wraparound porch that you could enter through the panoramic retractable glass doors. Once they were fully opened, the living room flowed onto the outside balcony.

The view was breathtaking. The balcony overlooked the city lights. There was a nice -size pool down below the main level with a Jacuzzi attached, and they also had a portable Jacuzzi that was situated far in the back by the cabana, which had an outside grill area. This home was every bit of my dream. This home was going to set the tone of the luxurious lifestyle I was preparing to embody moving into my third decade of life.

I was ready to start surrounding myself with people who lived like this on a regular basis. It was only fitting that my party be held there.

This party was costing me a little bit over $7000 for the decorations, the house rental, the DJ, the photographer, the alcohol, the food, my three different outfits, my hair, my makeup, the door attendant, the cocktail servers, and even paying the dancers that I hired to perform with me for the ending finale! This was going to be a night to remember. I had waitresses who were dressed in sexy lingerie to serve you dinner, drinks, and cake once it was cut. All of these things came out of my mind and vision as soon as I stepped into this house I was excited for everyone to come and enjoy all of my hard labor.

Now that I had taken out a loan for six grand to ensure I had enough funds to cover everything, I was no longer stressed to sell tickets to recoup some of the money I had spent preparing for this extravaganza. With all of the virtual party invitations and reminders that I sent out to all of my friends and family, everyone responded by letting me know if they were going to come or not. As of now, I have eighty-five people on the guest list who were confirmed. Just two days before the party, two of my maternal cousins let me know that they wouldn't make it. Of course, it was money related. Flights were too expensive, hotels were too high, XYZ. Being mentally prepared for none of them to show up, the last two confirmations didn't really bother me. It was no different in my mind when everyone decided they couldn't attend my first graduation and had nothing or no intentions of donating to my second. The fact that they weren't showing up to celebrate all that I had accomplished makes complete sense to me, regardless of their reason. Old timers have always said, "You make time for what you really want." No longer was I going to put myself in a position to let them make me feel unworthy just because they didn't make me a priority to support growth and development. I had over eighty people, some strangers, most of them familiars, who were willing and wanting to be a part of my celebration. So, hey, fuck 'em. What I'm starting to learn is that family is not just the people or the bloodline that you're born into but those who have your back and will always support you. From my experience, those you meet along your life's journey will become more like family than those who share your DNA. So instead of me harping on the fact that not one of my maternal family members, except Jason, would show up to my party, I decided to focus on all of the people that did!

Knowing that my ego prevented me from growing emotionally over the three years I refused to speak to my family after being criticized for my graduation fund and for harboring an ill perspective of them after nobody besides my parents showed up to not one but two of my graduations, I decided this time around regardless of who showed up and who didn't, I will only put forth an effort to be a part of people lives who do the same for me. Not only that, after intentionally choosing to retrace my path and find the flaws in my decision-making and the trauma that led to my self-protecting and destructive behavior, I was making it my mission for year 29 to learn more so that my discernment going into my 30's didn't cause me to feel like I was experiencing déjà vu from the previous two decades of my life. I was ready to feel content with life without needing any outside validation from family or a man.

When we repress our emotions or suppress our emotional content, whatever we are denying accumulates weight, or what I call vibrational density. This heaviness can take on many forms. But in all cases, it impedes your spirit's natural ability to shine.

–Panache Desai

Chapter

20

Chakras and Shadow Work

I won't lie, between dance rehearsal and working overtime to pay for this damn party, I've been slipping on my reading. I started this book about chakras back in February, which piqued my interest in retracing my past in order to heal. The book discusses the seven major chakras in our body, and I have only made it through the first three. According to the different metaphysical teachers I follow on the infamous YouTube University, the lower three chakras are where your shadow side, better known as your ego, resides. Until an individual learns to integrate the shadow version of themselves with the higher or light version of themselves, the ego functions in its lowest primordial nature, which is to protect you from danger, either perceived or real.

Even if you've never studied quantum physics, you've heard the expression before and learned in your basic physics class that everything is energy and energy cannot be lost or destroyed, only transferred; and that's exactly what your chakras are. Chakras are the energetic part of your physical body, the energy body that exists within you and extends beyond your physical body. Your energy body has layers that are collectively called your aura. Your aura interacts with your physical body as well as your energy centers. Those centers connect and support your physical and energetic body. These different chakras can be measured with scientific devices. Each chakra has its own frequency, which vibrates in accordance with the organs that vibrate on that same frequency. Therefore, because these things can be scientifically measured and because we know that everything is energy, and since everything is energy, everything has a frequency or a vibration, scientists and metaphysicians have come to realize that these energy centers not only influence but they control the physical, mental, and emotional aspects that makeup who we are.

As I learned what each chakra entailed, the organs that are associated with them, and the development of those energy sensors, as well as the different personality traits that are developed over a period of time, it began to become crystal clear to me that identifying the traits of my personality that were being expressed throughout my development was because of an imbalance in one or more of my chakras. The beginner's guide that I'm reading made it very cut and dry and simplistic as to how to understand whether or not your center was overactive or under active. Based on how you handle certain situations, the mind frame in which you process information, and the actions that you take when put in certain scenarios that trigger those centers indicated the health and stability of that chakra. Before I get into detail as to what the chakras are and how to identify your personality traits, let's talk about shadow work.

Shadow work is all about identifying the negative personality traits, mindset, beliefs, and actions that are part of your personality due to emotional or physical trauma you experienced which caused imbalances in your lower three chakras. In order to do shadow work, you must be willing to identify that, on some level or another, the things that go wrong in your life are because of you! Understanding that you are the common denominator in everything that goes well and everything that goes bad in your life is the first step to understanding how to do shadow work. Now, most people only begin the journey of shadow work when their life seems to be in shambles, which is typically when most religious people drop down to their knees and surrender to Jesus Christ or some other religious deity and ask for assistance to get them out of the rut that their life has been in or has become. Well, in the spiritual community, that's exactly when most people begin their shadow work.

They start to search for connections and patterns in their own life from their own choices that have led them to be in situations that they currently find undesirable. They do this in order to stop the pattern and change aspects of themselves so that the pattern no longer repeats. This has been my entire journey throughout this book with reliving all of the past traumas that I have been subjected to in my childhood that were beyond my control as well as acknowledging and identifying the choices that I made consciously that put me in multiple different situations and scenarios that were within my control as I got older.

The pivotal point in becoming wise to the realization of what your shadow was supposed to teach you begins with acknowledging negative traits derived from your pain. Understanding how things that were seemingly out of your control from your childhood, were actually necessary parts of your growth so you can learn to better react to situations once you are able to make choices for yourself. Once you come to a realization as to where the toxic trait began and you identify the toxic trait that you currently have, you can then move on to healing by releasing yourself from the patterns that have led you to the point in your life that you no longer desire to be.

The conscious community will explain that your ego is only meant to protect you as you develop in your formative years. Before the age of two, you have no sense of danger as an infant, which is why you depend on your parents for all your basic necessities of living. As children progress as toddlers, they will try anything, do anything, and put anything in their mouth without any fear because they are not yet aware of the dangers that are in their environment; so your parents are supposed to be there to protect you from you basically killing yourself. The more a toddler falls down the stairs or bump their head when they jump off the couch, the more their ego begins to alert them via intuition by suggesting not to attempt that same activity that has caused them pain repeatedly. So your ego begins to develop midway through your root chakra years in which survival, a sense of being, and family are what's being established during that time. However, if you are being programmed with toxic traits and behaviors from the people who are meant to provide safety and security around you, your ego, which is connected to your subconscious mind, begins to internalize that the toxic ways to handle situations moving forward are the correct way. So once you begin to learn about and heal yourself from the toxic traits that your ego has developed past your lower three chakras, only then will your ego work for you and not against you.

The Root Chakra

The root chakra is all about survival, physical and mental security, and family. It is largely responsible for how safe and secure you feel. This energy center is located at the base of your spine. From the years of zero to seven is when the emotional, energetic connection to yourself and the outside world is established. A few ways to identify whether your root chakra is in balance, ask yourself if you feel disconnected from the world around you. Do you have issues with your identity or old family wounds? Do you have a healthy relationship with your parents? Did your parents raise you? Do you feel secure in the knowledge that all of your basic needs, such as food, shelter, clothing, and love, will be met? Do you make decisions out of fear? Do you feel unsafe, and therefore, do you operate your life from the perspective of being constantly in jeopardy? These are all personality traits that are expressed or even mindsets that manifest due to blockages in your root because of unresolved trauma.

The organ that is connected and vibrates with the root chakra is your adrenal glands. The adrenal glands are located above each kidney; and they produce hormones responsible for regulating your metabolism, immune system, blood pressure, and your body's response to stress, just to name a few. Some common diseases which arise due to energy blockages in this center, are chronic lower back pain, which is where the root chakra is located. Also, obesity due to an over consumption of nutrient-lacking foods. If you grew up in an environment similar to mine where the basic necessity of food was lacking on a constant basis, when you become an adult that is now responsible for your own food, you could subconsciously overeat due to the fact your ego has been programmed to feel you are in lack. Therefore, you overindulge. Maybe you are the first person to run to the clinic each year to get a flu shot because it is suggested by the authorities on the television, yet you find that you get sick several times per year regardless of the vaccine. Others who never get a flu shot and pay little attention to the suggestions given to the masses via the media haven't had to use a sick day in years. The reason for this phenomenon is due to one person operating from a position of fear, which weakens the immune system, and the other person having a strong root foundation and is secure in knowing they are responsible for their health, which in turn strengthens the immune system. Emotionally, you may feel disconnected from your physical family, and you don't feel safe in large groups. You are insecure about your ability to stand up for yourself and to provide the basic necessities of life. If any of these things resonate with you, if you experience any health conditions listed or any health conditions that may be affected by the adrenal glands, that is a clear physical indication that, energetically, your root chakra is out of balance.

For me, my root chakra was negatively impacted by my mom and dad from their divorce and arguing all of the time. My sense of safety and security was further impacted as we bounced from house to house when they finally separated, which was around four years old. From four until seven, going from living in what was our home, although I didn't feel secure or loved in a healthy way, to then having to live with multiple family members reaffirmed the fact that I didn't feel safe and that all of my basic necessities were not met such as food, shelter, clothing, or love. I knew my mom loved me because she never left my side; but my dad, on the other hand, was nowhere to be found. The result of these traumatic events was that my subconscious mind and my emotional, energetic root center were being programmed from a position of lack. Therefore, when I became of a conscious age, I began to look for love with the bare minimum standards driving my attraction.

The Sacral Chakra

The sacral chakra is located just above the root chakra in your pelvic region. It is all about sexuality and creativity. It is developed from the years of eight to fourteen. The sacral chakra is most closely connected with the reproductive organs and the emotions affected during the hormonal shifts experienced as you grow through puberty. During these years, your creativity expands as you find ways of expressing who you feel you are inside. When this center is out of balance, you have little ability to feel pleasure, and you hold on to unprocessed anger. You may feel resentful and have relationship issues, whether platonic or romantic. You may have feelings of shame, money issues, or creating abundance for yourself. You may overemphasize the need to have material possessions in order to feel valued. The organs that vibrate with the sacral chakra are the ovaries and testicles. The appendix, bladder, hip, and kidneys are all affected by this energy center. Most people who have energy blockages in this area also have sciatic pain, lower back pain, gynecological problems, pelvic pain, impotence, uterine, bladder, or kidney problems. The emotional issues may present themselves as guilt, and issues with money, sex, power/control, ethics, honor, relationships, and creativity. These blockages tend to stem from traumas such as sexual abuse, rape, or issues around gender.

The way the blockages presented in my life due to the underdevelopment of my sacral chakra while I lived in unhappy environments was low self-esteem. My aunt and cousins impacted my confidence and self-worth by teasing me about my appearance, comparing me to other members of the family, and making it clear to me that I was the darkest in the family, which translated to me being weird in my adolescent mind. Because I was being teased for being different, I felt undesirable. Although I wasn't yet sexually active during my sacral development, when I began to be interested in males, I felt the need to be creative mentally, so I concocted stories in my mind that would allow me to entertain these individuals. The creativity I displayed when I wanted to be liked by a boy came from a toxic lack mindset. I was so creative in what I told myself, so I didn't miss out on potential affection due to my subconscious insecurities. It was one of the main reasons I even thought I needed to get a Brazilian Butt Lift. I thought I would finally fit in with the rest of the women in my family by having a plump backside, and in turn, the men I attracted would have no reason to cheat if I was the full package. I had brains, beauty, and breasts but no booty; so that was the first thing I thought I needed to fix to be the object of every man's desire.

The Solar Plexus

The solar plexus is all about self-esteem and willpower. It corresponds with your personality and your sense of self-worth. From ages fifteen to twenty-one is when this center is developed. The emotions you feel and the mindset you have during these years are all about needing a sense of control. You're moving out of your young adolescent teenage years and becoming a young adult. You're taking control of your life after having been under your parents' roof at least eighteen for most of us. You begin to create an image for yourself. A few ways to identify whether or not your solar plexus is out of alignment is you have an overarching need to dominate and control those around you as well as situations. You have a great need to keep up appearances as you function through the world with deep feelings of inadequacy. I embodied all these attributes unfortunately. You may not have respect for yourself, which may manifest in many ways as self-hatred. You have no sense of self-worth, and you constantly seek the validation of others.

The pancreas and the adrenal glands vibrate at the same frequency as the solar plexus. As you can see, these lower three chakras begin to overlap in the body parts and the emotions they control. Your root chakra also resonates with the adrenal glands, so if you have an imbalance in your root chakra, it is very likely that you will also have an imbalance in your sacral chakra as well as your solar plexus chakra. The parts of your body that are most affected by imbalances in your solar plexus are your stomach, upper intestines, liver, gallbladder, spleen, and the middle of your spine.

This chakra sits right above the sacral chakra. When they are energy blockages and imbalances in the solar plexus, physical ailments such as colon and stomach cancer, diabetes, indigestion, anorexia, adrenal dysfunction, fatigue, and hepatitis are just some of the ways that your physical body can manifest illness due to blockages in this energetic center. Mentally and emotionally, an out-of-balance solar plexus chakra is due to repressed anger issues with control, especially related to people in power. As for me, mentally and emotionally, the toxicity I was exposed to and had become used to enduring while my mom's boyfriend Vergil lived with us from fourteen is how my codependency toxic personality trait was expressed in all of my relationships that followed. My solar plexus was completely out of balance because I felt the need to be sexually active at a very young age, losing my virginity right before I turned fifteen. It was then reinforced by my need to control and dominate Little Man by not only using his illiteracy to manipulate him to be in a situation with me that prevented him from being a true father, but I also thought I could control his love for me by overly expressing how much I loved him. My feelings of inadequacy to be loved by someone I didn't have to teach was a manifestation of my own self-hatred. I gave my power to him by putting my life in his hands even when I knew better. As far as TJ is concerned, I developed a habit of smoking weed to keep up the appearance of being cool while dating someone who engaged in a behavior that I had no interest in participating in prior to the relationship. Most say it was peer pressure, but after you read the story, you know no one pressured me to take the first hit of that blunt on senior ditch day. I wanted to be accepted and appear cool instead of standing my ground and understanding that just being me is enough for those who really care for me. These are just some of the ways a lack of mindset will manifest in your daily life if no introspection is done to facilitate growth.

The Heart Chakra

The heart chakra is all about love and compassion. From age twenty-two to twenty-eight is when this energy center is developed. The heart chakra is located in the spine just behind your breastbone. This center is the connection to your physical and spiritual aspects. It is the gateway between when you move from your lower three survival aspects of yourself to when you rise to that pivotal point where you operate out of love and compassion for yourself and all of those around you. It is when you begin to transform from your lower nature to your higher self. When there are imbalances in your heart chakra, you have difficulty loving yourself or receiving love from a genuine place.

You don't feel deserving of love, so you typically manifest what I consider to be "struggle love". Struggle love is the type of love that causes you to compromise your morals, standards, principles, and values just to keep someone around who doesn't quite show you the type of compassion that you truly want. You may feel some level of depression. If you do happen to meet a guy or a girl who gives you everything you could possibly ask for, you may start to think, *what's the catch? What are they hiding? When is everything going to fall apart?* because you're used to struggle love.

The heart chakra affects the thymus gland, heart, lungs, arms, and hands. The thymus gland is responsible for the production and maturation of the immune cells in your body. Of course, the circulatory system is connected to the heart. The heart pumps blood throughout the body and circulates the blood through the circulatory system. Your lungs receive oxygenated blood from the heart. Your shoulders, arms, ribs, breast, and diaphragm are all connected to your heart chakra. It's very easy for me to identify nowadays just by looking at someone if their heart chakra is unbalanced. Their shoulders are hunched over. They have terrible postures. They smoke constantly, and their breast or chests are sunken in. That's a subconscious body movement to protect the heart center. It's a body posture that you may not even notice that you're doing, but now that you know what areas the heart chakra affects, stand up tall, push your shoulders back, and don't slouch and lean when you sit. If you are a smoker, do your best to cut back if you have no intentions on stopping.

Some physical ailments that are a result of blockages in your heart chakra can be congestive heart failure, heart attacks, heart disease, asthma, allergies, lung cancer, bronchitis, pneumonia, lung disease, breast cancer, and high blood pressure. Mental and emotional issues that develop due to an unbalanced heart chakra can present themselves as resentment, hatred, grief, self- centeredness, loneliness, and overly compassion. All of this is due to repressed heartache and unresolved grief.

During my heart chakra development twenty-one to twenty-eight, I yearned for love when I subconsciously manifested Tobias. Subconsciously, I was looking for a man who had strong family ties. A man who came from a family that showed and displayed the love they had for each other. I was in college at the time and feeling very little love from my family. Nobody called to check on me to see if I needed anything, and to top it all off, I had just broken up with my high school sweetheart, who couldn't find time to send me a birthday or Valentine's Day card. So clearly, I wasn't feeling any love from him. Of course, Stacey, my mom, was always in my corner. But as we've already discovered, I've never felt love from a man, not even my father; so I wasn't looking for any more validation from my mom. It was the men that I wanted to show me that I was special and loved, which led me right into the arms of DJ, my edible arrangement fling, who I used as practice to see if I really had what it takes to look for a sugar daddy that would give me affection without breaking my heart. Little did I know, I was starting to shut down my heart center because I was unable to attract a healthy relationship. So after my fellatio fraud, I decided that I would just have fun, and if I was going to have fun, I had to at least get something out of it besides a wet ass. With Jay, aka Mr. Border Patrol, I pretended to be something I wasn't, yet again to avoid the heartache and wound up feeling cheap and used. So next, it was my turn to use someone for a change, and that's when I manifested my Sugar-Free Daddy and set myself up for failure once again. Not only was he broke, he was the oldest man that I ever considered trying to love with the smallest dick I had ever seen. When I took over a year off to focus on myself and my career, I was determined not to make the same mistakes until the knight in aluminum foil by the name of Sweetz appeared, and I thought he was coming to save me from all the past heartache I had endured. He melted the walls I had built around my heart, only to show me why going against my gut would always be the wrong choice, every time!

After six months of solitude and repairing my ego, my female coworkers convinced me I should just have some fun and serial date with no expectations. So what did I do again, go against my intuition and get on a damn dating site! No true healing had to took place. Hell, I didn't even know how to heal at this point. But my ego had me convinced that I had learned my lessons and that I was wiser to make better choices when it came to men. Consciously, I thought I was ready, but little did I know that beneath the surface, my toxic programming was running the show. They say when you know better, you do better. Now that I had come across this new information, I was ready to give my all and apply it to my life. I had now made it halfway through the throat chakra chapter when I realized what needed to be done with my Bama Boo I met offline, who had now ran up his tab to damn near $3,000.

*Spiritual Work is not easy. It means the
willingness to surrender feelings that seem,
while we're in them, like our defense against a
greater pain.
It means that we surrender to God
our perceptions of all things.*

—Marianne Williamson

Chapter

21

A Cry for Help

Since I'm in the beginning of my throat chakra development, which began when I turned twenty-eight and until I turn thirty-five, it was time for me to speak my truth and proclaim to the universe exactly what I want in this lifetime. It was time to be honest with myself and those around me. I finally finished the chapter on the fifth chakra, the throat, which gave me the courage to call up the latest predator I had let into my life. I was ready to demand some sort of a repayment plan.

I was no longer willing to be that girl that gets screwed over and just sucked it up. Yes, I had been foolish to loan him money. One thing I knew for sure: Karma is a bitch, and I was ready to step in her shoes. I finally had a few days off, so I had time to refl ct on why I allowed my Bama Boo into my life.

I let my coworkers convince me that I needed to get back on the dating scene after picking up the pieces of my heart that Sweetz shattered. So I downloaded a few apps for Black people in my area. His profile was average. He had caramel skin, was shorter than what I'm used to dating, a guy with a few tattoos. His bio told me that he was a traveling construction worker from Alabama, which in my mind signaled that he wouldn't be here for very long, so I shouldn't and wouldn't allow myself to get romantically caught up. The plan was to just have some fun, go on some dates, enjoy each other's company; and if we liked each other enough, I might even get my rocks off a few times. Since he was a traveling construction worker, I knew he was making decent money, and being that he was raised in the South, I expected him to have Southern values and manners. Every guy I met and was intimate with during my stay in Alabama had a nice, long black snake, and I was hoping he was the same.

He was new in town, so after a few messages back and forth, I suggested a bowling spot where we could meet to hang out and get to know each other in person. Our first interaction was quite pleasant. I arrived on time; he was about five minutes late. When he walked up, we noticed one another, and we had on the same colors, grey and black. My shirt was grey, and my pants were black, his shirt was black, and pants were grey. If I had to describe him any other way, I would say that he was a T.I. look-alike before he had money. The bowling alley we went to had pool tables and a bar for us to order drinks and food. It was a nice vibe, and we had a good time. We didn't talk much, as far as getting to know each other or anything, both of our competitive spirits were coming out, and it was obvious that neither one of us had been bowling in a very long time. We joked and teased about how badly each other was doing. He ordered a few drinks for us and made sure to compliment how nice he thought I looked. By the time our two-hour slot for bowling was up, I told him that I didn't really care to go another round. We both had enough fun. We ate, we drank, we laughed, and we each won a game. It was a good first encounter. He walked me outside and held the doors as I went through. He gave me a nice hug and a small peck on the cheek and told me he was looking forward to seeing me again. For my first time meeting someone off an app, he wasn't doing very bad of a job impressing me. He had Southern values, and he paid for the entire date. He opened my door and was very much courteous and complimentary.

After our bowling adventure, we didn't talk much on the phone, but we texted. He worked days, and I worked nights, so in between time when we were both awake, we would let each other know that we were thinking of the other and just wanted to see how their day was going. It was just about two weeks since our bowling adventure before we saw each other again, which I was more than okay with, but that was also the first time I found out he smoked cigarettes. I pulled up to the house that he was sharing with the other guys who worked at the same company, who also came from Alabama. As he walked out of the house up to my car, he was smoking a cigarette. *Ewww*, was all I could think, but my lips said nothing. Even though I tried not to show it, he lost major cool points from that. I reminded myself that he wasn't my man and that I wasn't looking to be serious with him, so I wasn't going to mention anything regarding him smoking a square. I did, however, tell him that he couldn't get in my car with that, and he had to put it out. He didn't have a car yet, and the one roommate that did have a car, they all shared it to make their own errands. Once again, I convinced myself that he was a traveling construction worker, so I shouldn't expect him to have all the things a normal resident would have. In hindsight, I was once again making excuses for him in order to brainwash myself into overlooking things about him that I knew went against my normal standards when dealing with the opposite sex. I knew he smoked weed, and occasionally, I did too, so he rolled up a joint, and we sat there and talked for a couple of hours. He told me he had three kids. He said he was two years older than me, and all these facts consciously convinced me he would not be around long and that this was just gonna be a fling.

Our next few encounters were sort of the same as the previous one. I would pick him up, and we would either go to a park, smoke a blunt, or find something inexpensive to do. It felt nice to have some companionship again and to have someone tell me multiple times how beautiful I was and how happy he was to have met me. But I was getting bored with these car dates. I. If he wasn't going to wine and dine me, I thought about seeing if he could at least please me sexually. I know that should have been the farthest thing from my mind, given everything I just laid out about this guy, but it had been almost a year of celibacy, and I was craving some intimacy. Until now, sex was the one way I knew how to obtain that feeling of desire.

The fifth meet-up was a booty call. Against my better judgment, I allowed him to come to my house. I knew he had hella roommates as to why he didn't offer for me to come over there, but it never dawned on me to ask him why he didn't offer to get a hotel room. I really didn't want him to see my newly-built three-thousand-home and think I was about to be his sugar mama or something.

When he pulled up, he did everything he could not to let his jaw drop to the floor when he realized that I wasn't living with my mom and that this was my house. Not only was it my house, I wasn't renting it.; I owned it. That was one of the biggest mistakes I could've made. My cousin, who was living with me at the time, wasn't there, so I wanted him to be in and out like a thief in the night before anybody saw him. I hadn't had any random visitors, and I definitely wasn't planning to make a habit out of it. But boy or boy, just like most toxic Niggas, they make sure they lay down the best dick to try to mentally confuse the shit outta you, even though you know they ain't shit.

I saw all of his red flags, and I rode over the motherfuckers like we were playing Grand Theft Auto or Bumper Cars in real life. I told myself to ignore them because I wasn't looking for anything serious, ; but yet I was allowing him to penetrate me physically, spiritually, energetically, and, little did I know, mentally! He didn't have the biggest dick I've ever had, but man, did he know how to work it! He was the third person in the history of my sexual experiences to bring me to an orgasm. From his tongue game, and even when he began to penetrate me, his stroke simulated passion. It wasn't like he was ramming himself inside of me just so that he could get his rocks off. Nope, it was like he was really trying to fuck his way into my brain. I was more than satisfied after he finished pleasing me. It was like he came to lay down some daddy dick, put me into a sex coma, and leave. And that's exactly what happened. Little did I know he thought he had did all that he needed to do to work his way right into my wallet, cause not even two days later is when he asked to borrow the $250 I told y'all about. If the cigarettes and three kids weren't enough red flags for me to ignore, I knew this was a bad sign. Of course, he gave me a sob story, and my ego was screaming, "He already saw your house bitch. He knows how you live. He knows you got it! Do you really want to look like you broke? If he doesn't give it back, just don't talk to him again. It's only $250." Man, that ego will tell you anything it needs to keep you stuck in the same cycle of toxic behaviors until you learn your lesson and finally reprogram yourself for success.

Of course, I gave it to him, and two days later, he repaid me. I thought this was a sign of him being a man of his word. I probably was still a little high off the orgasms he had just given me a few days before. My mental had been disrupted because what I really should've been asking, besides why he needed it, was why none of his friends at home whom he lived with and came from Alabama with, and had known much longer than me, couldn't give it to him? Why was he coming to somebody that he had known less than three months, hell, just barely one month, for $250? It was hella suspicious, but I was just glad that I got it back.

The next three months seemed to be filled with a lot of fucking and no dates. He said he was saving up to buy a car since he would be here a few more months until his contract ended. Since he wasn't taking me on dates and I knew we were not in a relationship, I got back on the app and started exploring other options. Potentially someone who could arouse me more mentally. I didn't plan to make it a habit of sleeping with guys from these sites, and since Bama Boo had proven he could get the job done, I was willing to stick with one person for that aspect. His conversation was minimal, and the things we talked about didn't satisfy my curiosity about life and didn't cause me to address or think about anything worthwhile or of substance, so I began to look for more intellectual, studious kind of guys.

The two intellectuals I gave my time to were an epic fail. I met a guy who had his own remodeling company that he was working to get off the ground. He was into spiritual shit like crystals, meditating, moon cycles, and things of that nature. Since I was just starting to get into all of that myself, we had a lot to talk about, but he had no problem with letting me know that he wanted to be intimate with me from the very jump. He was very forward in his approach, the language that he used, and how often he brought up sex or made some type of sexual innuendo just during a typical conversation was beyond annoying. It was hard to speak to him over the phone because, somehow, everything came back down to sex with him. I quickly blocked him. The next intellectual I gave an opportunity to get to know me was a banker of some sort. He wore a suit and tie to work every day, was clean cut, had his own car and own home, had no children, didn't smoke, had great teeth, gorgeous dark -caramel skin; but he was an even bigger asshole than the spiritual remodel or guy! He would set dates for us to go out, and I wouldn't hear from him. He would blame it on work or something else, and on multiple occasions, I had to check him about the way that he addressed me, which was in a hyper-sexual way as well. At least with Bama, he didn't make me feel like a piece of meat. But at this point in time, that's pretty much all I was willing to give him.

By August, I would consider myself to be in a full-blown situationship with Bama Boo. We had been doing some major fucking for the past five months. He had finally secured him a car and was planning to move out of the house that he shared with six other people into a small apartment with him and his best friend that he came up here with. Now that he had a car, he wanted to come by more often, he even asked to spend the night a couple of times, which I wasn't comfortable with. It was starting to feel more and more like a relationship without the title and benefits. He told me about his kids and his baby mama and about his dad and his mom. He was just opening up to me in general about things that, honestly, I didn't care about.

One month later after buying his car, his car key stopped turning over the engine, and he needed a loan for $1,500. He begged and promised he would repay me. I wouldn't have even believed it cost that much if I hadn't spoken to the mechanic myself in person. I mean, he didn't have a luxury car or anything, but it was a foreign vehicle, and the key had a chip that needed to be replaced not only in the key but in the electrical wiring system of the car in order for his car to start. For some reason, I felt obligated to help him, and that reason was because I was allowing his essence to penetrate me regularly. I may not have had that amount of money in cash because all of the money I was making was going toward this party, but I did have a credit card I could put it on. Once again, my deep-seeded need to self-sacrifice in order not to lose someone, even if it was time to let them go, reared its ugly head; and I went ahead and swiped my card. You will never guess what happened next! Three days later, the contract he was working on came to an end. So not only had I just given him $1,500 of my money, it was looking very slim for me to get that money back now that he was unemployed and living in a hotel.

The morning he called me, I was just getting off work, and he asked me to stop by the hotel he was staying in, which was just about five minutes from my job, so I didn't have to go out of my way to see him. I wasn't expecting him to tell me all of this bad news. He now wanted to let me know that in addition to being laid off, his car was not starting after just paying $1,500 just three days earlier. I guess he thought that by telling me he had a job interview lined up for ten o'clock that morning that it would make it all better. But how the fuck was he going to make it back and forth to work with no car? I had no intention of giving him more money, and I let that be known. What he asked me was if I could take him to his interview, which was more like a formality because the company that had just laid him off referred him to another company that was still in need of workers for a project that they hadn't yet completed. So it was less of an interview and more of him filling out paperwork, taking the safety course, and getting the materials that they would need to start the job the next day.

My next bad decision came when I decided to loan him my car for a few hours so that he could handle his business. I had just worked a 12-hour shift and wanted to rest, but I absolutely wanted to make sure he got to the job so that he could begin working and be able to pay me my money back. I told him to come pick me up after their safety class, and things were complete. In my mind, I rationalized giving him my car so that he could pay me back what he owed me. Before my head could hit the pillow, he called to give me more bad news. Someone had side-swiped him in my fuckin' car! I had no idea how to process this. Here I am just about two months before my big party, and not only was I $1500 broker, but the car that I had worked so hard to pay off in a year and a half was now damaged in an accident that I hadn't even caused. To be honest, it wasn't terrible. It was a minor fender bender literally, they hit the driver-side fender and made a small dent, but that wasn't the point! It wasn't his car to fuck up, and now I'm feeling punished again for trying to help him so that he could repay me. When ultimately, it was just the universe slapping me on my ass because I had once again put myself in a position to self-sacrifice for someone who couldn't and wouldn't do the same. Not only was I not learning my lesson, I was constantly putting myself in a position to repeat the same self-sabotaging patterns, and the Saturn Return energy I was now in was making sure that I felt the harshness of my hardheadedness. He sent me a picture of the damage, and I sent it to a mechanic who, just by eyeballing it, said that it would be about a $750 fix.

He was more than a liability, and I was no longer interested in how well he could lay pipe. All I wanted was my money back, and I wanted it back before my party, which was now only two months away. I ended up taking out a loan for $6,000 to pay the rest of the party expenses and to pay off my credit card. I felt foolish, naive, and every other emotion you can imagine. This was my first time in my adult life I ever had to take out a loan, and it wasn't to get ahead, it was because I had put myself in positions to help others get ahead, which ultimately set me back. After I got approved for the loan, I immediately hung up the phone and called my Bama Boo to see when he would start making payments toward the now $2,300 that he owed me. $1,500 for his car, $750 for the repairs to my car, and $50 for the gas money that he used while using my car. He didn't answer, of course, so I made sure to text him. From all my years of watching *Judge Judy*, I knew that I needed to have something in writing to prove what I was saying if it came down to me having to take him to court. He called me right back, probably after seeing my message to inform me that he was going to be giving me my money back, he just didn't have it right now and that he was probably gonna have to go back to Alabama because the company that he borrowed my car to start with wasn't gonna need their services for too much longer.

I found that highly suspicious that a company would go through the trouble of hiring, training and doing background checks to only use their services for two weeks. In my opinion, he was running back to Alabama so that he could escape his financial obligations he had to me! I was furious! I hung up in his face as I began to cry! I had to release the emotions that were building up inside. I had to release the idea of control over the fact that I had no way to make him stay. His financial obligations to me were even more reason to run back home, where he claimed a job awaited him.

It was now less than thirty-five days before my party, and Bama had been gone for about two weeks, and as I sat on my bed and finished chapter five on the throat chakra, I knew what I had to do. My final call to ask for a payment was null and void. I even threatened to sue him if he didn't agree to a repayment schedule! This muthafucker had the nerve to call me a bitch and a few other names that I choose not to say right now and told me that I wasn't ever getting shit and hung up the phone in my face! I was overwhelmed with frustration, anger, and self-pity. I began to cry hysterically! I was no longer going to be a victim. But I damn sure knew I needed the intervention of a power higher and greater than my own to help me with this one. I knew I needed to get it right this time. I needed to be specific because words have power, and I wanted to only speak into existence what I truly wanted. I sat up on my knees in my bed; and with tears streaming down my face, snot dripping onto my pillow and sheets, and my head buried in my hands, I let out the loudest scream that swelled up from the pit of my stomach from the sadness I felt for myself from bearing and carrying around all the pain and hurt that has ever happened to me, and I called out to my higher self:

> *"Divine creator, ancestors, higher self, and spirit guides, I know I have been accepting less than I deserve! I have given my body, time, energy, love, and money to multiple men, hoping to keep them around, praying that they love me and validate all of my insecurities! I have been seeking love outside of myself that I should've been giving to myself all this time. Divine creator, I now know my worth, and I know I deserve a man who will value my mind and not use my pain to cause more harm. I'm ready to forgive myself for not knowing how to love myself or even what healthy love looks like. From now on, I will only entertain the man designed for me. Universe! Divine creator! My higher self, send me my other half! My twin flame, my soulmate, my* husband, *the man who will love me despite my flaws; who will nurture me,; care for me mentally, emotionally, and financially. I want him to be from the south with gentleman values. At least six feet tall and two shades darker than me. A beautiful smile, and a few tattoos but not in weird obvious places. He needs to make good money. He doesn't have to*

be as educated as me, but he must be willing to learn new things and be open-minded. I want him to be spiritual, not religious. A family man. I don't mind if he has at least one kid. I want him to worship the ground I walk on and be loyal and faithful to me and honest always, and to desire me and only me. I want him to have a sense of humor and be willing to spend his money on me. I want him to be sensual with soft lips and enjoy pleasing me orally. I want his dick to be at least seven inches with a moderate girth. I want him not too much older than me, and on the same level in life so that we can build together. I want him to have some unresolved mommy issues that I can help him work through because I know I'm still working through some of my daddy issues. I want him to be the best friend in male form that I never had in my dad. The only person I want to call when life gets rough, and the first person I want to call when life is going well. I thank you for all of the previous lessons, and I thank you in advance for all of the many blessings! Ase'."

I wiped my face, blew my nose, and mentally prepared myself to never receive a dime of money back from that scumbag. It was now out of my hands, but I trusted that what was owed to me would find me, and the karma he had coming to him will find him as well. But for now, I needed a nap because I was literally drained after that prayer!

By three methods we may learn wisdom:
First, by reflection, which is noblest;
Second, by imitation, which is easiest;
and third by experience, which is the bitterest.

—Confucius

Chapter
22

Scorpions in the Sand

W hen I awoke from my nap, there was a text message waiting for me. My cousin, who recently moved to AZ earlier this year, invited me to her birthday dinner in two weeks. She asked me to give her a call because she had some tea she wanted to drop on me. After that good cry, I could use a little cheering up, so I washed my face and did my best to take the frog out my throat from all that crying and called her. When she answered, all I heard was, "Biiiitch, I got something to tell you! I know you and your little Bama Boo haven't been working out well, but my old homey from college just moved here, and he works about fifteen minutes from my house. He's an engineer. He was telling me about his homeboy who just moved up here from Alabama that's working at the same company as him. After he and I did a little catching up, you know I had to put you on, cuz! I want you to meet him, so I invited him to my birthday dinner. Do you think you can make it?" Although I was in no mood to tell her about what just went down, I considered meeting this friend of a friend she was eager to tell me about. Y'all know how the saying goes: "The best way to get over one man is to get on top of another." I had no intention of sleeping with anyone else anytime soon, but I could use the entertainment of another man, possibly just to get my mind off everything that I had just experienced. Regardless of whether he showed up or not, I wasn't going to miss my cousin's birthday dinner. I would be lying if I said I wasn't intrigued by the little information I did hear from the conversation about him. She didn't know much about the guy, but she promised she would get more information from her friend later that evening. She asked me to send her a photo, and she would ask for one of him as well. I sent her a few recent shots so that she could choose the one that she thought would be best to send her homey so that he would know exactly what I look like and whether or not he wanted to show up or not. I didn't have much time to focus on the tea because I had to pull myself together for rehearsal tonight. There were only three more rehearsals left before the big day, and I was more than excited that it was finally coming together. I needed some inspiration tonight because I was supposed to have a solo part in this performance, and I didn't yet know what I was gonna do.

Rehearsal went well, but at the point in the song that was designated for my solo, I just told them to let the music play and that I'd figure out some moves to do before the big day came. Mentally, I wasn't in the mood to be sensual, enticing, seductive, and all those other adjectives that my solo was to embody. I just wanted to make sure that we were all on the same page and on the beat when it came to the parts that we had to all do together. So I mustered up enough energy and put on a brave face to get through the two-hour rehearsal, but that's about all I had energy for.

Boxes and boxes were coming to my house with cake plates and plastic champagne cups, and little napkins that coordinated with the theme of the party. I was starting to get excited even more than I had been while planning it because the day was quickly approaching. The DJ had been solidified and paid, and the photographer had been solidified and paid. My backdrop had come in the mail as well as the stand that it would be on for people to take pictures in front of. All of the little final details that I had conjured up in my mind were finally starting to come together. I was even going to have a wardrobe change three times throughout this party. I mean, who did I think I was?! Although I wanted it to be magical for everybody else, this is gonna be magical for me no matter who is in attendance. This was me celebrating me in a huge way with all the people who deemed me important enough to show up.

My three outfits consisted of an all-black semi-sheer jumpsuit with gold rhinestones that I would start the night with. For the performance, ohhhh, that outfit was spicy! I had fishnet stockings, a bodysuit that barely covered anything, and some nipple pads because the girls were gonna be out. It was something that you would see in the most classy upscale brothel you have ever been to. Just imagine what the waitress would be wearing, yeah, that was my outfit. I'm a 38 double D, with a size -eight pants. Thighs that was thick as cold grits and this ass…huh, I paid enough for it, and it's set up and was plump and voluptuous, and nobody could tell I wasn't born with it because it complimented my frame as if I had grown it over these past twenty-eight years. My hair appointment was set. I will be rockin' this twenty-two-inch weave that was copper colored with curls. Even the makeup artist was coming to the mansion to do my make up before the party. I was truly going to feel like a celebrity that night.

The anticipation overshadowed the humiliation and embarrassment I felt for everything that had went down with that ignorant muthafucker Bama. As I hung up each outfit in my closet, I envisioned how bomb I was going to look when the night finally came. I quickly snapped out of it as I realized that I was running late for my cousin's birthday dinner and needed to hurry up. I chose a nice simple sweater dress. It was black ribbed cotton material with a red -and -white patch across the chest, nothing too fancy. It wasn't my birthday dinner, and I also didn't wanna look like I was putting too much energy into it, knowing that someone was supposed to be showing up that I was supposed to meet. At dinner, I sat next to her college friend, who was pretty good company; and as it turned out, his birthday was the same day as my party. Of course, I had to tell him all about it and invited him. My cousin had already told him, but we were having dinner conversation, so why not mention it again. His coworker/buddy was a no-show to dinner. I went about my night and pretended as though I had no idea that I was supposed to be meeting someone.

The next day was Sunday, and I was off with nothing to do, so I decided to do a game night. I invited a couple of the dancers that would be performing at my party, a couple of my coworkers, and my cousin; and I told her if she wanted to, she can invite her college friend because, as of right now, the game night was female dominant; and we would need some extra male present. She told me she would invite them. I received a text message from her apologizing that she wouldn't be able to make it but that she'd see me later next week. I didn't have his number, of course, and I wasn't expecting him to apologize for not making it to a game night. I mean, I had only met him the day before, so it really didn't matter if his presence was there or not.

The game night was a bust. Nobody was really available to come out. I mean, it was Sunday, so most of the regular Monday through Friday work nine-fivers were preparing for the week, getting their kids ready for school, meal prepping, and everything else. So I rolled me a joint, sat on the back porch, and chilled until I was ready to go to sleep. It was a nice, quiet night for me, so I wasn't trippin'. I had to work on Monday, but I'm a night shifter, so it wasn't like I had to wake up early or anything.

Just around three thirty the next day, I was preparing to get ready for work. I usually squeeze in about an hour's nap before my twelve-hour shift just to ensure I have enough energy to get me through the night. It was about four o'clock when I got a call via social media from my cousin's college friend asking if I was busy and if he could stop by for a second. He said he was at a sports bar up the street from my house, and he wanted to just stop by because he felt bad for not making it to the game night the day before. I told him that was fine and that I didn't mind if he stopped by 'cause all I was doing was kind of chilling before work, but if he was coming, he better hurry up 'cause I would be lying down soon. So when the doorbell rang twenty minutes later, I was expecting to see him, but when I opened the door, he had somebody with him, and I was completely confused. Not only did he not mention that he was bringing somebody he barely knew me, so why do you think that it was a good idea to bring somebody to my house without asking? The shock of the second person didn't allow my brain to put two and two together. This had to be the guy they wanted me to meet at my cousin's dinner. Kendal introduced his friend as they entered the foyer of my home.

Then it all made sense. They had been planning this meet and greet since her birthday dinner when he didn't show up. Why didn't he just tell me that he wanted me to meet his homeboy when he asked to stop by? Thank goodness ya girl wasn't looking like a bum during this ambush. I had my hair braided up into a bun, my eyebrows were newly waxed, and my toes were freshly painted. I had on this striped, colorful sundress that hugged my curves in all the right places. I was looking like a whole snack, as the kids would say, so I didn't mind too much that he showed up; but it would've been better if I was prepared. Now that I had invited them in, I was checking the dude out. He was about four inches taller than his friend, slightly under six feet. He was about two shades darker than me, and he had some dark black Ray-Ban sunglasses that he finally took off after he entered the house. He had a nice low profile Boosie type haircut with the little swivel sponge curls at the top. He had one tattoo that I saw off the rip. It was on his neck. I couldn't exactly read what it was. It was old and faded, but I was checking him out from head to toe. His mustache was well groomed, and his lips were thick and looked like fluffy brown pillows. When he spoke, I could hear his Southern accent. His teeth were white against his brown pillow lips. He had a slim, athletic frame. He had on a multicolored outfit as well. I want to say he had on a Puma sweatsuit with a shirt and jogging pants and some multicolored gym shoes that complemented the colors of his sweatsuit. All I could think was, *Wow!* The universe does work in mysterious ways. We went on the back porch to chat a bit. He told me he was from Alabama, and I could tell by how thick his accent was that he must had just left.

I had to let them know that it was time for them to leave so I could get ready for work, but I appreciated them stopping by. We exchanged numbers before he left. As soon as I went upstairs to start getting ready for my shift, I had to call my cousin 'cause, baby, this man was checking off so many boxes from the prayer that I just put out three weeks prior! I couldn't believe it! He was from the South, almost six feet, about two shades darker than me. Handsome with pillow lips and a beautiful smile, a few tattoos, but not in weird places. I hadn't asked him any questions about himself really, so I didn't yet know the full dynamics of his home life, but I was excited to get to know him. This had to be the guy I asked the creator for. By the time he texted me before I left for work, we set up a first date for a week later.

While at work, I did my best to try not to check my phone to see if he had finally put my number to use, but I was anxious and excited to hear from him. About two days later, I remember him sending me some messages on a social media app. He said he was looking forward to our first date and asked me if there was any place in particular I wanted to go. I recycled my last meeting place from Bama Buster and suggested, "Hey, let's go bowling." We went bowling with my cousin, and a few of his coworkers met us there. We had a nice outing with low pressure because we had people there that we knew in case things went left. I was analyzing and probing him with questions to see if this really was the guy that I asked the universe to send me.

The following week, he asked to see me again, but this time we were alone. I was a movie buff, and turns out he was too, so since there were some new things out in the theater, we had a movie date. Once again, he was the perfect gentleman. He paid for everything, held my doors when we walked in and out of the theater. He didn't open the car door for me, but I gave him a pass on that one. I was enjoying the attention and the time and effort he was putting into me.

After the movie, we sat in his car for a while, smoked us a blunt, and we were able to talk a little more and find out some more information about one another. Come to find out, this man's birthday is the day after mine. He's a year older than me, which technically means we were born on the same day of the week, Monday, just one year apart. Sounds a lot like my other half to me. All of his attributes and physical qualities were starting to add up, and I was getting more and more excited about getting to know him with each date. You already know I had to invite him to my party! I still didn't have a male to dance with during my routine and solo, so I asked him if he would be my dance partner because we were only a week and a half away from the party, and seeing as how he was new in town I knew whatever plans that he had for his birthday wouldn't be at all in any way as much fun as this party was going to be. So I told him to be there or be square in my cocky Scorpio persona.

Eighty guests had already purchased a ticket, and a few people from social media inboxed me asking if they could pay at the door. So I was expecting just under 100 people to be in attendance. As you know, none of these tickets were from my aunts, cousins, or sisters. I purchased a plane ticket for my dad so he could be there. The mansion was about thirty-five minutes from where I currently lived, but everyone who was coming to town stayed at the mansion. So if $200 a night per person for the experience wasn't worth it, they were welcome to find a hotel nearby. Only one of the three exes that I invited said he would be there from out of town. You guessed it, Sweetz! The same dude that broke my heart after I found out he had cheated on me with his baby mama. To be honest, he was really the only one that I cared about showing up, especially now that I had this new Boo on my arm. I knew he would be jealous and eating his heart out when he realized and saw how I was thriving, happy, sexy, and another man had my attention. I wasn't really expecting him to show up either. You know people give a lot of lip service these days, so I'll believe it when I see it. According to the Eventbrite checklist, he had not yet purchased his ticket, so the only way he was getting in was to purchase a ticket at the door.

The day we moved into the mansion, which was a day before the party, I decided to throw a little taco night for my guest. This was like the pregame to the big day. Everybody was impressed by the house and was excited to see how the party unfolded. Of course, my new boo, Tommy, showed up. He seemed a little shy, probably because he was around folks who had known me my entire life, and here he was, less than a month into trying to make an impression without knowing if he was stepping on anyone's toes or not. I told my home girls to lock the door after their guest left because I needed to lay down and rest. Since I was leaving, Tommy left, and when I woke up the next day, he called to see if I had slept well and asked if he could take me out to lunch before the party began. He knew that a lot of people would be in attendance, and he just wanted to have a little more alone time with me before things got crazy. I mean, are you serious? This guy was saying all the right things, doing all the right things, and looking damn good while doing it! He was definitely making an impression, and he seemed to be checking off all of the boxes. He wasn't cheap, he was willing to spend his money on me. Man, everything that was going on between us had me convinced he was the answer to my prayer.

I returned to the mansion from lunch with him on cloud nine before I even began to get ready for the party. My home girls were down in their rooms getting dressed. The people who lived here in the city who weren't staying at the mansion arrived a few minutes earlier than most of the guests. I had hired two different girls to serve drinks, and I had another girl at the front door with the guest list, checking out names and taking money from anybody who didn't have a ticket. The balloons were blown up and situated around the living area. The couches were moved and pushed back so that people had somewhere to sit. The main floor was open and inviting for dancing. The DJ was set up in the furthest corner, with music bumping. The patio doors were pushed completely open, so the fall warm night air was coming through the whole house. The cake was set up in the kitchen off to the side so that it didn't get interrupted by guests passing by. The food was staying warm in the heated drawers that were built into the island. The drinks that were being served were kept in the formal dining room, which no one had access to. Most of these people were under the age of forty and probably hadn't even seen the inside of a mansion, let alone know what to expect from a mansion party. I think I pulled it off ery well.

When the guest walked to the right, near the stairwell, there was the photo booth where my photographer had everything set up real nice. I did my best to make sure I got a picture with everybody that came through those doors. The party was to begin at 10:00p.m. and end at 2:00a.m. For the first two hours, we were to mix and mingle and eat a little bit of food. Take pictures and selfies, and the plan was when the clock struck midnight, the performance was to begin. The closer and closer it got to midnight, the more nervous I got. My coworkers, associates, friends, neighbors, mom, stepdad, and cousin Jason were all in attendance; and I had to strut my stuff in some burlesque lingerie and do a whole dance routine in front of all of these people. In my mind I could do it, but it took about three shots and a couple of hits off a vape pen for me to actually get the courage to step out with nipple pads and fishnet stockings on to gyrate, shake, and twirl this ass in front of all these people. I may be a Scorpio, but I was nobody's hoe. I always kept it classy and freaky behind closed doors, but it was time for me to step into a new phase of my life, and I had planned this night down to the T. I had rehearsed and rehearsed, so it was time for me to get up there and show my shit.

My dance partner was looking quite scrumptious with these camel pants and a black button-down shirt that had gold speckles on it. I mean, together, you would have thought we had been dating for years. Although I was looking like a full meal, he was definitely looking like a snack, and all the single ladies in the room wanted to know if that was me and if they should fall back. When the time came for me to perform, my home girl Lisa, whom I've been ten toes down with, let me know that Mr. Sweetz himself had actually made it! He hopped on the flight and brought a couple of his homeboys with him to attend my party, and when I looked out into the crowd that was gathering and circling around the area where we would be performing, I could see the shock on his face. He was smiling to see that I knew he was there, but it was also a look of "OMG, I really lost her, and I think that dude she was dancing in front of got her." I did my best not to make eye contact with too many people as I performed for the crowd. And when the music slowed down, and it was time for all the spotlights to be on me! Internally, I froze. I forgot every step that I was planning to do. There was a lot of rolling around on the floor, and I shook my hair from side to side. I slowly rolled my neck the way I see all of the strippers do on TV. I teased Tommy by winding in front of him. I popped my ass up, dropped it down on his lap, and slowly rolled my body up. It was definitely a strip tease, not only for him but for everyone else that was in the room. Everyone's phone was out recording me, and I did my best not to think of any of that. It was the longest minute-and-a-half section of this performance that I could possibly remember. When it was over, it was an unheard sigh of relief. The other two girls joined me, and we continued to perform for the guest. All I could hear was, "Get it, bitch" and "Yes, PJ, do yo shit," and that kept my confidence high! I was smiling so hard, and my cheeks hurt the next day. My mom was in the background, being my biggest cheerleader, of course, egging me on. Oh my goodness, I was more than a celebrity! The night was magical. The feeling was electric, and this was everything that I wanted it to be. I deserved this party. I deserved to feel the excitement that I felt by performing and stepping outside my box and stepping into the new woman that I was becoming.

Once the performance ended, it was time for wardrobe change number three. It was a nice sparkly black -and -gold bodycon dress. There was no way I was spending another minute in that performance outfit. I felt like everyone was devouring me in their mind, which to some degree was the whole point, but I'm not accustomed to being visually fucked by everyone in the room. Since it was approaching 1:00 a.m., the liquor had ran out, and I was ready to sing "Happy Birthday" and get these folks on out. After the cake was cut and everybody ate, the guests began to leave, but I was looking for Mr. Hubby To Be. I walked most of my guests out to the car. I saw his car but not him. I walked outside on the patio and asked if anybody had seen Tommy. I decided to go upstairs to my room, take off my shoes, and get comfortable. If his car was here, he was around somewhere he would eventually turn up, I figured. By the time I opened the door to my room there he was lying there waiting for me. I knew at that moment I was finally ready to give him some of me, even though it had only been about a month since we met. We had just shared a moment in front of the whole party. The chemistry was there, the attraction was there, and you already know I had been mentally checking off the boxes from my prayer. So I took a bath, and because I was prepared to intertwine with his spirit, I put on my second negligée on. I wanted him to see me as the vixen that I felt I was. I was lying there in the bed waiting to be devoured, and boy oh boy, did he not disappoint! I did my best not to scream as I climaxed again and again. He made sure that I was pleased before he even thought about penetration. When I saw what he was working with, ohhh that Alabama black snake had me curious. With each stroke, it got more intense. He took his time and was patient with the way he maneuvered inside of me. I threw my head back, arched my spine, and allowed him to go deeper and deeper inside. With each stroke, he led me to believe that he was who I cried out for.

Over the next few months, we spent every free second we had together. We talked, laughed and shared stories about our past and hopes for the future. To my understanding, we were both spiritual people, and I finally had someone to discuss my views and perspectives on what's considered normal in the world. Although he was a weed connoisseur, he didn't smoke squares. He had been a semiprofessional athlete for some years now, so he ate well and exercised often. All the things I struggled with, he seemed to be good at, and vice versa. After hearing about his childhood, I knew he had some mommy issues that I hoped my love, compassion, and empathy could help him get past. I don't know if you ever heard of the saying, "Don't be so spiritually high that you're no earthly good." Well, that proverb was about to take on a whole new meaning for me.

I was deep into my spiritual seeking at this point, but you see, knowledge and wisdom are two totally separate things. Intellectually understanding something is one thing, but genuine wisdom only comes from being placed in a situation in which that knowledge is challenged and you actually apply the information you have and overcome the challenge. One day, while texting at work, he shared something about himself that also checked a box on the prayer list. But this check, had I been wiser, I would have seen it was a big fat red X, that should have sent me running for the hills. Instead, my ego convinced me that I had been prepared for this confession earlier in my life. I thought to myself if this was the only downfall he had. It seemed to be an easy fix, in my opinion. At that moment, my old programming had reared its ugly head. I was ready to go into fix him mode rather than understanding that no matter how many green checks he had, this red X should be a deal breaker. Logically, I told myself, he was hardworking and appeared open-minded; and maybe, for a change, he just needed someone like me to be in his corner and help him through this. My insecurities, fear of abandonment, and lack mindset were about to rear their ugly heads if I didn't put an end to whatever was developing between us.

I was surely going to fail this test if I didn't. See, the universe had given me exactly what I asked for, but what I didn't know was that some of those things I asked for on that list were spoken from a lack mentality and were indicative of me needing to focus more on my healing! I couldn't see that at the time because the man on the other end of the phone presented himself to be 80 percent of what I asked for, and I wasn't giving that up without a fight.

Epilogue

Proverbs 4:7 says, "Wisdom is the principal thing; therefore get wisdom: and with all thy getting get understanding." It has been my earnest desire to provide you with great details into the thought process of a young woman who desired to break the generational curses she was born into. The curse of poverty, single -parent household, a family riddled with addictions of many kinds, and even feeling as though she wasn't beautiful by the standards of her family first and society later. The accumulation of trials in her childhood provided for the perfect storm, which led to subconscious insecurities that went on to affect her throughout her life.

While searching for the answers to what would truly make her happy after realizing that money couldn't do it, a large home couldn't do it, and even an elaborate party couldn't do it. The answer became apparent that she needed to learn to love herself before she could attract anyone to add to that love. The problem is when you're broken, even during your healing stage, it's easy to cling to attributes in individuals that you have never experienced before, which can cause you to ignore the negative characteristics you have seen before.

In the world we live in today, females are glorified more for being hoes with low morals and little self-respect, and we wonder why the male and female dynamic is toxic and continues to perpetuate self-centered behavior. The heart centers of women have been closed off, and they have now chosen to embody their more masculine attributes. Women are disconnected from the essence of womanhood and need to take a deep dive into their past to locate where their pain began in order to heal it!

The gems that were dropped in this book are worth more than diamonds and gold if you decide to do the work and retrace your life. By seeking to better understand yourself and why you make the choices you make begins the Shadow Work journey. This is no easy feat and will require a level of honesty with yourself that you may not have ever done before. True happiness begins when you are able to accept yourself and all the mistakes of your past and use those lessons to make you a better person today! Instead of blaming others for your unhappiness, PJ challenges you to retrace your life and release yourself from the shame, pain, and poor decisions of yesterday so that a new you emerges tomorrow!

PJ began the process of healing her inner child by acknowledging the pain of her shadow that manifested with many poor choices with men, which led to low self-worth and poor financial choices. Although she's on the right track, she is one more lack -driven decision away from putting it all together and gaining the wisdom to emerge as the Phoenix from the ashes!